Front Cover design by Luis Stephenberg

"Towards immortality and eternal youth" is th̶— —————— —erne's
gravestone monument at the Madele̶—————————————— It was
commissioned by Verne's son Michè̶—————————

Jules Verne, the "Father of Modern ———————————— **ortal**
and eternally young **across three ce**——————— *ᴚhe Sea: The*
Adventures of Jules Verne's Mathia̶—————ᴅᴑrf, **we pay tribute to Verne**
who inspired pioneers throughout the world for generations.

Here, we take Verne's 1870 ultimate prediction of communication with
our friends of the watery deep to its outer limits. In fact, communication
with these friends was heralded throughout the world when in 2003,
America used dolphins to clear mines designed to hamper the invasion
from the port of Unn Qasr in southern Iraq.

For the first time, a pioneering research Preface underscores why
and how Verne proclaimed *Mathias Sandorf* his greatest epic science
fiction masterpiece. His dedication of the original work claims "…I
tried to make of *Mathias Sandorf* my Monte Cristo of extraordinary
science fiction adventures."

Verne drew his Austrian heroic character, Dr. Mathias Sandorf, from
the reality of the battleground of Germany's conquests of Austria and
France during the 30-year period prior to World War I.

Advance acclaim for Masters of the Sea

"In Masters of the Sea: The Adventures of Jules Verne's Mathias
Sandorf, author George Rios has been masterful in the English
language translation and adaptation of this epic. It is a work well
worth reading."

Richard Warren Rappaport, Esq.
Entertainment Attorney and Partner
Adorno & Yoss LLP

"Having read *Journey to the Center of the Earth* and *Twenty Thousand*
***Leagues Under the Sea* as a child, it is refreshing to discover as an adult**
that the novel Jules Verne considered his greatest, *Mathias Sandorf*, has
been translated and adapted for a modern audience, and is available
to science fiction readers like me."

Georges Ph. Rios
Senior Editor
Thompson Reuters

Masters of the Sea

The Adventures of Jules Verne's Mathias Sandorf

George J. Rios

iUniverse, Inc.
New York   Bloomington

Masters of the Sea
The Adventures of Jules Verne's Mathias Sandorf

iUniverse books may be ordered through booksellers or by contacting:

iUniverse
1663 Liberty Drive
Bloomington, IN 47403
www.iuniverse.com
1-800-Authors (1-800-288-4677)

ISBN: 978-1-4502-1198-7 (sc)
ISBN: 978-1-4502-1734-7 (ebook)
ISBN: 978-1-4502-1735-4 (dj)

Printed in the United States of America

iUniverse rev. date: 8/4/2010

Preface

To say a literary work is singular and preeminent is one thing; to prove it is another. In the world of great art, each masterpiece comes with its own provenance that provides the professional documentation attesting to its authenticity. In the case of Jules Verne (1828–1905), who is regarded as "The Father of Modern Science Fiction" and who wrote sixty-five novels, there are several important factors that have mitigated against simply declaring one work above all others as his greatest. The following discussion and analysis will reveal why *Mathias Sandorf I and II* is not recognized as Verne's greatest novel in the United States.

We shall examine why Verne deserves attention, his prophecies, the effect of poor English translations on his thoughts and visions, and how, with no autobiography, research must be conducted to affirm the conclusion that his character Mathias Sandorf, in the two books of the same title, is drawn from reality and is Verne's favorite character.

After more than one hundred years since Verne's demise, many Americans do not even realize his works were written originally in French. With a little nudging, we may get a response related to the motion-picture interpretations of his works from the 1950s and '60s, such as *Twenty Thousand Leagues Under The Sea, Journey to the Center of the Earth*, and *Around the World in Eighty Days.* Yet, Verne made some of the most remarkable prophecies of the nineteenth, twentieth, and twenty-first centuries.

Verne's scientific forecasts preceded reality, sometimes by more than a century. Verne's influence and stimulus on explorers and scientific inquiry are legion. His predictions were artistically and cleverly wrapped in more than eighty science fiction works, the most notable sixty-five of which are titled *Les Voyages Extraordinaires.* In our time, hardly a year goes by that Verne's prophecies and influence are not relevant. For example, Verne believed in "cellular rejuvenation," noted in *Twenty Thousand Leagues Under the Sea* and *Mathias Sandorf I and II. The New York Times* feature story of Thursday, June 7, 2001, "Study Finds Heart Regenerates Cells," exploded the longstanding dogma that held damage to the heart is always irreversible and that the heart cannot grow new cells.

In the United States, Jules Verne unfortunately has been relegated to the status of a mere storyteller for children. This has resulted in an inability of Americans to consider some of his more mature, thought-provoking concepts, compared to Europeans, and an unclear focus on his greatest characters or his best works. Before examining the reasons for these shortcomings, one must explore Verne's prophetic contributions.

Verne's Prophecies

Verne predicted with mathematical precision the escape velocity needed by a rocket or missile to wrest free from the earth's gravitational pull. He placed the departure from earth in Florida and thus foresaw the first man on the moon as an American. The foregoing represents a powerful triple prophecy: accuracy of thrust, country, and even the state. He also foretold the television medium that enabled millions of people all over the world to share in this great adventure. Commander Neil Alden Armstrong launched for the moon on July 16, 1969, and landed on the moon on July 20.

In connection with the conquest of air, Verne wrote about circumnavigating the world in a balloon, which Bertran Piccard of Switzerland and Brian Jones of Britain realized on March 20, 1999. Verne also foresaw the development of parachutes and heavier-than-air craft (what we know today as airplanes). He understood that airplanes would become military weapons, but he also envisioned the peaceful commercial development of passenger service. The dangers of the misuse of science became a trademark of his greatest works, including *Mathias Sandorf I and II.*

Verne anticipated the lighting of cities with electricity even before Thomas Edison developed the light bulb. Furthermore, he anticipated that electricity would provide the means for heating, cooking, ventilation, and security and motive-power for an array of vehicles and industrial endeavors. He foresaw the telephone and storage batteries while yet a young man. His idea of "electric stun guns" (today known as Tasers) came to fruition in the 1970s. The misuse of this weapon made headlines in New York City on March 29, 1983. The story featured Judge Lawrence Finnigan's sentencing of police officers Pike, Gilbert, McCorey, and Steven for stun gun abuse. "Don't Tase me, bro!" is an expression that became popular in 2007. Presently, the department of justice is investigating more than two hundred deaths associated with Tasers.

Verne anticipated the development of French "separatism" in Canada, the industrialization of China, the emergence of the African peoples, and the demise of Darwin's theory of evolution as a result of advances in molecular biology, biochemistry, and genetics. Also, harnessing thermal energy from the sea and solar power fascinated him, and both are in widespread use today.

With respect to military weapons, Verne foresaw the military-industrial complex that President Dwight Eisenhower warned of and that many subsequent administrations have watched carefully, especially military budget scandals. Verne warned of gas bombs, which have been used since World War I. He envisioned torpedoes, intercontinental missiles, underwater weapons, and other war armaments capable of annihilating entire cities. The atomic bombings of Hiroshima and Nagasaki fulfilled his tragic forecast in *Les Cinq Cent Millions de la Bégum.*

Verne predicted weather forecasting and the development of scientific devices to accomplish this. He likewise espoused the study of ocean currents and the exploration of subterranean passages. Verne foresaw new, surprising habitats and species. In 1890, the Devil's Hole, a geothermal aquifer-fed pool in the Amargosa Desert of Nevada, was discovered, and in it was a twenty-two-thousand-year-old species of pupfish living at ninety-two degrees Fahrenheit, a temperature that would kill many other marine species.

Verne foretold of the widespread use of submarines and the technique of "driving" a submarine down deep along inclined planes. He anticipated the formation of new islands, explaining in great detail how these would be formed. He foresaw a future culture whose archeologists would discover the sunken city of Atlantis. Additionally, he wrote of underwater lenses and photography, optics, and uses for the chemical selenium. His studies of light refraction also foretold of three-dimensional talking-and-moving pictures and projections so lifelike they could fool the senses, as in his novel *Carpathian Castle*. Thus, Verne predicted the motion picture industry. This vision encompasses virtual reality as well. Interestingly, Louis and Auguste Lumiere of Lyon, France, made the first public film screening of a motion picture, but they saw no future in it.

Verne's character, Captain Nemo, explored the North and South Poles in his submarine, the *Nautilus*, reaching the former via a passage under the ice, in *Twenty Thousand Leagues Under the Sea*, published in 1870. American Admiral Robert Peary and Matthew Henson, with four Inuits, conquered the North Pole on foot in 1909. Roald Amundsen reached the South Pole in 1911. A nuclear submarine reached the North Pole in 1958 in the fashion described by Verne.

Above water, Verne anticipated the development of the hydrophobe; then, he took us back under to submersible housing and laboratories. These "submarine towns," of which Captain Nemo dreamed, would not become reality until ninety-nine years later. In 1969, four scientist-aquanauts lived for two months in submersible dwellings off the island of St. John in the Virgin Islands.

Verne saw the ocean as a limitless resource for mankind, capable of providing food for the starving and medicine for the infirm. He studied cellular rejuvenation and the regeneration of entire limbs, which in his day was termed *"redintegration,"* applicable to certain species of fish (e.g., starfish). Additionally, Verne warned of the extinction of certain species and the effect this would have on our oceans and in turn, on us.

Verne invited mankind to domesticate whales and dolphins so as to use them symbiotically as a shepherd uses a sheepdog. This concept is unveiled via his character Professor Arannax, who suggests exactly that in *Twenty Thousand Leagues Under the Sea*. Farfetched? Visit any Sea World in the United States to catch a glimpse of the domestication of, and the communication with, whales and dolphins. Communicating with marine life is part of a continuing, serious study by the militaries of several nations. For example, during the 2003 war with Iraq, the United States used dolphins to clear underwater mine fields. Images of these dolphins in action were televised worldwide. And for those of us who are old enough, who can forget the popular television show of the 1960s, *Flipper*?

In 1943, another Frenchman fulfilled yet more Verne predictions. The world-famous explorer, Jacques-Yves Cousteau, helped invent the aqualung, precursor of the self-contained underwater breathing apparatus (scuba), and used it to excavate a vessel under the Mediterranean Sea near the island of Grand Congloué. In 1959, Cousteau invented the first small, submersible, battery-powered diving saucer, propelled by jets of water, which safely submerged a crew of two down one thousand feet. Perhaps more significantly, however, Cousteau lived for what Verne wrote about: sea exploration, the wonderment of marine life, and the need for mankind to live in harmony with nature.

In 1963, the United States lost a brand new nuclear-powered submarine, the *Thresher*, 220 miles east of Cape Cod, Massachusetts, with 129 crew members on board. It took one and a half years for a Navy search team to locate her resting eight thousand feet down.

The search required a Verne-like bathyscaphe, the *Trieste II,* to locate her.

In 1986, the world marveled at the discovery and subsequent exploration of the *Titanic,* which sank in 1912 carrying more than fifteen hundred passengers to their death. The *Titanic* lies at 41° 46′ N, 50° 14 W′ in the Atlantic Ocean. In fact, *Time Magazine's* cover story of August 11, 1986, is replete with Verne's predictions in operation. For example, only submersibles envisioned by Verne could submerge to this depth and capture the wreck via Verne-like cameras. The deepest recorded dive occurred on January 21, 1960, when Jacques Picard and Lt. Donald Walsh dove in the *Trieste* down to a depth of thirty-five thousand feet, or the equivalent of ten Empire State Buildings stacked one on top of the other. Verne's Captain Nemo holds the record at 52,800 feet.

Verne's visions included submarine warfare, electric stoves with heating coils, electric generators, electric high-beam searchlights, and even seaweed cigarettes. In his recently discovered *Paris in the Twentieth Century,* written in 1863, he describes automobiles, elevated trains, fax machines, and the advent of the typewriter. While current critics agreed with his original publisher that the work was not fit for printing, it is interesting that even his worst, which was published in 1996 in more than thirty languages, including English, earned millions.

Like a jewel in a beautiful setting, Verne saw the sparkling gem of science and set it among novel and interesting characters for the enjoyment and education of adults and children alike. Verne shaped like a gem-cutter some of mankind's most enduring dreams: to walk on the moon, to explore space, to investigate the Earth's core, to discover Atlantis, to probe the seas, and finally, to communicate and live in harmony with marine life. Clearly, Verne's visions are not just for children, and they are as relevant today as they have ever been.

Translating Verne

Jules Verne has never been fully appreciated as an adult novelist, or for the most part, translated well in English due to a variety of causes deserving attention. According to several experts, who are highlighted below, he has been the victim of poor translations. Even Verne himself acknowledged that the translations of his day were poor.

- In 1874, Edward Roth, a Philadelphia schoolteacher, prepared a preface to Verne's moon novels in which he lamented that for six years "not a single work of Jules Verne issued from the American press, except *Five in a Balloon* ... containing so many ... mistakes ... it must have been done in a hurry." Although U. S. publishers promptly responded to the situation, Roth correctly observed that in their rush, they issued "hasty translations of Verne's works by English hands," which "through ignorance, incapacity ... or prejudice ... omitted some of Verne's best passages." (Miller, 1976, Forward, p.xx). Roth's solution unfortunately exacerbated the problem when he tried to "improve" on Verne by adding situations that were purely his own to the published Verne-Roth moon stories.

- In 1972, Jean Cheneaux noted that Europeans know a better "adult" Verne *in comparison* to Americans. In his *The Political and Social Ideas of Jules Verne*, he strongly laments this historical reality.

- In *Billion Year Spree: The True History of Science Fiction*, Brian W. Aldiss notes the poor quality of English translations, which "diminish his chance of better critical appraisal ... a good translation of his best novels might effect a re-evaluation of his vast *oeuvre* ...." (Miller, Afterword, P. 357). Miller observes that, "Some of Verne's best books are crudely abridged in English. Others are simply not yet available in our language. What is available is often badly translated, full of literary errors that are not Verne's. Passages omitted from these standard translations are often Verne's most heavily political, philosophical, and scientific. They include some of Verne's finest literary efforts, too. These cuts, often subtracting 30 to 40 percent of Verne's text from the English editions, naturally weaken his story line, his characterization, his humor, and the integrity of his ideas." (Miller, Forward, P. ix).

- In 1976, Professor Walter James Miller from New York University picked up on the underlying challenge of these authors. He wrote *The Annotated Jules Verne: Twenty Thousand Leagues Under the Sea* and *From the Earth to the Moon* and criticized the English translation of Lewis Page Mercier and Eleanor E. King. Just for *Twenty Thousand ...* Miller made six hundred annotations, adding up to a 23 percent longer and far more accurate text than anyone had previously produced. Although Mercier graduated from Oxford University, spoke French, and was considered highly intelligent, Professor Miller demonstrates that Verne's grasp and control of the French language was, simply put, far beyond the translation capabilities of Mercier. In fact, Professor Miller notes that Verne's writing challenged even the educated elite of Europe. Professor Miller's work has been widely admired and is considered by many to be the finest translation and restoration of Verne's writings ever undertaken. In Professor Miller's own words, "Hence today we have, ironically, at least two kinds of translations of Verne—some that give us less than Verne wrote and some that give us more." (Miller, Forward, P. xx).

Since Professor Miller's work on Verne, there has been a resurgence of interest all over the world in Verne's novels, especially in the English-speaking world. Hopefully with this renewed interest will come better translations of his works. Although our work may be criticized for not being a pure translation of *Mathias Sandorf I and II*, it was never meant to be; it is an adaptation.

- In 1886, George Hanna published the first English translation of *Mathias Sandorf I and II* with Sampson, Low, Marston, Searle, and Rivington. The most recent English Version was done by Edward Brumgnach in 2005. Wesleyan UP will publish in its "Early Classics of Science Fiction" series in 2010. In itself, this appears to imply Hanna's work was lacking. We have yet to see how the reviews of the newest work will unfold.

Discovering Verne

Prior to his death in 1905, Verne destroyed most of his private papers and letters, leaving little in the way of autobiographical writings. The only "official biography" of Verne was written by his niece, Marquerite Allotte de la Fuye, in 1928. Allotte alone had access to Verne's remaining papers and incomplete final novels. In *Jules Verne: Sa Vie, Son Oeuvre* (his life, his works), Allotte approached Verne's life chronologically in tandem with most, but not all, of his works. Unfortunately, because it was published twenty-three years after Verne's death, it is unclear which characters and works *he* thought were his greatest. This presents a considerable challenge of proving *Mathias Sandorf I and II* is Verne's greatest novel. Although much is known about Verne, there are things about him that people may be unaware of. Verne was a private, reticent, and sensitive man. He wore a mask in social and even family life, saving his deepest feelings, opinions, hopes, and fears for his writing. His closest friends corroborate this in Allotte's biography of Verne. She notes his mysterious side is very secret ("son coin de mystére est fort secret"), but nothing would make of him an outgoing person ("mais rien fera de lui un expansif"); and he had a blend of coolness and sensitivity ("mélange de froideur et de sensibilite"). Allotte discusses Verne's sensitivity, claiming he had too much and he masked it ("Il en avait trop. Il la masquait"). Allotte also reveals that Verne expressed himself through his characters.

Allotte's biography has been criticized as distorting historical facts, such as when she makes no mention of who shot Verne in 1866, relegating this to an "accident," when in fact he was shot in the leg by his own nephew, Gaston Verne. Allotte also makes no mention of Verne's mistress, perhaps trying to protect some family secrets.

We know from various sources that, in order to remain in Paris close to the literary circle he admired, Verne misled his own father, Pierre. Pierre Verne believed Jules would take up law and financed his studies accordingly. Earlier in life, Pierre boarded the ship *Coralie* and told Jules he could not go to sea. Jules was thirteen. It was at this time that Jules promised the family to have adventures only of the mind: I'll no longer travel except in my dreams (*Je ne voyagerai plus qu'en rêve*) (Allotte, 1928, P. 22).

Allotte underscores how Verne often drew from his contemporaries, his own past, personal travels, and life. This is very important for the understanding of the unique place *Mathias Sandorf I and II* held in Verne's heart. Several examples of Verne's propensity to draw from reality come to mind.

- When Jules and his brother Paul crossed the Atlantic Ocean on the *Great Eastern* steamship in 1867, Verne reportedly took copious notes and asked numerous questions of the crew. Remember that the *Great Eastern* was in the process of laying the cross-Atlantic cable. Thus, divers recounted to Verne their sights at the bottom of the ocean. This was converted by Verne into two of his novels, *Twenty Thousand Leagues Under the Sea* (1870) and *A Floating City* (1871) (Allotte, 1928, p. 84).

- Verne's close friend Felix Tournachon was a photographer interested in aerial photographs, and he built a balloon to that end. The cartoonist Honoré Daumier sketched a famous printed caricature of Felix, high in a balloon above Paris snapping pictures with a camera. Tournachon had a pseudonym, Nadar, which, according to experts, became the anagram for Verne's character Michael Ardan (Allotte, 1928, p.88), who conquers the skies in the lighter-than-air gondola in *Five Weeks in a Balloon* in 1863. Verne went airborne again in a balloon with his characters in *The Mysterious Island* in 1875.

- Verne drew from contemporary life when he wrote *Master of the World* (1904), which was published just one year after Orville Wright's historic flight of December 17, 1903. In fact, Robur, the main character in *Master of the World*, appeared in *The Clipper in the Clouds* (1886), published well before that historic flight.

- Upon the death of his brother, Paul, in 1897, Verne wrote *Les Frères Kip* (*The Kip Brothers*) in his memory (Allotte, 1928, p. 202).

- Verne's warm friendship with the famous cave explorer Charles Sainte-Claire led to yet another great adventure story, *Voyage to the Center of the Earth* (1865).

- To support a permanent circus in the city of Amiens, Verne resurrected two great characters from *Mathias Sandorf II* (who were originally in a circus)—Pescade and Matifou—in *Petit Bonhomme* (1891).

- Verne's desire to go to sea as a youth is reflected in *Capitaine de Quinze Ans* (*Captain at Fifteen*) in 1878 and *Around the World in Eighty Days* in 1873. This latter sea voyage novel may well confuse American readers who have seen the motion picture with the same name. This motion picture was originally produced by Michael Todd, starring David Niven and the great Mexican comedian Cantinflas. What most Americans never realized was that, under poetic license, Mr. Todd actually merged two Verne books into one. That's right! *Five Weeks in a Balloon,* written in 1863, was merged with the 1873 steamship voyage of *Around the World in Eighty Days*. In addition, characters have been completely annihilated, a ship substituted by a balloon, ten years magically blurred, and a limited exploration of Africa converted into a tour of the world.

- Other sea adventures attesting to Verne's personal travels include *Les Enfants du Capitaine Grant, The Adventures of Captain Hatteras,* and *A Floating Island.*

Beyond his novels, Verne's personal life is replete with his love for the sea. For example, Verne was born on an island, Feydeau, in the harbor at Nantes. Islands are in many of Verne's works. The island Verne was born on has been described as "looking like a ship churning through the waters." In speaking of the bay where he berthed his yacht, Allotte says, "Jules Verne adores that bay" (*Jules Verne adore cette baie*) (Allotte, 1928, p.114). Allotte writes of "his nest upon the waves" (*son nid dans les vagues*). During his life, Verne purchased three yachts, naming them all after his only son, Michel—the *Saint Michel I, II,* and *III*. After several weeks on land at Amiens, Verne wrote to the shipbuilder Babin, who was at the time outfitting Verne's third yacht, "I already have an overpowering desire to see my *Saint Michel* again" (*J'ai déjà une envie furieuse de revoir mon Saint-Michel*) (Allotte, 1928, p. 157). For Verne "breathes with the sea, she is to him like a living being, he notes her character and physical attributes" (*respire avec la mer,* comme *elle est il en note le caractère et pour lui en être vivant, la physiologie*). Whenever he was able, Verne wrote aboard his yacht: "The imaginative things he wrote of, sitting on a seaweed mattress on the *Saint Michel*" (*L'imaginatif qui 'ecrit, assis sur le matelas de varech du Saint-Michel*).

When one compares Verne's love for the sea with that of his characters, it is impossible to separate Verne from them. Captain Nemo remarks: "Professor, is not this ocean gifted with real life? (*Voyez cet océan! N'est-il pas d'une vie réele*) (Miller, 1976, p.115). The intimate connection between Verne and his characters with respect to their shared love for the sea is best captured in *Mathias*

Sandorf I and II and in *Twenty Thousand ....* In *Twenty Thousand ...,* in a quote regarding Captain Nemo, "He exploits, with Nemo, the infinite domain of the seas" (*Il exploite, avec Nemo, le domaine infini des eaux*). In fact, Verne himself wrote, "If I am not always that which I should be, my characters will be that which I would like to be" (*Si je ne suis pas, toujours, ce que je devrais être, mes personages seront ce que je voudrais être*) (Allotte, 1928, p.151). Dr. Fournier wrote that Verne's personality was intangible. "His real self is in his novels" (*Son vrai lui est dans ses livres*) (Allotte, 1928, p.211).

Exploring this symbiotic relationship with his characters even further brings us to an 1854 photograph of Jules Verne taken by his friend Nadar. In the now-famous pose, Verne has his arms crossed on his breast. This pose is identical to that of both Professor Aronnax and Captain Nemo (as can be seen in the engraving in the original edition of *Twenty Thousand ...* in 1870). We know Verne modeled for the engraving artist, Riou, in that pose, and this pose appears in his works. For example, Professor Aronnax assumes this pose when he looks from the deck and reflects nostalgically: "I devoured with eagerness the soft foam which whitened the sea as far as the eye could reach" (Miller, 1976, p.27). And when one of Nemo's sailors dies saving him, the unforgettable undersea burial includes Nemo standing, "with his arms crossed on his breast ... in prayer" (Miller, 1976, p.168). Thus, we see several facets of Verne's own nature in both of these characters.

Professor Miller documents how "Aronnax, like his creator, Verne, is a great lover of figures of speech and of classification." Here, Verne pays homage to his own father, who possessed these traits. Then, Professor Miller highlights "Verne's autobiographical delight in his writing as manifest in the passages devoted to New York." In *Twenty Thousand ...,* Professor Aronnax receives a telegram from the Fifth Avenue Hotel. Verne and his brother stayed at the Fifth Avenue Hotel after arriving in New York on the *Great Eastern* (Miller, 1976, p.13).

Verne developed hundreds of characters. However, we need not seek him out in all sixty-five novels. There are a select few characters Verne identified with the most. According to Allotte, "At that time in his life, Jules Verne is not at all sorry to be Nemo (*Twenty Thousand* ... 1870), *Antékirtt* (emphasis ours; *Mathias Sandorf* 1885), Michel Ardan (*Five Weeks*, 1863), Robur Master (1904)" (À cet âge de sa vie, Jules Verne n'est point fâché d'être le Nemo, *l'Antékirtt*, le Michel Ardan, le Robur ...) (Allotte, 1928, p.155).

Here, Allotte, who chronogically noted roughly twenty novels, violated her own approach. Allotte should have listed Ardan first since *Five Weeks* ... was published in 1863. Nemo chronologically arrives in 1870 in *Twenty Thousand....* Then come Antékirtt and Robur. Why does she list Verne's top four out of sequence as published? Perhaps we will never know. At any rate, Antékirtt is the secret identity of Mathias Sandorf. However, in our adaptation, this name does not appear at all. Why? We decided to transpose the *Count of Monte Cristo* revenge-after-twenty-years plot. In so doing, our hero Mathias Sandorf returns after twenty years not knowing who his enemies are. As a returning hero of the Austrian revolution, Mathias Sandorf is targeted for death by his old enemies. As their efforts fail, our hero uncovers who the enemies of a free Austria are.

In America, the combination of secrecy during his life, the delay of twenty-three years for the first biography with its noted liabilities, the litany of abuses by translators who added and subtracted, the indifference of publishers, and the cinematic liberties taken all converge for a very clouded picture of Verne. These factors also leave open the quest for Jules Verne's greatest science-fiction work. Can we accept Allotte's choice for first place? We think not. Our analysis, which follows, will introduce the character who is closest to Verne, drawn from reality and the one Verne most admired—Mathias Sandorf.

Jules Verne's Greatest Novel

The dedication of *Mathias Sandorf I and II* by Jules Verne to Alexander Dumas Jr. in memory of Alexander Dumas Sr., who died in 1870, is the strongest piece of evidence that this was his greatest novel. This is the only such dedication of all sixty-five novels. Within the dedication, Verne underscores in his own words that *Mathias Sandorf* is his *Monte Cristo* of extraordinary travel adventures. Dumas Sr. was the author of the original *Count of Monte Cristo*. Indeed, while Dumas wrote many other great works, his greatest was this one. In accepting the dedication, A. Dumas Jr. indicates the unique relationship between his father, A. Dumas Sr., and Jules Verne when he writes that "literarily speaking, you are more his son than I" (Verne, 1885, Book II, p.1). A. Dumas Jr. was well aware that his father served as a literary father figure for Verne. We shall explore this further to add weight to the importance of both Verne's declaration and dedication.

When Jules Verne was a twenty-year-old law student in Paris, he enjoyed the hospitality of the Dumas family, especially A. Dumas Sr.'s cooking. A. Dumas Sr. fancied himself to be quite a chef. At this time in history, Dumas Sr. was enjoying the fame and fortune associated with having written *The Count of Monte Cristo* and the three novels of *The Three Musketeers* (1843), the sequel, *Twenty Years After* (1845), and *Le Vicomte de Bragelonne* (1848). Dumas Sr. was at the pinnacle of literary success and held the distinguished position of director of the *Théâtre-Historique de Paris*. At this time, this theater was one of the most celebrated in the world. For the premiere of the play *The Three Musketeers*, Verne's own words capture his enthusiasm best: "I just saw the premiere of *The Three Musketeers*. I was in the Dumas box." And: "It's truly a delight to be in direct contact with literature" (*C'est vraiment un plaisir d'être en contact immediate avec la literature*) (Allotte, 1928, p.35).

Allotte has described Verne's reaction to this experience as "completely glorious" (*tout glorieux*). Equally interesting is Allotte's insight that "already, Jules Verne dreams of being performed at the

Théâtre-Historique thanks to the friendship of A. Dumas Sr." ("*Déjà, Jules réve d'être joué au Théâtre-Historique, grace à L'amitie du père Dumas*) (Allotte, 1928, p.36). Allotte informs us further that "for this purpose, he prepares some far-reaching works.... He counts least on a verse act ..." (*a cet effect, il prepare des oeuvres de grand envergure ... Il compte moins sur un acte en vers ...*) (Allotte, 1928, p.36). When Verne presented these works to A. Dumas Sr., it was *Les Pailles Rompues* (*Broken Straws*), which was world premiered by A. Dumas Sr. on June 12, 1850, when Verne was only twenty-two years old. Other works followed—*Les Savants* and *Qui Me Rit*—which were also shared with A. Dumas Sr., according to Allotte. A. Dumas Sr. enjoyed the latter work so much that he broke out in a hearty laughter. He endorsed it wholeheartedly.

Around this time, Jules concluded his law studies. His father Pierre sent for him to return home, expecting him to initiate his law practice. Jules lovingly and respectfully declined. In effect, Jules turned away from a solid, guaranteed profession with financial stability. His father disapproved and would repeatedly insist that Jules had made a tragic mistake and should reconsider his decision. But Jules Verne was compelled to write, and he would repeatedly find support and encouragement from A. Dumas Sr. Indeed, he discussed and sought guidance from A. Dumas Sr. relative to what became Verne's trademark and signature formula for success. He asked A. Dumas Sr. what he thought about combining the scientific inquiries of his day, the future, and great adventure characters, and how the public might receive this. A. Dumas Sr. declared "the idea of his young friend as great. The latter was strengthened in his resolve" (*immense l'idée de son jeune ami. Celui-ci est reaffermi dans son dessin*) (Allotte, 1928, p.44). Thus, we know A. Dumas Sr. changed Verne's life while encouraging him to believe in himself and his own unique literary vision, which has delighted the world for well over one hundred years.

Later in life, as Verne captured the imagination of a world-wide audience, A. Dumas Jr. nominated Verne to be a candidate for *l'Académie* (one of forty immortals charged with producing the official French dictionary and preserving the language). Allotte reminds us that this came just on the heels of Verne's greatest success in France, the publication in 1885 of *Mathias Sandorf I and II*. While Verne declined the honor, this moment marked a peak period in his literary life. Therefore, it deserves special attention. While experts agree, we find that Allotte has best captured this when she notes: "In the eyes of the witnesses of his life, the period, which extends from 1872 to 1886, was the zenith of Jules Verne's fame and fortune" (*Aux yeux des témoins de sa vie, la période, qui s'étend de 1872 `a 1886, fut l'apogée de la gloire et de la fortune de Jules Verne*) (Allotte, 1928, p.147). Importantly, a careful review demonstrates that Verne produced nearly twenty volumes during this timeframe. Allotte underscores that his writing was at "its full tide" (*sa meilleure veine*) and that "he is at the crest of his life" (*il est au sommet de sa vie*) (Allotte, 1928, p.172). Verne himself recognizes this when he writes: "My life is full, no room for boredom. It's nearly all that I could ask for." (M*a vie est pleine, aucune place pour l'ennui. C'est à peu près tout ce que je demande*) (Allotte, 1928, p.147). Thus, A. Dumas Sr. was at the start of Verne's career and a great supporter until he passed away. The "Dedication" in *Mathias Sandorf I and II* both honors the memory of his greatest literary backer and contains Verne's own declaration that this is his greatest novel.

Inside *Mathias Sandorf I and II*

In our quest for documentation that would prove *Mathias Sandorf I and II* is Verne's greatest novel, we additionally decided to examine the character Verne most admired. Would we find Verne within this adventure? We were not disappointed in the least that *Mathias Sandorf I* opens in the bay of Trieste (*au bord de cette baie*). This plunges us into the setting where Verne was most at home—his birthplace in a port city and the berth location of his beloved *Saint Michel* yacht. *Mathias Sandorf II* opens with "The Mediterranean is beautiful" (*La Méditerranée est belle*) (Verne, Jules, *Mathias Sandorf II*, p.1). Verne's love for the sea has been noted earlier. These locations are reflective of Verne's own soul and spirit of sea adventures.

Mathias Sandorf I chapter 1 begins with "A Messenger Pigeon" (*Le Pigeon Voyageur*). We believe it is not a stretch of the imagination to see Verne's fascination with flight so pronounced in so many novels. However, a second strong possibility is apparent. We believe Verne drew a parallel with the reality of his time. In order to circulate quickly Verne's latest writings, his publisher, Pierre Hetzel, developed a messenger-pigeon service on November 8, 1874, eleven years before Verne wrote *Mathias Sandorf I and II*. During Verne's prime the demand for his work was feverish to say the least. We then examined the lead character, Mathias Sandorf. Was he real or fictional? In 1884, Verne sailed into the Mediterranean on his *Saint Michel III*. While in Italy, Verne met the archduke of Austria, Louis Salvadore de Toscane, brother of a banished prince whose pseudonym was Jean Orth. This prince disappeared for many years, giving rise to much speculation. Could Louis Salvadore be Étienne Bathory, the "direct descendant of a line of Magyar princes"? Could Salvadore's exile relate to the twenty years Mathias Sandorf is away from Austria? Louis Salvador spent most of his life aboard his own lavish yacht, *La-Nixe*. Thus, both Salvador and Verne were yachtsmen. However, Salvador refused to set foot on Austrian soil while Prussia (today, Germany) ruled her. This self-imposed exile was not at all unlike Verne's own experience aboard his first yacht when he patrolled the coast of France during Prussia's invasion of both France and Austria. We find that Salvador and Verne became close friends and communicated from 1884 until Verne's death in 1905. One letter of 1904 notes: "Salvador always writes me" (*Salvador m'écrit toujours*) (Allotte, 1928, p.191).

Louis Salvador also shared Verne's fascination with the sea. Salvador was the author of a document that charted the Baleric Islands, a province of Spain in the Western Mediterranean. The islands included Ibiza, Mallorca, and Minorca. Verne wanted to have the document published with credit going to Salvador. Notably, it is the Mediterranean Sea that serves as the home of Salvador and the setting for *Mathias Sandorf I and II*. Verne's own nostalgic love of the Mediterranean was best captured fifteen years earlier in *Twenty Thousand* ... when Verne wrote: "The Mediterranean, the blue sea *par excellence,* the great sea of the Hebrews, the sea of the Greeks, the mare nostrum of the Romans ... embalmed with the perfume of the myrtle...a perfect battlefield in which Neptune and Pluto still dispute the empire of the world!" (Miller, 1976, p.224).

Salvador and Verne shared a common enemy—Prussia. While *Mathias Sandorf I and II* deals with Prussia as oppressor of Austria in the novel, we can easily discern a parallel from Verne's personal life. Remember that on July 19, 1870, war broke out in Europe, pitting France and Austria against Prussia. With a, "Good-bye, Dad!" (*Au revoir, papa!),* Verne was called up for coast-guard duty. His first yacht, the *Saint-Michel I,* was overhauled and outfitted with a cannon. Moreover, twelve soldiers were placed on board. From the Crotoy Bay Verne loved (*J'aime cette baie*), he patrolled the North Sea on lookout for Prussian vessels. Verne wrote of this time: "We shall therefore be able to give the Prussians one hell of a trouncing" (*Nous allons donc pouvoir donner une bonne rossée aux Prussiens).* "I am still in Crotoy ... the Prussians have the deplorable custom of burning and pillaging the countryside" (*Je suis toujours au Crotoy .... Les Prussiens prennent la déplorable habitude de brûler et de piller les campagnes).* Here, Verne was reflecting on how glad he was that his own wife and children were in the city of Amiens. When Paris came under siege, Verne lost friends and relatives. Even his publisher, Pierre Hetzel, and Hetzel's son fought at the barricades. Meanwhile, the royal family of Austria was banished, providing Verne with strong personal motives for respecting and also memorializing Louis Salvador in *Mathias Sandorf I and II.*

Real and Imagined Cruises (Croisières Réelles et Chimériques)

This is the title Allotte gave to chapter 18 of her biography of Verne. She was very much aware that Verne's third yacht—with which he sailed into the Mediterranean Sea in 1884, just prior to writing *Mathias Sandorf I and II*—had been commissioned by the Marquis de Preaulex. However, this was to be the third luxury yacht for this seventy-year-old Marquis, and it was being prepared in Nantes by the very best shipbuilder in France, Babin. Upon learning it was for sale, Verne concluded the deal in just twenty minutes (Allotte, 1928, p.157). However, it would take two more years of construction to make her seaworthy. Allotte claims that Verne placed his own yacht into the novel *Mathias Sandorf*: "His *Saint-Michel* is embellished, expanded, improved, and becomes the *Ferrato*, the amazing yacht of Doctor Mathias Sandorf" (... *son Saint-Michel s'embellit, s'amplifie, se perfectionne, et deviant le Ferrato, yacht mirifique du docteur Mathias Sandorf*). Allotte goes on to say: "Here, Jules's imagination soars and the sumptuous interior of the *Ferrato* leaves the casual elegance of the *Saint-Michel* far behind" (*Ici, l'imagination de Jules se donne librement carrière et le faste intérieur du Ferrato laisse loin en arrière les sobres élégances du Saint-Michel*) (Allotte, 1928, p.158). The only entire chapter in Allotte's biography devoted to one of Verne's novels is this chapter. Thus, more evidence of the importance of *Mathias Sandorf I and II* is underscored by Verne's biographer.

During his voyage into the Mediterranean Sea, Verne was at the peak of his popularity and at almost every port, he was feted and toasted by governors, royalty, and hundreds of people. He was greeted with lavish parties and shown numerous sights that stirred his imagination (Allotte, 1928, p.168). As we know, he made copious notes and even rough sketches. Upon returning to Paris, 110 of his sketches were refined and incorporated as graphics in the first publication of *Mathias Sandorf I and II*.

At Malta, Verne was not only celebrated but also taken on a tour of the worst "quarter," known as the Manderaggio. It is here that Verne saw the incredible mix of peoples of the Mediterranean Basin, some of whom became key characters in *Mathias Sandorf I and II*, such as Andrea, Luigi and Maria Ferrato, Sarcany, Zirone, and Carpena. At Algiers, the bay itself forms a large and a small peninsula well known even today as Pointe Pescade (small) and Pointe Matifou (large)—and, again, two more characters are drawn from real life (Allotte, 1928, p.169).

On the sea, Verne almost perished due to a great storm that actually sank another craft. Only the arrival of a pilot ship kept his *Saint Michel III* from being dashed upon the reefs. In *Mathias Sandorf I and II,* a ferocious storm serves as the backdrop for Mathias Sandorf's escape from Pisino Prison. Later, a Mediterranean storm assails the *Ferrato*, driving the vessel onto a reef. So, it is clear that Verne incorporated his experiences during the Mediterranean voyage into *Mathias Sandorf I and II* (Allotte, 1928, p.168). Verne notes a severe storm which Miller labels a tsunami or tidal wave initiated by an earthquake (Miller, 1976, p.334).

Allotte also notes the special audience granted by Pope Leo XIII. Since Verne was born and raised as a practicing Catholic, he was particularly touched by the words of the Pope. In fact, the Pope brought tears to Verne's eyes, complimenting the author on the "purity, the moral and spiritual merit" (*pureté, la value morale et spiritualiste*; (Allotte, 1928, p.169) of his works. Many of these qualities undergird the heroes of *Mathias Sandorf I and II.*

The Adaptation of *Mathias Sandorf I and II*

Our adaptation reflects numerous additional Verne experiences and desires as well as predictions not generally known in America. Even when we deliberately veered from the original text, we developed Vernian themes and expanded on them. For example, Verne wrote in a much earlier novel, "Why could we not share the life of the fish that populate the liquid element, or better yet, the life of the amphibians who, for hours on end, can live on land or at sea, as their whim determines?" (Miller, 1976, p.220). In our work, Chinese characters swim often with fish and other marine life, and for long periods of time. Verne was personally aware through direct experiences that fish species communicate with great ability and over great distances. For example, Verne wrote of hundreds of a fish species called Argonauts: "As if at a signal the whole fleet disappeared under the waves. Never did the ships of a squadron maneuver with more unity … several times ten or twelve whales united tried to crush the Nautilus by their weight" (Miller, 1976, p.273).

We know that Verne catalogued numerous species of fish during his life and conversed with hundreds of travelers and explorers about marine life. We also know Verne was fascinated with giant sea creatures, which are featured in his novels. For example, Verne wrote about the Kraken, a giant squid that, at the end of the twentieth century, was discovered by scientists, who thought they were extinct. Verne described it as "the largest and most surprising of all the animal creation." Verne wrote about the narwhal, which was hunted for its ivory tusk and oil. Its hard-as-steel ivory tusk had been taken from the bottom of pierced ships. Verne wrote about cachalots, with the male of this species having zebra-like stripes on the back of its head. Verne wrote about the manta ray, with its white belly and gray-spotted back. Verne wrote about mollusks, some of which form pearls, and electric eels. All of these sea creatures are featured in *Mathias Sandorf I and II*.

Verne even wrote of a man with desirable amphibious qualities in *Twenty Thousand....* He named him Nicholas of Cape Matapan, surnamed Pesca (the fish), well known in all the Cyclades. Verne described him as "A bold diver. Water is his element, and he lives more in it than on land, going from one island to another, even as far as Crete" (Miller, 1976, p.220). Our work features cranial expansion during a ritual that permits for maximizing the brain's power so as to communicate with fish. Thus, our work embraces Verne's "man of the waters ... genie of the sea ..." the label Allotte gave to Captain Nemo (Allotte, 1928, p.121.) Additional evidence that *Mathias Sandorf I and II* reflects Verne's life presents itself if we are open to it. Take, for example, the first attempt to kill Mathias Sandorf. In this scheme, the merchant ship *Trabaculo* is deliberately launched ahead of schedule to assassinate our hero while making it appear to be an accident. Only the amazing strength of Verne's Herculean Matifou keeps Dr. Sandorf's yacht from destruction. Here, we believe Verne drew from his own personal experience once again. Verne knew firsthand of the numerous incidents that befell the *Great Eastern* on which he sailed, including sabotage. The *Great Eastern* also suffered a launching accident, which took weeks to clean up, thus delaying Verne's voyage to the United States (Allotte, 1928, p.116-119).

How far need we travel to see in the trio comprised of Pierre Bathory, Matifou, and Pescade, the parallel to *The Three Musketeers*, written by A. Dumas Sr., a man he admired so much? Surely, one would not ascribe this portion of his literary adventure purely to coincidence.

Even more relevant Vernian themes are manifest in our adaptation. For instance, as mentioned earlier, Verne was a student of *"redintegration,"* now known as the regeneration of tissues and limbs. Before 2001, cellular rejuvenation of heart tissue was considered impossible (Altman, NY Times, June 17, 2001). In *Mathias Sandorf I and II,* the restoration of an entire limb and the brain operation on Pierre Bathory simply apply Verne's vision of the possibilities in this area.

Verne ascribed to the ideas of his good friend Arthur Mangum, of the French Academy, relative to "the laws of harmony and equilibrium." In our adaptation, we introduce the Chinese "Chung and Ho," similarly "Yin and Yang." Verne was also fascinated with islands and coral reefs. Early in life, one of Verne's teachers believed her husband was a castaway on some deserted island, a recurring theme in many of Verne's novels, including *L'École des Robinsons, A Floating City, L'île à Hélice,* and *L'île Mystérieuse.* Moreover, we know that one of Verne's favorite novels was *Robinson Crusoe.*

Finally, we note that the special Verne pose discussed earlier, with arms crossed on his breast, emerges twice in *Mathias Sandorf I and II.* Of all sixty-five novels written by Verne, it is *Mathias Sandorf I and II,* drawn largely from his personal life, that he was closest to and that he declared in his "Dedication" as his greatest work. Scholars can pick from among his many novels. Some may wish to cite readership, money earned, or choose a personal favorite. However, on what basis can we dismiss the evidence provided here relative to Verne's being so integrated with *Mathias Sandorf I and II?* In the years following the publication of *Mathias Sandorf I and II,* he never claimed any other work as his *"Monte Cristo* of extraordinary science-fiction adventures."

Conclusion

We would be misleading our readers if we suggested that our adaptation was a scholarly word-for-word translation of the original. It is not and was never intended to be so. Since our work was never intended to meet that standard, we decided to present the characters and the action in an easy-to-read sentence structure throughout. Our readers will find that they do not need a handy dictionary to enjoy the work, nor will they need to read lengthy descriptions of species, scientific terminology, geography, and events. We strove to emulate two styles of writing—that of Ernest Hemingway's approach in *The Old Man and the Sea*, and that of Ian Fleming's pictorial approach in his James Bond series. Where we adapted from the original, it was to reconcile situations, invert plot, introduce Vernian themes through new characters, avoid coincidences, and otherwise strive to maintain a fast-track focus on the action for a contemporary audience.

For example, in the original text, Verne has our hero dangling from a lightning-rod cable perched high atop Pisino prison during a fierce thunderstorm, with the roaring Foiba River below. Just then, Verne breaks from the action with a lengthy footnote on electrical currents and conduction. Verne's footnote elaborates how it is possible for a person to be electrocuted even at a presumed safe distance from a lightning bolt or rod. He then expands this footnote further by citing a real situation that occurred in 1753 when a man named Richemann was electrocuted. Then, the footnote continues with a detailed explanation of what happens when an electrical circuit is broken. Clearly, no such explanatory footnote is needed for a contemporary reader.

Another example of how we modified the original entails an eighteen-page, highly complicated deciphering of the secret coded message attached to the messenger pigeon in chapter 1. Verne, we know, was dazzled by ciphers. However, we substituted a simple Bible passage to trigger the action of the Austrian rebellion against Prussian occupation. Here again, we believed there should be no break in the action. Last, Verne takes his readers on a twelve-page tour of old and new Trieste of his era before describing the arrival of the messenger pigeon. Although we have eliminated this kind of detail from our adaptation, we kept great faith with Vernian themes, having been inspired by his wondrous visions and story-telling.

Many artists in various fields are not celebrated for the work that they themselves have chosen as their masterpiece. We believe that Verne has suffered a similar fate with *Mathias Sandorf I and II.*

We note that this character, Mathias Sandorf, was drawn from real life thirty years before the famous Von Trapp family fled Germany, giving rise to *The Sound of Music* film and introducing America to the beautiful settings of Austria. Today, the most popular tours in Austria are the locations of this story and film.

We hope that this adaptation of Jules Verne's *Mathias Sandorf I and II* will illuminate more of his convictions and evoke a better appreciation of our world, with a view to taking better care of the things in it. The future of mankind—our food, medicine, energy, and peace—may well rest on our ability to continue to heed the warnings within Verne's immortal science-fiction adventures.

Bibliography

Aldiss, Brian W. *Billion Year Spree: The True History of Science Fiction.* Garden City, New York: Doubleday and Company, Inc., 1973. Company, 1941.

Allotte De La Fűye, Marguerite. *Jules Verne Sa Vie, son Oeuvre.* Paris: Hachette, 1928.

Altman, Lawrence K. "Study Finds Heart Regenerates Cells," *New York Times.* New York: Thursday, June 7, 2001.

Chesneaux, Jean. *The Political and Social Ideas of Jules Verne.* Translated by Thomas Wikely. London: Thames and Hudson Limited, 1972.

Cousteau, Jacques-Yves. *The Ocean World of Jacques Cousteau.* New York: The World Publishing Company, 1973.

Miller, Walter James. *The Annotated Jules Verne Twenty Thousand Leagues Under the Sea.* New York: Thomas Y, Crowell Company, 1976.

More, Marcel. *Nouvelles Explorations de Jules Verne.* Paris: Gallimard, 1963.

Murphy, Jamie. "Voyages to the Bottom of the Sea," *Time Magazine.* New York: Time Inc., August 11, 1986.

Verne, Jules. Numerous Vernian and reference works.

1

A Messenger Pigeon

It was a clear afternoon in May of 1867, several miles north of Trieste, Austria. An emerald forest forms a link there with an Eastern spur of the Alps. Millions of evergreen pines converge into dense green foliage. There are no large beasts of prey, so these mossy woods teem with frolicking rabbits, foxes, squirrels, and deer that dart playfully among the conifers. Under the luxuriant foliage, the forest floor is carpeted with colorful flowers. Thousands of narcissus, lilies of the valley, primroses, hepatica, sunflowers, and morning-glories offer up fragrances that permeate the air. A joyous chorus of birds resounds through this glorious temple. The beautiful harmony beats on, like the pulse of eternity—until it is sacrilegiously interrupted.

The symphony reluctantly dies down. In its place is heard the beating and flapping of countless wings, rushing frightened upward, a rising flutter like an army on the march. Suddenly, streaking down out of the blinding sun at 180 miles per hour, six peregrine falcons tear into the flock of fleeing birds. These trained demons particularly chase after the beautiful feathered herons, flamingoes, and birds of paradise. They strike with clenched talons, ripping, slashing, and rending defenseless with the force of their impact.

The sky fills with bloodstained feathers. Death cries are cut short by the thud of falling bodies. Finally, a piercing whistle signals the massacre is over. Then silence prevails. The marauding falcons hover in the blue sky, the fierce orbs of their alert dark eyes contradicting their lofty bearing and nobility.

In a forest clearing below, fifteen aproned men busily collect the fallen birds with routine deftness, separating the feathers into large baskets. Trailing behind them are two bowmen, three women, and seven uniformed horsemen, their mounts richly harnessed. All but the two bowmen are gaily attired, as if they were on a Sunday picnic.

It was during the reign of Elizabeth I that feathers began to occupy an important place as accessories for women. Among the aristocracy of Austria, feather-gathering forays had become quite popular as a result. The women now busied themselves with the feathers, holding them up for inspection, giggling. One woman picked out a particularly attractive pair, while a second smiled in delight when she found matches for the pure white and jet-black male ostrich feathers adorning the brim of her hat. A third woman greedily snatched up more feathers and began attaching them to her already filled bonnet. Satisfied with the attentions of her two friends, she replaced her hat on her head with a flourish, evidently convinced she was beautiful. The horsemen, afraid of being considered discourteous, smiled dutifully.

The falconers blew their high-pitched whistles and the falcons began returning to their heavily gloved hands. Soft leather hoods called rufters covered each falcon's eyes, and soon the party was ready to depart. The two falconers dropped back and looked skyward, where a lone falcon stubbornly refused to obey the signal that the hunt was over. She hung in the air, her hooked bill toothed and notched, while far below, her master, Sarcany, narrowed his dark eyes. A fairly handsome man of twenty-five, he now looked cold and deadly. His Sicilian companion, Zirone, peered on with utter indifference.

Sarcany had no other name. He probably hailed from Tunisia or Tripoli, or some other North African region. Although his features were more white than black, no eye could discern on his face the inner stigma of contempt, dislike, and disgust that had bred within him a perpetual state of revolt against society. If physionomists claim—and they are right in most cases—that all deception shows against oneself in spite of cunning, Sarcany would give a categorical refutation to the proposition.

Looking at him, no one could tell what he was or what he had been. He did not provoke the aversion that greets thieves and rogues, and so he was more dangerous. His diverse experiences had taken him to many parts of the world and exposed him to a wide variety of people, including one of the wealthiest families of Trieste—that of Silas Toronthal, the banker.

Unlike the departing group, whose laughter may have been directed at him, Sarcany had a functional approach to his apparel. He dug his heel into the earth, as if to strike back at their laughter.

Zirone was thinner and shorter than Sarcany. A soldier of fortune, without faith of any kind and subservient to no law, Zirone was at the disposition of the first person who paid him well or the second who paid him better. He was as capable of giving bad advice as taking it, and certainly of assuring its execution. Where he was born he might have said, if he knew.

Some time ago, back in Sicily, the luck of a bohemian life had brought him together with Sarcany. Since then, they had stayed together through thick and thin, trying by hook and by crook to make one good fortune from their two bad ones. Zirone sported a full, cheerful, deep brown beard and a thick mat of dark hair. He had trouble concealing his natural deceitfulness, always betrayed by his half-closed eyes and swaying head. He wisely sought to conceal his true nature with constant chatter and a cheerful demeanor.

Today, Zirone sensed Sarcany's dark mood and spoke with considerable tact. Like a stoic sergeant, through gritted teeth, Zirone said, "Our luck is as bad as that falcon's hearing. You know what I'd like?"

"A girlfriend?" Sarcany replied.

Ignoring this jibe, Zirone continued, "I'd like to see your banker friend, Silas Toronthal, produce a fistful of money—a wad big enough to choke a horse. If we don't come up with some dough soon, our creditors are going to eat us alive, just like those falcons devoured those birds. Surely you know something that might give you a bargaining position, or a hold on that banker?"

Zirone noted carefully that Sarcany was still steely-eyed. "Listen to me well, Zirone. For the last time, I repeat, we can hope for nothing further from Silas Toronthal. He didn't become a successful banker by giving his money away. The few favors I did for him are filed under *accounts closed*. What I hold over him is best forgotten, since it would cause me even greater trouble. Besides, if I did have a grip on him, he'd already be paying capital, interest, and interest on the interest."

Sarcany looked up as if the subject had not changed. "As for the falcon, she hears better than you or I," he said. "She's as stubborn as a nagging wife."

During an all-night spree, with a last roll of the dice in a seedy gambling house, Lady Luck had turned her back on the pair, draining their purses. Providence was apparently in no hurry to come to their assistance, so they had decided to search for better luck by joining this excursion. They were motivated by the free lunch and the chance to make some interesting—if not immediately profitable—contacts.

Sarcany's thoughts now turned away from the previous night to the modest hotel near the Santa Maria Maggiore church, in the old part of Trieste, where they lodged. He was thinking of the hotelkeeper, who was yet unpaid and obviously annoyed by watching their debt grow day by day. A faint smile curled at the corner of his lip. "The hotelkeeper must be wondering how we have managed to stay out of his sight for an entire week now," he said.

Zirone smiled knowingly in response. He noticed a quick movement in Sarcany's eye and turned his attention in the direction of his gaze.

"Look," Sarcany cried. He pointed to a large cluster of trees as a small pigeon flew from behind them. The pigeon rose over the tree line above the clearing.

"That pigeon seems near exhaustion," Sarcany said. "See its erratic flight?"

Zirone now had the pigeon clearly in sight as it haltingly rose and dipped. Both men froze in the clearing as the pigeon rested briefly on the lower branches of a tree. In seconds, it was off again. The falcon too saw this plump, easy prey and began her deadly dive, intent on one more thrilling kill before her day came to an end.

A skilled archer, Sarcany quickly threaded his bow, took aim, and launched a pointed shaft that darted skyward with tremendous force. In the same instant the falcon struck the pigeon, grasping it in her claws, the arrow pierced her heart. It killed her instantly and brought both birds tumbling to the ground.

Zirone rushed to where the birds had fallen. With a perplexed look, he loosened the talons from the pigeon. "The pigeon lives," he said in amazement.

"Good. Hold him fast and look at his leg," said Sarcany as he stepped ruthlessly on the dead falcon, retrieving his arrow with a tug.

"Why, there's a message tied to its foot!" exclaimed Zirone.

"That's right," replied Sarcany. "This may well be the change in our luck we've been hoping for."

Zirone unfolded the note, and both men examined it with keen interest. The message it bore was written in some sort of code. There were five columns of letters and numbers:

G	E	L	N	D
2	J	R	2	S
2	K	2	C	E
N	E	J	2	P
E	S	I	J	L
E	D	H	J	A
O	J	M	N	H
Z	H	Z	M	

"Doesn't look like our luck's changing at all," Zirone muttered. "I can make no sense of it."

Sarcany examined the note shrewdly. "Were this a love note, there would be no change in our luck," he said. "But this message requires a cipher, codebook, or grille, which in these times means something interesting is afoot—and it might well be turned to our advantage. Treat the pigeon gently, Zirone, while I make a copy of this cipher."

Zirone examined the pigeon's wings, which he found to be without lesion or rupture. Sarcany took a small notebook and pencil from his pocket and busily duplicated the message.

A half-hour later, Sarcany and Zirone had fed the pigeon and refastened the note to its leg. Since the pigeon had been coming from the north it was most likely heading for Trieste. In order to know exactly where the pigeon was heading, they needed to be at the highest point overlooking the city. Therefore, they returned to the metropolis and ascended to the Cathedral of Trieste, perched on the highest hill. From their vantage point in the belfry, a panoramic view of old and new Trieste—the number one port city of the Austrian empire—stretched out before them. Wherever the pigeon flew they were sure to see its destination and learn the location of the recipient of the message. With a gentle caress, Zirone said, "Go now, little messenger pigeon. Show us the way to good fortune." Almost as if in reply, the pigeon cooed. Perhaps it was the pigeon's way of saying thanks for its rescue. Zirone released the bird, and it fell quickly. For a moment they feared it could no longer fly. Then the pigeon, with its long wings and powerful muscles, caught the wind and rose confidently straight out over the city. The pigeon's instinctive sense of direction took it toward its original destiny.

"Ha, ha!" exclaimed Zirone as he carefully watched the flying dot. The pigeon was silhouetted against the whole city, the crimson sun that descended slowly toward the azure waters of the Adriatic, and the clouds that hung like cream puffs.

Sarcany voiced his apprehension. "There is an outside chance the pigeon was not heading for Trieste but for some point further down the coast."

"I see it! I see it still! Look!" cried Zirone. The pigeon descended swiftly to the top of an elegant old house and disappeared into an attic window. The house was near the old hospital and the public garden of Bellini. This public garden, one of the most famous and beautiful in Europe, boasted a wide assortment of flowers, fancy slopes, running waters, and terraces shaded by neatly trimmed trees. Thousands of pigeons congregated here, ensuring that no one would notice one occasionally slipping in and out of a nearby residence.

It did not take long for the two men to find the house, after quickly crossing Trieste on foot. As they approached, they saw that the house was a feudal château. They noted the owner's name on the gatepost:

DOCTOR MATHIAS SANDORF

Careful not to arouse suspicion, they set up a vigil from the Bellini garden. The location offered them perfect cover, while providing an unimpaired view. Shortly, they noticed an elderly manservant leaving the house and returning about an hour later with Count Ladislaw Zathmar. Within minutes these men were followed into the house by Professor Étienne Bathory. But for the servant, whose name Sarcany did not know, the others were distinguished citizens of Trieste and easily identifiable. Sarcany had made it his business to know the landed gentry.

Satisfied with their vigil, Sarcany and Zirone returned to their residence, carefully avoiding their hotelkeeper. When they entered their room, they noticed that an envelope had been slipped under the door. As Sarcany opened it, he spoke calculatingly to Zirone, "Surely something is afoot. Dr. Mathias Sandorf is of high birth and one of the wealthiest men in Austria."

Sarcany started to laugh as he read the letter, fanning the money inside. He read it aloud for Zirone's sake: *"Here is enough money to cover your creditors, with a little left over to get you to Sicily. Leave, and I hope I never hear from you again."* It was signed only *S*, for Silas Toronthal.

"Good Lord!" cried Zirone. "One should never despair of men of finance."

"Precisely," Sarcany responded.

They were interrupted by the sound of a key turning in the door lock. The hotelkeeper entered with an air of confidence, having caught up with them at last. He was a short, stubby fellow, very neatly attired, the picture-perfect innkeeper. "So ..."

Before he could continue, Sarcany interjected, "Well, there you are! We thought you were on vacation. Zirone, I told you there is no other concierge in all of Europe with so big and trusting a heart as our hotelkeeper. A lesser man would certainly have demanded payment by now. We appreciate your patience."

Sarcany counted out the money they owed and pressed it in the stunned hotelkeeper's hand, then gently steered him out and quickly closed the door.

Zirone could not contain the laughter he'd been stifling; it sprayed forth in spite of his effort to cover his mouth. After settling down, Zirone inquired of Sarcany, "So then, we will use this money to leave Trieste?"

With a cunning look on his face, Sarcany replied, "No ... we'll stay!"

2

Mathias Sandorf

Dr. Mathias Sandorf was a Magyar who lived for one purpose only: to see his country, Austria, made free. His wealth derived from gold, silver, minerals, and precious stones from mines in the Central Alps and lead from Carinthia. Part of his fortune currently financed a revolution against the German occupation.

Dr. Mathias Sandorf was thirty-five years old. He was lean, yet muscular, with a proud and noble head. His face was warmed by a few well-worn wrinkles characteristic of his pure Magyar lineage. A perpetual smile played on his lips, and his firm, calm eyes signaled a frank and generous nature. It has been said that there exists a great analogy between the Magyar and the French character, and Mathias Sandorf was living proof. He was honest, just, and a devoted and loyal friend. He had not allowed his wealth to spoil him. At the University of Pesth, the Academy of Sciences at Presbourg, the Royal School of Mines at Schemnitz, and the Medical College of Terneswar, he had distinguished himself by graduating all his courses with highest praise—summa cum laude. A life of dedicated study had enhanced and solidified his natural qualities, making him a unique and very wholesome man. As a result, all those he met, especially his teachers, held him in the highest regard. Everyone respected him, and he had many friends throughout the country as well as abroad. But at present, his countenance betrayed the fact that his country was in turmoil.

The Franco-Italian War of 1859 had dealt a terrible blow to the Austrian army. Not only was Austria stripped of her Italian possessions but it was also subordinated to Germany, whose troops were everywhere. Italy offered to stay neutral in exchange for Venetia. Austria was at first too proud to make this sacrifice, but ultimately, it signed a treaty with Napoleon III on June 12, 1866, promising to surrender Venetia after the war.

Austria then had to fight a war on two fronts—the Seven Weeks' War. Although Archduke Albert won a barren victory over the Italians at Crustoza, the main Austrian army was completely routed by the Germans at Sadowa on July 3, 1866. By August 23, Austria surrendered in Prague. Only by the grace of Bismarck did Austria remain a great power. As a result of the war of 1866, Austria became the second "sick man of Europe". Austrians tried to retain their pride, but they had been dealt a devastating setback. Each Austrian patriot felt stigma in his or her blood.

The more extreme German nationalists, with the backing of the German Reich, proposed that Austria should become exclusively German in character. As with the Bach System of 1855, German bureaucrats tried to make Austria a centralized German state.

Originally, the approximately five million Austrians were made up of Egyptians, Tartars, Spaniards, Finns from the north, and the Huns of Attila. These origins were controversial but of little importance. What most mattered was that, by the 1800s, these people did not regard themselves as Slavs or Germans. They had practiced their own Catholic religion since the eleventh century; their language was developed in the fourteenth and sixteenth centuries; and they had evolved their own Tirolian customs. While their language was not as rich as German, it had already replaced Latin in their laws and ordinances. This language was their mother tongue: soft, harmonious, poetic, concise, and energetic. The Austrians were not about to give up their culture without a struggle.

On the heels of the German takeover, Dr. Mathias Sandorf was spared a quick death because of his exceptional skills as a surgeon, which had earlier kept him out of the military. He was also a member of a distinguished family and well loved by the average Austrian. The Germans believed they had enough problems without killing Dr. Sandorf and making him a martyr. Not wishing to offer the Germans a ready excuse to kill him, Dr. Sandorf had also wisely studied the developing political situation and had never stepped out of line. He was joined in his efforts by his wife, Savarena, who was also a Magyar. Equally dedicated to Austria's independence, Savarena was active in the underground movement, traveling from place to place with various groups. It was dangerous, but under the German occupation, everything was perilous. At present she was with a group of partisans in Pesth.

Trieste was the center of the underground movement. Many meetings were held there. Two of Dr. Sandorf's closest friends were Count Ladislaw Zathmar and Professor Étienne Bathory. Both were patriots like himself. They were older than Dr. Sandorf by fifteen years and had arrived at his home to finalize plans for the upcoming insurrection. The only other person in the house was a very old and loyal servant named Borik.

Étienne Bathory was a direct descendant of a line of Magyar princes who had occupied the throne during the sixteenth century. Since then, the family had been dispersed and lost in numerous intermarriages. It would have shocked his ancestors to know that one of their last descendants was a simple professor at the Academy of Sciences at Presbourg. He was, however, astute enough to resign when the Germans took over. Now, as a private teacher of teachers, he managed to live modestly with his wife and ten-year-old son in an apartment at Palazzo Modello (actually the Hotel Delorme) on the Grande Piazza.

Count Ladislaw Zathmar had retired from business and lived on a small estate at Lipto on the Danube River. He was a rugged-looking individualist, with lines of experience that clearly marked his face.

But when one looked closely, one could picture him as a clergyman, or even a saint, for he radiated goodness.

The group met in Dr. Sandorf's study, which was dominated by a large Elizabethan fireplace. Two walls were entirely covered by bookshelves, which, upon close inspection, would have revealed a broad, impressive collection of books. A large, hand-crafted mahogany table was bordered on three sides by a very comfortable French bombé sofa, a love seat, and two chairs with footstools. A rather impressive cabinet held one corner together. Heavy maroon drapes covered the two patio doors and a window at the side of the house facing the walled garden. A circular lamp hung from the ceiling with all of its candles lit. The marble floor evidenced the age of the house, and reflections from the flickering fire danced across it. An empty space where a painting used to hang was the only indication that something was missing. This space formerly held a portrait of the king of Austria that had been confiscated by the German army.

Étienne Bathory arrived late, having just sent his wife and son, Pierre, to France to visit Pierre's grandparents. He seemed to be lost in thoughts of them.

Count Ladislaw Zathmar asked, "How was your trip?" His tone made it obvious that he hoped all had gone well. Étienne Bathory's smile was all the reassurance he needed.

"All our messages have been received, and all is ready," Dr. Sandorf informed them. "The messenger pigeons need only carry the final signal and the hour, and all the partisans will rise up, to be followed by the people. Even our friends in Transylvania are eager to help."

"Yes, everyone is ready! We, too, are ready!" Étienne replied. "All will rise up on the signal. All our simultaneous attacks will surprise and confuse the Germans."

"I estimate that within two hours, we should be in command of Buda and Pesth," Count Ladislaw joined in. "In roughly half a day, we will control all of the principal estates of Theiss, and in one day the government will be ours. Then our Austrian brothers and sisters will have regained both their pride and their independence. Our friends presently constitute a majority in the Diet, so the new government should be able to immediately direct the affairs of state."

Borik, the servant, poured bright red native wine into their glasses. "If money is the nerve of war, it is also that of conspiracies," he remarked.

Dr. Sandorf gestured for Borik to join them in a toast and said, "If our friends are willing to sacrifice their lives for the independence of our beloved country, I can certainly sacrifice my fortune. To success!"

All spoke as one: "Success!"

3

Silas Toronthal

Several years earlier, Silas Toronthal, a twenty-eight-year-old banker, was involved in some questionable dealings that required the services of a ruthless yet capable soldier of fortune, Sarcany. The two men formed an alliance based on greed, and both had proven themselves capable of anything. Silas had an image of propriety to maintain, so Sarcany never approached him in public, but he was never far away. For a while now, Silas had tried to disassociate himself from him, but Sarcany, knowing his former dealings, sought to continue a relationship of sorts.

Silas was exceedingly rich and by all rights should have been. After all, speculation with large merchant fleets, his ties with Lloyd's of Austria, and a general scarcity of banks had brought his bank a tremendous amount of money. As a member of the Austrian aristocracy, however, the Germans kept him under close surveillance.

Sarcany had been aware for some time that he was an embarrassment to Silas, so he usually came around only when he needed money. And once again, he felt certain that the coded message could be parlayed into money. So he decided to make his way to the home of Silas late that night, knowing that Silas's wife was very sickly and would undoubtedly be asleep.

As Sarcany walked to Silas's house, Silas was enjoying a good smoke with his large and expensive pipe. Two things contributed to his good spirits. First, he was delighted that the Germans found his banking skills and social connections useful. Second, he had learned that Sarcany's creditors were becoming impatient. Silas decided that if he settled Sarcany's debts he might be rid of him once and for all. To that end, Silas had sent Sarcany a letter with enough money to liquidate his debts and leave town.

Although Silas perceived himself as still being his own man, nothing could be farther from the truth. His involvement with the Germans had changed him considerably. He no longer looked people squarely in the eye and treated people with disdain. He now had very few friends.

Even his wife had noticed the transformation, but she was more concerned with their social status, so she said nothing to him. Instead, she held lavish parties and convinced Silas that they had to live in the luxurious apartments of the Hotel of Acquedotto. She was older than Silas by some years, and her frail heart had aged her. Although some thought it a good marriage, it was more a marriage of convenience. She enjoyed a wealthy lifestyle, and Silas was seen as a settled, trustworthy banker. She had retired to bed earlier in the evening, as she often did due to her illness, leaving Silas to whatever amused him.

As Silas smoked his pipe and savored a glass of chardonnay, there was a faint tapping at the door. His cheerful expression withered from his face, and he quickly descended the spiral staircase that was a special feature of the duplex apartment. He gave his red housecoat a tug and tightened the sash to hide the beginning of a rather generous waistline. Silas paused at the hall mirror to ensure that his white wig was on straight. As he opened the front door, he impatiently said, "You again! What do you want now? Didn't you get my letter? I sent you enough money to leave Trieste. Why haven't you gone? What do you want from me?"

Silas was about to close the door in his face, but Sarcany braced himself against it. In a firm, insolent, and provocative tone he said,

"Hear me out for five minutes. If you don't think what I have to say is worth your consideration, I'll leave and you'll never see me again."

"From here or Trieste?"

"From here and Trieste!"

"Tomorrow?"

"Tonight!"

Silas reluctantly allowed him to enter the house, carefully closing the door behind him. As they made their way to the study, Silas said, "This had better be good, is all I have to say." Silas sat in his huge leather armchair and relit his favorite pipe. This pipe was inverted and had debuted in the grand court of Habsburgs' Maria Theresa in Austria in 1770.

Sarcany sat down on the edge of another chair. "I think there is a conspiracy developing from which we can both prosper," he began.

"*We?*"

"Yes, we."

Silas, visibly annoyed, said, "Just how in the hell do you see me involved in any of your affairs, least of all a conspiracy?"

"Hear me out," Sarcany said. "It's my way of trying to pay you back for all the money you've given me."

Silas let this remark pass without comment. Sarcany explained quickly about the messenger pigeon and everything that had transpired earlier in the day. If Silas was interested, he did not show it. However, when he heard the name of Dr. Mathias Sandorf, he puffed harder on his pipe. He very quickly recalled and tabulated the doctor's account in his head. He knew that Dr. Sandorf was worth millions.

Sarcany could not read through Silas's stare and perceived himself to be making no headway.

After several moments passed, Silas asked calmly, "Well, how much will it cost me?"

"Nothing. I don't want your money. I need your assistance in presenting this uncovered conspiracy before the German Commander Von Brun."

Silas got up and made a futile effort to control his anger. "This message may be nothing at all, and you have the nerve to ask me to go to the Germans with some scribbling, nonsensical message? Not on your life."

"But if I am right about this conspiracy, think of what it might mean."

"What, that Dr. Sandorf gets arrested, and then the Germans smile my way more often? It is far too risky."

"No, no. His fortune," Sarcany replied. "If we denounce him as a conspirator and he is condemned, the German policy is to reward informants. His property and fortune will be turned over to us. With my reputation, the German commander would not even give me a hearing. But you …"

"No. Your five minutes are up, and I haven't changed my mind," Silas said. "What you have here is a hunch, and not much of one. You have no real proof. Now you said, and I intend to hold you to it, that this is the last I shall see you."

Sarcany showed him the copy of the message as he had transcribed it. "Here is proof!"

After Silas examined the note he said, "This still isn't proof."

Sarcany realized that in spite of Silas's curiosity being raised, the conversation was over. It was hopeless to try to convince him to speak with the German commander. Silas escorted him to the door and closed it firmly without a farewell.

Each stood for awhile on opposite sides of the door. One thought passed through their minds simultaneously: what exactly did the message say? Sarcany resolved to find out its meaning.

Silas then opened the door and mindful of Sarcany's resourcefulness, simply said, "When you find out what the message contains, we'll talk again."

Both smiled knowingly at each other, for once again they had renewed their unlikely friendship, even if for the last time.

4

The Message Deciphered

As often happens in regions close to the sea, a chilling mist hung heavily like a low cloud all over Trieste. You could barely see Dr. Sandorf's house even from the gatepost as the last light was extinguished by the lamplighter, marking nightfall. This was the night of the following day. The distant Center Square clock could be heard striking twelve times. It was late and the sort of foul night that would keep everyone indoors—everyone except Zirone and Sarcany, who had waited all day for this moment. After the lights had been out for about an hour, Zirone scaled the wall next to the gate with ease. He was clearly not a novice at this type of thing. Quickly, with sureness of purpose, he waited in the shadows under the parlor window until the clock in the Center Square struck two. Then, deftly, he forced the window latch and slid into the house.

Once inside, he proceeded stealthily about the house, stopping here and there to listen attentively. Nothing stirred. Silence prevailed. Actually, Dr. Sandorf and Borik were sleeping peacefully upstairs.

Borik nearly jumped out of bed when he heard the loud crash of a downstairs glass case. Although he was disoriented, it sounded like it came from the study. Borik reached into his night table where he always kept a pistol ready. He descended the main staircase and quietly entered the study. Without the fire in the fireplace, the study was pitch black, like the inside of a mine. He heard soft footfalls and noticed a blurred shadow slipping out of the house. As he stood with his back against the wall acclimating his eyes, he could hear his master descending the stairs. On the way down, Dr. Sandorf would notice Borik's open door and realize that he was up and investigating. Borik was one of those remarkable old men who had long ago stopped fearing for his own life. His only thought was for his master's safety. He cried out, "He is outside!"

Both men went to the window and saw a vague form slipping over the wall pulling a sack after him. Borik fired in the form's general direction, but it was too dark to hit his mark squarely or to give chase.

"Let him go," cautioned the doctor. "We'd best stay put on such a foul night. Let's get some light and see what's missing."

Borik struck a match and opened the gas valve on a lamp, which quickly illuminated the entire room. He said, "Yes. No telling what might be out there on a night like this."

Dr. Sandorf asked, "Is anything missing?"

After a quick inspection, Borik said, "The silver candlesticks, and some plates are gone; that's all. Just a burglar."

A pensive Dr. Sandorf replied, "Perhaps, and perhaps not; you never can be sure." He crossed the room to a large wall of books and examined the Bible there carefully. Satisfied, he closed the window and said, "We'll report the theft in the morning."

"Yes, sir."

Minutes later, the lights went out in the house and all was quiet as Trieste slept.

Meanwhile, downstairs in the darkness, the clock struck four as the hall closet door opened and Sarcany stepped out from where he had been hiding. Everything had gone according to plan, except for Zirone getting shot at. Sarcany lost no time reaching the Bible and under match light, examined the pages inside. The silence was deafening, and his heart began to pound loudly. In between the last pages, he found what he had come for—a grille that would decipher the message. He grinned happily.

Sarcany returned to the hotel where he hoped he would find Zirone. He realized Zirone might have been wounded and was apprehensive about entering their room. He hesitated for a moment, thinking that Zirone might be dead or the police might be waiting for him. Sarcany listened intently at the door for several minutes until he heard Zirone cursing inside. He entered and found Zirone tending to his wound. The bullet had grazed Zirone's buttocks, which meant he would not be going to any plays for several weeks. It was more of an annoyance than anything else, and Sarcany was relieved.

A visibly infuriated Zirone said, "Next time, I'll hide in the closet. That doctor can shoot."

Upon examining the location of the flesh wound, Sarcany could not contain his laughter. "Actually, I think it was Dr. Sandorf's old butler who shot you."

"I knew it, I knew it; now I'll have to put up with your ridicule on top of everything else," griped Zirone.

Sarcany went to the dresser and extracted a traveler's Bible that was inside. He opened it ceremoniously as if he were going to read at Zirone's funeral. It was just as Zirone thought, Sarcany intended to rib his friend and have some fun at his expense. Then, in a more serious manner, he handed the grille to Zirone, saying, "You get to decipher the message."

Zirone asked, "How?"

"You see how the grille has a small box cut into it, with a number near this opening?"

"Yes. So what?" replied Zirone, still puzzled.

Sarcany explained, "Place the grille on the index to the Bible there on the contents page. See, the opening serves as a small window through which the precise book of the Old Testament is signaled out. Then, the numbers on the grille make sense. It's brilliant."

In a discerning tone, Zirone replied, "Yes. I understand. The opening reveals the J in column two and the numbers are nine/thirty-two on the grille."

Contents

The Old Testament

Genesis	Exodus	Leviticus	Numbers	Deuteronomy
Joshua	Judges	Ruth	1 Samuel 1	2 Samuel 2
1 Kings 1	2 Kings 2	1 Chronicles 1	2 Chronicles 2	Ezra
Nehemiah	Esther	Job	Psalms	Proverbs
Ecclesiastes	Song of Solomon	Isaiah	Jeremiah	Lamentations
Ezekiel	Daniel	Hosea	Joel	Amos
Obadiah	Jonah	Micah	Nahum	Habakkuk
Zephaniah	Haggai	Zachariah	Malachi	

The opening in the grille permitted only the word *Judges* to be seen. Then the numbers 9/32–33 made sense.

Zirone turned the pages of *Judges,* finding chapter nine, verses thirty-two and thirty-three, and read aloud, "Come by night with an army and hide out in the fields; and in the morning, as soon as it is daylight, storm the city …"

5

The Arrest

Borik prepared to leave the house early the next morning in order to report the theft. He greeted Count Ladislaw Zathmar and Étienne Bathory, who were just arriving at Dr. Sandorf's home as he was leaving. "Good morning. Make yourselves comfortable. Dr. Sandorf will be right down. I'm off on an errand."

It was not far to the local Austrian police station, and Borik enjoyed walking. As he entered the station, he went to a large desk where an Austrian lieutenant listened to his story and made out a report. When the lieutenant finished taking down the report, he motioned for Borik to wait and entered a rear office. Through the open door, Borik noticed Silas Toronthal with Sarcany. To him they seemed out of place there, but he dismissed the thought.

As the lieutenant closed the door, Borik noticed that a German officer, Commander Von Brun, stood at the window facing out. The lieutenant went to his own captain, who sat behind a desk, and prepared to present Borik's report. But before he could speak, Von Brun turned from the window and barked, "You will make your report to me." He stood waiting, his medals gleaming and uniform immaculate. He had distinguished himself at the Battle of Sadowa and was rewarded by being put in charge of the garrison at Trieste. The lines in his face, his square jaw, and manner were stoic.

"The servant, Borik, from the house of Dr. Mathias Sandorf has just reported a theft at the doctor's house," said the lieutenant.

Von Brun issued his command, "You and your captain will accompany the servant to the home of Dr. Sandorf. Your captain has his orders." The orders, of course, were to arrest Dr. Sandorf. Now he could be arrested under the pretext of investigating the robbery.

As the two officers left the room, Von Brun said to Silas, "The Austrian police will accompany the servant, Borik, to the home of Dr. Sandorf. A strong force of German troops will follow close behind. You two will come along to identify the conspirators."

The plan was, once inside, the Austrian police would get everyone into one room and make an immediate arrest. It was an effective strategy, especially since Dr. Sandorf would think they were there about the robbery. The captain, the Austrian police, and Borik arrived at Dr. Sandorf's home. Borik led them to the study, where Dr. Sandorf was talking to Count Zathmar and Étienne Bathary. After the captain gave the signal, he immediately placed a pistol to Dr. Sandorf's back and whispered, "Please do not resist. There are many Germans outside who would not hesitate to kill you." Dr. Sandorf was stunned. The Germans entered with heavy manacles and proceeded to chain the prisoners. The captain protested, "They are not animals; there is no need for chains." He was completely ignored.

Von Brun entered with Silas and seemed to take some satisfaction in the fact that it was a fellow Austrian who would point out the conspirators. "Is this Dr. Sandorf?" Von Brun inquired as he stared at Count Zathmar.

"No," replied Silas. "He is the doctor," as he pointed out Dr. Sandorf.

"And how do you know him?"

"He comes to my bank regularly and has done so for many years."

"Fine."

By now Dr. Sandorf had regained his composure and not knowing the circumstances of his arrest, asked, "What's the meaning of this outrage? How dare you enter my home in this manner."

Von Brun looked at him coldly, went to the book collection, and took out the Bible. He surreptitiously slipped the grille back in the Bible. Then, he sadistically struck Dr. Sandorf in the stomach with the spine of the Bible. Dr. Sandorf doubled over in pain. The others struggled against their captors but were easily restrained from doing anything. Dr. Sandorf looked icily at Silas as he and the others were led from the house. The chains made walking difficult.

Von Brun ordered, "Search the house from top to bottom. I want the names of all of his friends. I intend to stamp out this conspiracy. I will put them all in chains." As Von Brun left the house, he reassured Silas, "Do not be afraid of him. He will soon be in no position to harm you. You are going to be very wealthy. You'll see how generous we Germans are."

The captain approached Von Brun and said, "We have jurisdiction here according to the Treaty. These prisoners belong to me."

Von Brun replied, "Here is your prisoner," as he pointed to Borik. "File an official complaint, if you must."

Borik was left to assist with the house search since he was considered of no consequence in the conspiracy. The others were all escorted to a small coach drawn by four horses. Normally, these small, horse-drawn coaches had windows, but the Germans had modified this particular coach so that no one could see in or out of it.

"I wonder where they are taking us," said Étienne apprehensively.

"I don't think it will be to the converted Château in Trieste," replied Dr. Sandorf.

The coach was sealed from the outside and took off immediately. Inside, it was dark and stifling. The prisoners were disoriented, with no idea where they were being taken. They really had no idea where they were going.

"They changed the horses while you were both sleeping," said Dr. Sandorf as his companions awoke from the heat-induced drowsiness of the confined quarters.

"Is it my imagination or is it cooler now?" asked Étienne.

Doctor Sandorf replied, "I've been listening carefully since we entered the coach, and I think I know the general direction in which we've been heading. I believe we've been moving north of Trieste because initially I could hear the sound of the surf on our left. The tilt of the coach has been unmistakable for most of the trip. We've been heading up into the mountains. I think the horses had to be changed because the trip has been steadily uphill."

"The coolness would also suggest we are up in the mountains," noted Count Zathmar.

All listened for any clue as to their whereabouts over the endless clippety-clop of the hoofbeats.

"I wonder how our plan was discovered," pondered Dr. Sandorf. "After the robbery last night, I checked my Bible and there was nothing missing … unless …"

Count Zathmar finished his thought, "Unless someone else was in the room and saw you check the Bible."

Étienne joined in, "And why did they ask Silas the banker to identify you? And who was the other man with them? Do you think one of them may have been the man in the room? And then what, they cut a deal with the Germans?"

"Perhaps," said Dr. Sandorf. "Maybe they were given a reward of some kind."

Count Zathmar said, "The Germans have enough to convict us. We can expect a quick military tribunal and absolutely no mercy."

Dr. Sandorf thought differently. "If they were going to bring us before the tribunal, my friends, it would not have been necessary to leave Trieste." The others nodded in agreement.

After a pause, Étienne asked, "So where are we going?"

"I fear the worst," said Dr. Sandorf with a note of pessimism in his voice. "The message arrived only yesterday. I do not believe there is a traitor among us. And I think we are the only ones who have been arrested … so far."

"You mean we are to be tortured until we identify the others?" asked Étienne rhetorically. "That would explain why we are being hurried out of Trieste and removed from Austrian jurisdiction."

"Precisely," said Dr. Sandorf. "My instincts tell me that we are in for a very bad time. We must try to escape before it is too late."

Count Zathmar asked, "Escape from where?"

Almost painfully, Dr. Sandorf replied, "From Pisino Prison."

6

Pisino Prison

Pisino Prison was an infamous bastille—actually a converted feudal fortress—high atop the mountains of Trieste. No one had ever escaped from it. The fortress rose hundreds of feet at the end of an abrupt precipice. Below, the cliff plunged down a rocky slope to where the Foiba River ran into a gorge. This gorge narrowed into a gauntlet of rocks, which extended about three miles in length. At times the Foiba ran completely underground as it passed underneath two mountains. Eventually, it emptied into the Adriatic Sea. Overlooking the Foiba at the crest of the cliff there rose the prison with only one turret. It was higher than the rest of the fortification and resembled a giant needle pointing skyward.

The coach took most of the day to arrive and by that time, the three captives were sore and haggard. They descended from the coach. Each in turn was unshackled. Von Brun watched closely. Behind them, they could see the huge drawbridge being raised, cutting off any hope of escape. They stood facing the far side of the fortress where the giant turret stretched, cold and forbidding.

In spite of his weakened condition, Dr. Sandorf made a very careful inspection of the fortress. He knew that the Germans would certainly torture them in order to ascertain their contacts throughout the country. He knew that the Germans would not be satisfied with just the three of them and that the rumors about how brutally prisoners were treated were probably not exaggerated. Von Brun appeared to read Dr. Sandorf's mind, for he cautioned, "There is no escape from Pisino."

Étienne Bathory and Count Ladislaw Zathmar realized that Dr. Sandorf had been correct in his assessment. Pisino Prison might well be their tomb.

Inside the prison, Von Brun took great pleasure in demonstrating why the prison was escape proof. He showed them a security measure designed to discourage them. "You will note that we have somewhat modified this portion of the fortress. For example, the narrow walk-bridge ahead was borrowed from a local ravine in the mountains. Once we are across, it will be disconnected on the far end. Any prisoner who tries to escape will be impaled on those spikes below."

Dr. Sandorf remained consistent in his careful observation of the prison. There were guards almost everywhere, except at the rear of the fortress where the turret rose. They were heading in that direction when they made a sharp left turn.

The three captives noticed that Von Brun and the guards had allowed them to move slightly ahead of them. All of a sudden, two huge German shepherd dogs appeared out of nowhere and without warning, reared on their hind legs ready to bite them. Only their restraining chains kept them from reaching the three captives. Having come upon these creatures so suddenly, it was not at first apparent that they were fastened. Moreover, these dogs did not bark or make any noise.

Von Brun enjoyed his little joke. "I had their vocal cords removed because I found their incessant barking a nuisance. I keep them half-starved so that no one can get by them."

"Charming," said Dr. Sandorf.

The dogs were pulled back from behind by their chains, permitting the group to pass. As they were about to enter a staircase, a long flash of lightning silhouetted the turret. A lightning rod was attached to the turret, its cable swaying to one side. Dr. Sandorf looked at the darkening sky behind the turret. It was clear that a bad storm was heading their way—a premonition of what was to come.

The three prisoners were taken down a long staircase, deep into the fortress, into what could only be described as a chamber of horrors. As they descended, an acrid smell greeted them.

"What is that smell?" remarked Étienne.

Count Zathmar responded, "It is the stench of torture. That's human misery we smell."

Dr. Sandorf knew only too well what awaited them and resolved to do all he could to escape. His thoughts turned to the reality that they would be tortured until they gave the Germans the information they wanted. Once they had it, they would be swiftly executed. If escape were possible at all, it would have to be soon—while they had their strength and their wits about them.

Since the cells were full of prisoners, they were taken to a dungeon and fastened with chains to the walls. Each hand was shackled separately, rendering them helpless. The key to their locks was carried on a ring by an exceptionally tall and strong-looking guard.

Von Brun had accompanied them to the dungeon and issued the order, "They are not to receive anything to eat or drink until I say so. Understood?"

The tall guard with the key stood at attention and responded, "Yes, sir; absolutely clear!"

Von Brun left the dungeon to attend to a matter, but he soon returned.

As a result of his medical practice, Dr. Sandorf was an exceedingly good judge of physical characteristics. Thus, he noted that the tall guard would be a formidable opponent in a fight. Yet, it appeared that this guard was very self-confident. Perhaps self-confidence would be the weakness to be turned to his advantage.

As thoughts of escape raced through Dr. Sandorf's mind, Von Brun ordered, "Take this one since he is the oldest of the three. Strip him to the waist and tie him to the rack." Von Brun cunningly believed that sympathy for Count Ladislaw Zathmar might lead them to talk. "These methods are avoidable if you choose to cooperate."

The rack was made ready for Count Zathmar. His struggles to avoid being strapped into the foot and hand harnesses were in vain. Von Brun said, "The rack is a particularly painful apparatus. Once on it, a person can't even scratch himself if he itches. It is designed to tear the arms and legs from the torso. The muscles and sinews at the joints bear the brunt of the discomfort and are the first to go. However, breathing becomes almost impossible after a while. You can avoid all this by simply giving me the names of the others. We just want the names of the others and you will all be set free." Count Zathmar knew this was a lie as they stretched him until he passed out. He never said a word.

Dr. Sandorf had never written down any of the names of the co-conspirators, and the messages between them were always encoded. He knew every last one of them, though, and wondered if he would be as strong as the count when his turn came. Suddenly, Count Zathmar groaned. They poured a bucket of water over the count to revive him, only to mercilessly stretch him again and again. As the hours passed, they lost count of how many times he was revived.

Dr. Sandorf strained against his chains helplessly until his wrists were scraped and raw. He wanted to help his friend but could do nothing. He gritted his teeth and began to survey the dungeon. He saw several implements of torture that could serve as weapons, but how was he going to get out of his shackles? Étienne, too, was thinking of escape and their tortured friend.

At Von Brun's gesture, some guards set about heating coals in the fireplace. Then they placed the hot coals on two trays. Von Brun made a point of teasing his captives. "We've improved on the rack since its invention."

Neither Dr. Sandorf nor Étienne was aware at first of how the simmering coals were to be used. The guards appeared unphased as they placed the trays of hot coals under Count Zathmar's feet. Count Zathmar was delirious by now, so he did not notice these preparations. Suddenly, as the guards slapped the trays to his feet, he lurched from the excruciating pain that seared through him. Within seconds he passed out. The trays were removed, and Von Brun examined him to see if he was still alive.

"He's alive, but he will be out for hours. We will wake him in a little while. He will be much more willing to talk after this, I'm sure. If he dies first, then you two will be next."

Dr. Sandorf said nothing as the hate welled up in him. He noticed how Von Brun curled his nostrils, offended only by the smell of the burnt flesh and the count's stubbornness and absolute silence. Von Brun decided to leave the dungeon with two guards at his side. Only three guards remained inside the immediate area while two others stood guard at the main door. At the head of the stairs, which they had descended, Dr. Sandorf recalled that no additional guards had been posted.

Dr. Sandorf's senses seemed to sharpen as his mind searched for a means to escape. Anything would be better than the slow, torturous death on the rack. Dr. Sandorf examined each guard with deliberate care. He noticed that each carried weapons. He recognized the weapons as Nikolaus Von Dreyse needle guns, adopted by the Prussian Army in 1848 as the standard rifle.

The cocky, tall guard carried only a sidearm. This sidearm was an unusual weapon for these times, and Dr. Sandorf recognized it from his gun club as a type of flintlock—a *miquelet*—having an exceptionally strong and simple lock with an external mainspring and a battery pan cover made in one piece. His mind recalled many details of this sort of weapon. The flint would be held in a vise on one end of an arm, known as the cock. The other end of the arm was pivoted on the lick plate so that the flint-bearing end could be swung in an arc in the direction of the steel. The steel was also called the battery. When the trigger was pulled, the cock, impelled by a strong spring, moved forward in a short arc. The flint, held in the jaws of the cock, struck the steel a glancing blow, producing a shower of sparks that dropped into the priming powder in the pan. It was, he thought, the same principle used in lighting household fires. The weapon could only be fired once. Then, it would require reloading.

Dr. Sandorf took all this in from his position against the wall to which he was shackled. He noted, too, that anyone standing in front of him would, of necessity, block the view of the other two guards. The situation was as desperate as the thin plan Dr. Sandorf was fashioning.

Dr. Sandorf knew that sooner or later, under Von Brun's orders, it would be his turn on the rack. He knew that now was the moment for action. He anticipated that the tall, over-confident guard would be the one who would come for him since this guard's hands were the only ones not occupied with a rifle. Dr. Sandorf slumped as though he was sleeping. However, he allowed most of his weight to hang from his left-hand shackle. As he hoped for, the tall guard, thinking him asleep, decided to unshackle his right hand first so that he would not have to hold Dr. Sandorf up. The tall guard was then forced to lean across him, blocking the view in order to place the key into the left lock. Being exceptionally aware of anatomy, Dr. Sandorf knew that certain pressure points could cause paralysis. He ruled paralysis out, opting instead for a death blow. Trying to grab for the gun, which might get caught in the waistband, would reduce his chances for success. However, in those few brief seconds, Dr. Sandorf was conflicted; sworn to save lives, he had a little difficulty contemplating taking one. But as soon as he peered out through half-closed eyes at the charred feet of Count Zathmar, he found all the resolve he needed.

As the tall guard leaned across to unshackle him, Dr. Sandorf's right hand drove up swiftly in an arc, gathering tremendous speed. His hand was open and his fingers stiffened. Like a knife, his hand dug deeply under the guard's ribcage. Dr. Sandorf felt the twelfth rib—one of two floating ribs not attached to the sternum—as it broke and like a sharp nail, ripped into the heart. The tall guard gasped, looked surprised into Dr. Sandorf's eyes for a second, and died upright. Dr. Sandorf's timing was impeccable. Just as the key turned in the left-hand lock, the guard collapsed into Dr. Sandorf's arms. As he had hoped, the two other guards had not seen a thing.

Dr. Sandorf yelled for the two guards, "Help me get him to a chair. I'm a doctor. It appears he is sick." Dr. Sandorf caught both guards completely by surprise. He handed the dead guard to them, and their hands were occupied with the weight of their fallen comrade. He was actually surprised that his plan had worked so well thus far. Dr. Sandorf was able to draw one of their Von Dreyse pistols and position himself where he could cover both guards. He did not wish to fire the pistol, for the discharge would alert the garrison, but neither guard was willing to take a chance. He had one of the guards quickly release Étienne Bathory, who lost no time gathering the two rifles. Then, Étienne freed Count Ladislaw Zathmar and helped him regain consciousness. The two guards were shackled to the wall, and gags were placed in their mouths.

Étienne helped Count Zathmar, who could hardly walk. Meanwhile, Dr. Sandorf climbed the stairs, opened the door, and marched the next two guards back into the dungeon at gunpoint. They, too, were shackled and gagged.

As the three mounted the prison stairs, they came to cells filled with prisoners. They quietly released all the prisoners, who seized additional guards and armed themselves. But this part of Dr. Sandorf's plan backfired. Once released, the forty or so prisoners rushed up the staircase into the courtyard, drawing fire. Several guards and prisoners were killed in this exchange. However, the entire garrison was alerted. It would only be a matter of time before all the prisoners would be either killed or taken captive.

As Dr. Sandorf, Étienne Bathory, and Count Zathmar slowly followed the wake of death, they noted fallen guards and prisoners whose throats were bitten and slashed by the silent guard dogs. But the guard dogs had in turn been shot. There were shouts and additional shots ringing out throughout the fortification. From where—upon their arrival at the prison—they had made a sharp left turn, they could now see the last of the prisoners successfully taking the machine guns and entering the courtyard door, heading toward the front of the fortification. Meanwhile, the mountain storm that had been brewing earlier was in full fury now, and rain fell like bullets throughout the fortification.

Dr. Sandorf said, "The poor devils. They will never get across the walk-bridge."

Étienne asked, "And what about us?"

At the direction of Dr. Sandorf, they stayed in the shadows rather than follow the others and entered the narrow tower, which they began to climb. Dr. Sandorf recalled his entrance into the courtyard and the flashes of lightning that had revealed the lightning rod and cable at the top of this tower. There was no way for them to know, however, that the lightning rod cable descended about one hundred feet and stopped there, dangling in the air. Beyond would come another eighty-foot drop into the roaring Foiba River.

The storm had gathered force, and the thunder mixed with the crackling sounds of gunfire. The prisoners had run amok in the fort, and a few had even managed to reach the small, narrow drawbridge. The Germans had pulled it up, and in their haste, several prisoners had not been able to stop in time. These poor souls had hurtled onto the sharp spikes.

As the three ascended the tower, the sound of gunfire diminished, leaving only the sharp crack of continuous thunder. "Will they come for us now?" asked Étienne.

Dr. Sandorf said, "Von Brun may believe us to be among the dead. It will take them a while to check all of the bodies. Once they realize we are not among them, they will come looking for us. We don't have much time."

"We have another problem," said Étienne. "The only window is barred."

Dr. Sandorf felt the bars and explained, "It looks like the bars and the mortar are very old and worn by the weather. Luckily, they have not been reinforced at all. We must pry the bars apart with something."

Étienne, without even thinking about it, had picked up a coal stirrer made of wrought iron to be used as a weapon. "Will this do?"

Dr. Sandorf was delighted. "You bet. Besides, we don't have any choice."

They gently set Count Zathmar down on the stairs and quickly began prying the bars loose. Through the barred window, the rain and thunder bellowed loudly in their ears. They strained vigorously, taking turns with the coal stirrer in the narrow space, and succeeded in removing the bars. Now they could squeeze through the window to the lightning rod cable.

It was then that they heard the booming voice of Von Brun. "Come down, Dr. Sandorf. I know you are up there! Come down!"

Dr. Sandorf ignored him momentarily, saying to the others, "Von Brun will not be too eager to enter the narrow staircase, which is easily defended. He may not know how many weapons we have either."

Dr. Sandorf shouted through the thunderclaps, "Come and get us, Von Brun. We'll be waiting."

"Count Zathmar's injuries are too severe for him to hold onto the cable," said Étienne. "We can't carry him. What are we going to do?"

The Germans entered the tower and could be heard ascending the spiral staircase. Time was running out fast.

With great difficulty and pain, Count Zathmar spoke. "You two must escape. There is no hope for me. You must go. Go for Austria. Go to avenge me. I will delay them as long as I can. Give me the pistol."

As Dr. Sandorf placed the pistol ever so gently in Count Zathmar's hand, he realized that his friend planned to use the pistol on himself.

"I wish there was another way. By God, how I wish there was another way." They embraced as Dr. Sandorf continued, "My friend, you will be avenged. Austria will be free." Étienne hugged the count good-bye. Then, Dr. Sandorf and Étienne scrambled out the window.

After several tries, as the wind and storm tried to wrest Dr. Sandorf from the tower, he grasped the lightning rod cable and began to climb down. He looked down but could see nothing except darkness. Étienne followed, but Dr. Sandorf could barely make him out due to the fierce rain stinging his eyes. The cable was slippery, forcing them to wrap themselves tightly around it as they descended. This was extremely difficult. Occasionally, they encountered the remnants of the bolts that were used to hold the cable in place against the fortress wall. These bolts permitted them a toehold and a moment to breathe and recoup their strength.

Above, inside the tower, the guards rushed in, and Count Zathmar was barely able to get off a shot with one of the rifles. The discharge of the rifle could barely be heard above the storm. He immediately dropped the first rifle and fired the second one.

Two guards fell backward into their ascending comrades. Soon, two more guards advanced, hugging the wall. One guard feinted a rush. Count Zathmar fired and missed. Because Count Zathmar was right-handed, he had to hurl the rifle and then retrieve the pistol in order to kill himself. Just as the pistol came up, Count Zathmar was pierced in the shoulder by a bayonet. His pistol discharged against the wall. Additional guards subdued him.

The guards continued cautiously up the turret, expecting to find the others. Von Brun stooped, hovering over Count Zathmar. Thanks to a flash of lightning, he noticed the window with no bars. The two guards who had mounted the tower returned and with a gesture, indicated no one was in the turret. Von Brun had a guard squeeze through and look out the window. As lightning flashed, the guard screamed, "They are climbing down the cable! Give me a rifle!"

With difficulty, the guard maneuvered the rifle and braced himself with his feet against the sides of the narrow aperture. Then he steadied himself for a shot.

Count Zathmar mustered all his remaining strength, pushing one of the nearest guards down the stairs and lifting the coal stirrer from the staircase. He rammed himself into the small window crevice and stuck the coal stirrer forcefully between the legs of the extended guard. The guard screamed in pain and fired in reflex, missing his target. His leg grip on the window gave way, and he plummeted out into the storm.

Below, Dr. Sandorf and Étienne heard the shot and saw a dark figure tumble past them, clawing at empty air. His death cry was barely audible as he disappeared below into the roaring Foiba River.

On the staircase, another guard drove a sword into Count Zathmar. Von Brun rebuked the guard, "You fool, we could have made him talk; the others will die in the gorge." He quickly stooped to examine Count Zathmar's wound, finding that it was indeed fatal. Count Zathmar smiled at Von Brun, knowing that he would reveal nothing. His pain left him with death. Von Brun stepped over him and looked out the window. The raging storm made it hard to see anything or adjust to the darkness. However, the night sky lit up with intermittent lightning flashes, which offered blinking glimpses of the two fugitives below.

Dr. Sandorf and Étienne Bathory were clinging desperately at the very end of the lightning rod cable. They were roughly eighty feet down with another eighty feet to go. The heavens roared above them while the hell of the Foiba River screamed below. The Foiba was swollen by the rains and crashed furiously into the walls of the gorge.

Suddenly, a great white light illuminated the entire night sky for an instant. A jagged bolt of lightning zigzagged down out of the hovering, dark storm clouds. Like a crooked finger of death, the electric charge struck the cable at the top of the turret. The steaming electric current instantly turned the cable white hot. Both Dr. Sandorf and Étienne were forced to release the cable, falling eighty feet into the roaring river, which eagerly swallowed them up.

7

The Foiba River

Dr. Sandorf and Étienne were underwater for a long time before they came gasping for air to the surface. They were saved from being dashed against the rocks only because the river was swollen by the heavy rains. Ironically, the water had cushioned their fall. The Foiba River swept them into the gorge with blazing speed. They were being tossed like ragdolls while the chilling cold water began to quickly sap their strength. In the gorge, a constant roaring of the waters joined with the thunderclaps. They were quickly descending from the mountaintop toward some caverns. Their vision alternated between several intense seconds of flashing lightning to the pitch darkness within the caverns. As they floated further into these impenetrable caverns, the thunder and lightning from the storm became fainter.

Étienne's hands were badly burnt by the bolt of lightning, and he was semi-paralyzed. He cried out, "Help! Help!" but the river covered him like a cold blanket. He would have drowned but for the strong arm of Dr. Sandorf, which held him fast. With one arm, Dr. Sandorf pulled Étienne's head above the water; with the other, he made an effort to swim with the torrential river. Only the immense speed of the current buoyed them up. Even with this small assistance from the river, and his iron will, it was soon obvious that swimming for two under these conditions was going to be short-lived. Yet, Dr. Sandorf refused to set his friend adrift. His arms ached, his lungs screamed for more air, and he bore the brunt of blows inflicted when the river dashed them against the rocks. By some miracle, Dr. Sandorf held on, refusing to succumb to the powerful Foiba. It is amazing what the human body is capable of when a strong moral force unites with a determined will and a physically fit person. Nevertheless, this situation could not continue. Amazingly, fifteen minutes later, Dr. Sandorf and Étienne were still together.

Dr. Sandorf was almost asphyxiated with all of his strength sapped when he felt Étienne slipping from his grasp. Only a superhuman effort enabled him to regain a firm hold on his friend. Now Dr. Sandorf was almost hallucinating. His thoughts were random, and he could not see or hear.

Suddenly, a violent shock tore at his shoulder. They had been hurled into a huge rock that protruded in the center of the gorge like a hump just outside one of the caverns. Dr. Sandorf grasped at the slippery surface and managed to get a handhold. He mounted the stone and lifted Étienne onto it, too. They lay on the stone for a few precious minutes gathering their strength. Soon the ever-rising water would cover the top of the rock and once again sweep them away.

"We're lost," gasped Étienne desperately.

"No. Don't give up."

The two men managed to kneel on the rock, watching how the water struck and parted on each side of the great stone. A high wave was formed on each side of them, and they were able to make out the gorge ahead as lightning flashes illuminated it. It looked like an open, hungry mouth waiting to devour them. As they glanced back they could see the walls of the gorge and a huge black form like a dark cloud coming directly toward them. The object was roughly one hundred feet away. The form looked like a huge battering ram with spikes. As it rapidly drew closer, they realized that it would strike the rock with tremendous force. Étienne murmured, "May God help us!"

As often happens, lightning had struck one of the great old trees high in the mountains, uprooting it from the earth. The Foiba had swept the great tree along, and it was the huge root end that now rushed toward them. Just as Dr. Sandorf realized what it was, he saw a slim chance and cried out above the roaring to Étienne, "I think God is listening. Hold fast; when the tree strikes, it must pass on either side of the rock. We must try to get on it as it passes. Do you hear me? We will ride the tree through the caverns."

Étienne understood. The gigantic tree crackled with the vibration of striking the boulder and slowed for several seconds before drifting to the left of the great stone. As the enormous tree came alongside, they leapt onto it, clutching the bent roots and huddling behind this natural barrier. Dr. Sandorf quickly fastened the strong roots of the tree around Étienne, lashing him firmly. The huge old tree again gathered speed and raced down the gorge, buffeted by rocks on every side. Several times, the tree struck rocks just below the surface and at these times, it rose about ten feet above the water, sailing forward forty to fifty feet in the air. Dr. Sandorf took these moments to glance ahead, hoping to see the end of these rapids. They clung in desperation to their only hope of surviving the river.

A long time passed as they entered and exited the numerous caverns before the torrent emptied them into a rather large lagoon. Quite literally, the last cavern spit them out into the lagoon. This lagoon looked like a small lake due to the flooding, but it was actually an estuary. The storm was beginning to wind down.

Dr. Sandorf had contemplated heading toward one of the nearby shores, but he thought Von Brun would search for their bodies. Instead of going ashore, they stayed with their lifesaver, the tree. At one point, as they neared the shore, Dr. Sandorf threw their shirts into the water so that the Germans might find them and think them dead. They tore their shirts off so that if recovered they would not appear to have been unbuttoned. With indications of their wounds and blood on their shirts, one would be hard-pressed to believe they had survived. In the meantime, they rode the tree down the main current into the

Adriatic Sea. It was not long thereafter that both realized how wise this decision was.

Von Brun was shrewd, and having underestimated them once, he had decided to check the river. Although he believed it was a thousand-to-one chance that anyone could survive the rapids, he decided to lead a search party. Von Brun had telegraphed ahead, and some German troops had galloped through the night to where the gorge emptied. The soldiers were spread out on both shores with torches. They searched for any indication of footprints leaving the Foiba. They also looked in the brush along the shore for their bodies. The early morning shoreline was dotted with torches. The troops carefully made their way to the coastline where the estuary narrowed considerably.

Dr. Sandorf thought the great tree might be noticed at this point, so they submerged themselves under some trailing branches. Sure enough, the tree was seen and several torches held high as it passed. They held their breaths underwater for as long as they could and were not seen. When they were finally forced to surface, they could just make out some of the German troops' voices murmuring in the dark.

The storm finally subsided completely. The fierce current drove them well away from land. They were well out in the Adriatic Sea, tired, cold, and hungry. A few hours later the sky cleared, revealing one of the most beautiful mornings along the seacoast that the two had ever seen. The sun broke through the thinning clouds and warmed their nearly frozen bodies. Soon they saw a small boat that had ventured forth in anticipation of a good day for fishing.

8

Andrea Ferrato

The fishing boat that picked them up was owned and run by Andrea Ferrato, who sailed with his son, Luigi, daughter, Maria, and a sailor named Carpena. Andrea Ferrato was an excellent boat builder and fisherman. In fact, he had built the thirty-foot craft himself some fifteen years earlier and maintained it in good condition. His boat was like himself, unpretentious and durable in a rustic sense. Luigi and Maria were in their twenties. Andrea's wife had passed away several years ago.

It was Luigi who first noticed the two fugitives huddled on the huge tree and maneuvered the small craft alongside. Once aboard, they were quickly wrapped in blankets, and Maria brewed some hot coffee, which they drank eagerly. As they drank the coffee, Dr. Sandorf looked them over carefully.

Andrea Ferrato was about forty-two years old, with a very serious but melancholy, weather-beaten face. He had large, dark, expressive eyes. He had strong, broad shoulders and looked very fit under the simple garb of an Adriatic fisherman.

Maria was beautiful, in a very direct way. She was slim and very well proportioned. She had ardent dark eyes like her father, long, chestnut brown hair, and a vivacious personality. She seemed calm and confident in a mature and serious way. She was going to make some lucky man a wonderful wife, thought Dr. Sandorf. In fact,

Maria had already received a few offers, but she was devoted to her brother and father, especially since her mother had died.

As for Luigi, Dr. Sandorf could tell that this was the son of a fisherman. He appeared determined, valiant, hard-working, and acclimated to the fisherman's rugged existence. He was just getting into his prime. He had a shaggy head of dark hair, giving him somewhat of a Samson look. He seemed audacious and fearless. Luigi adored his sister and worshipped his father.

Thanks to Andrea Ferrato, both Maria and Luigi knew how to read, write, and count and were relatively well-educated. The only other person on board was Saint Carpena, a hired hand who could not keep from staring at the two fugitives through his narrowly set eyes. Carpena was about thirty-five, not particularly attractive, but rugged like the others. He never met Dr. Sandorf's eyes directly, and it was impossible for the doctor to size the man up as he did the others. To Dr. Sandorf, Carpena seemed somehow out of place. Carpena was not very sociable either.

Andrea Ferrato knew they were fugitives because he had overheard several German troops talking on the dock just before setting sail. Moreover, he was very familiar with the currents in the area, so he surmised that they must have come from the Foiba. He made certain that his children asked no questions, and he himself made no inquiry. He saw two patriots in distress and did not hesitate to help them. Like many Austrians, he hated the German presence but was in no position to do anything.

Maria liked both men immediately and fussed over them considerably. She served them salted pork, hot fish, bread, and plenty of wine. Carpena appeared to look on her attentions jealously, misunderstanding her friendliness. Maria felt a strong aversion for Carpena, for she had noticed his ill-intentioned looks on several occasions. In fact, Andrea had given him a week to clear out and find another boat. Carpena had met Andrea in town and had also overheard the Germans. Unlike Andrea, Carpena admired the Germans and considered his countrymen weaklings.

The day passed by with a good run of fish. Dr. Sandorf and Étienne slept throughout the day unmolested. When Dr. Sandorf opened his eyes, he was close to the cabin window and overheard Carpena and Andrea talking.

"I want to speak to you, Andrea."

Andrea replied, "We have nothing to discuss."

"Yes, we do. I must speak with you. I insist."

Reluctantly, Andrea said, "Well, what is it then?"

Carpena seized the opening, "I know you do not approve of me, but I must speak to you about Maria."

"Not another word."

Carpena persisted, "But you know I love her, and my only desire is to make her my wife."

"Carpena," Andrea interjected "You have already spoken to Maria and she said no. Now you have spoken to me and I say no."

Carpena continued, "But she is young, and this decision should not be hers alone."

Now Andrea was really annoyed, "Young or old, the answer will still be no."

"And this is your last word?"

"If it is the last time you bring up the subject. If you mention it again, you will get the same answer."

Dr. Sandorf felt awkward at having overheard this exchange. Then, as he came on deck, Andrea informed him, "We'll be making for port in the evening when most of the catch has been sold. Less people around." All on board nodded knowingly.

When they docked at the port of Rovigno, Luigi tied up the craft and then helped his dad, Maria, and Carpena unload the catch of the day. Meanwhile, both Dr. Sandorf and Étienne remained hidden below deck.

After the number of people on the pier thinned out, Luigi came with clothing in a duffel bag and fetched them. They ambled along through the nearly deserted village and were not conspicuous in any way. They arrived safely at the home of Andrea.

Andrea's house lay behind the shelter of a large boulder abutment some five hundred feet beyond the walls of the fishing village of Rovigno. Here, his home was protected from the winter winds and sea spray. They cherished the additional privacy this afforded them. The house was made of simple wood and had only one level divided into four chambers, two in front and two in the rear. Three of these rooms served as bedrooms, and the fourth was a combination kitchen, work room, and dining area whose most distinguishing feature was a rather large stone fireplace. The furniture was very simple wood kept immaculately clean, thanks, of course, to Maria.

Earlier in the evening, before Luigi had brought Dr. Sandorf and Étienne to the house, Andrea had spent a while in town speaking to his usual friends at the local tavern. Carpena had gone with him, but only to drink. Andrea heard the latest gossip about the increased German presence in town.

Meanwhile, Maria was busy preparing dinner at the house for everyone. Carpena decided to leave the tavern and to profess his love for Maria once again, still hoping to win her over. He surprised Maria in the large room. Before she could stop him, he had his arms around her and was trying to kiss her.

"You've been drinking. Stop! Don't come any closer."

Maria was backing up around the table with Carpena in pursuit. She picked up a rather large kitchen knife for defense only because it was the handiest thing around. She was young and strong as well as virtuous, and Carpena was unsure of what to do next. His pride was injured at being held at bay by Maria. She merely wanted to protect herself by threatening him. She could not really conceive of stabbing him. However, Carpena rushed her and both sprawled on the floor. Without intending to, Maria struck out by reflex and accidentally cut Carpena's cheek. Carpena sobered up rapidly as he got up, backed off, and looked at his wound in the mirror. He took a handkerchief from his pocket and held it to his bleeding face. It was a nasty gash.

In a rage he warned her, "You'll pay for this. Just wait and see; you'll be sorry."

Maria replied, "When my father and brother return, it is you who will be sorry for being a pig."

Carpena scowled but had nothing further to say. He bolted out the door nursing his bloody cheek.

Later, upon her father's arrival back from town, she related what had transpired with Carpena. Andrea vowed to make Carpena pay. Just as he said that, Luigi walked in with Dr. Sandorf and Étienne. Maria returned to preparing dinner. Andrea turned to the doctor and said, "We need to talk. Your friend Count Ladislaw Zathmar is dead, and the German Commander Von Brun is convinced you are both alive. He has posted a reward of five thousand florins for your capture."

Dr. Sandorf replied, "You are all in great danger. You have done enough for us. We must leave now."

"Where will you go? The area is filled with German troops," said Luigi.

Maria insisted, "Well, whatever you decide, it will have to wait until you've eaten. You're not going anywhere on an empty stomach. Now, everyone eat."

As they ate dinner they discussed what to do, and it was finally agreed that the best chance for escape lay in Andrea Ferrato sailing them down the coast under cover of darkness. They were pouring some brandy around ten in the evening when there was a crisp knock at the door. Andrea answered the door, opening it just a little bit, and stood shocked for a moment. Carpena was with German troops. Moreover, Carpena's face looked terrible with the scar now swollen and out of place on his cheek. Carpena had gone to Von Brun for the reward and for some misplaced modicum of revenge.

Von Brun and two of his soldiers barged in forcibly. Once again, surprise had aided the Germans. Von Brun held a steady pistol in his hand and smiled fiendishly at Dr. Sandorf and Étienne.

"Good evening, Dr. Sandorf. How nice of you to still be alive. I have such delightful plans for you."

Von Brun had recaptured his prize and was already savoring what would come next. But of all in the group, the least attention was directed to Maria, who stood by the stove boiling a large caldron of water for the coffee. She quickly lifted the caldron and threw its contents directly at the Germans and Carpena. Von Brun ducked, discharging his pistol into the floor. As for Carpena, the hot water had scalded his sensitive scar, and he posed no threat at all as he cringed cowardly in a corner. Étienne slammed into Von Brun, knocking him aside and managing to bolt the door. Luigi landed a blow directly on the nose of a guard, knocking him out cold. Luigi then turned toward the other guard while Dr. Sandorf traded blows with Von Brun. Von Brun was a veteran of many battles and was able to draw his sword. Luigi took the fallen guard's sword and tossed it to Dr. Sandorf. Dr. Sandorf, having been trained in fencing at the finest school in Austria, held his own. The exchange was fast and furious. At almost the same time, the remaining guard headed for the door to enable the other soldiers to enter. Maria threw the knife, which penetrated his throat, felling him at the door. Suddenly, Von Brun was facing two pistols and Dr. Sandorf's blade. He gave up his weapon.

The band fashioned a daring escape plan. They held pistols to the heads of Von Brun and the remaining guard and walked through the ranks of soldiers outside. These soldiers dared not fire for fear of striking Von Brun. They marched through the streets filled with villagers responding to the shots. They boarded Andrea's fishing boat. Luigi untied the craft while Maria scooped up two sacks of provisions. They set sail at once with the two Germans between them and the soldiers helplessly watching from the pier.

At roughly one thousand yards from shore, Andrea asked, "What shall we do with these two?"

With the shoe on the other foot as it were, Von Brun and the guard feared for their lives. With a gentle push, Dr. Sandorf shoved them off the deck, offering a parting remark, "I presume you can swim?" Von Brun and the other soldier hit the water, sputtered, and indeed began to swim for shore. On the shore the villagers were laughing, while the troops watched hopelessly. On the deck, all were smiling with relief. But several minutes later, these smiles turned to sadness when, peering through the darkness, they observed the burning of Rovigno. The distant gunfire signaled to them that Von Brun would leave no witnesses to his humiliation. His evil nature would not permit it.

"Now that we are fugitives, we should sail for France where Étienne's wife and son are staying. From there, we can make our way back to Austria and reconnect with the underground," said Dr. Sandorf. Von Brun had not yet played all his cards, however. As the small craft passed the island of Malta, they were intercepted by three German gunboats. Von Brun had telegraphed, giving a complete description of the fishing boat to all German vessels in the Mediterranean. Moreover, he boarded a gunboat and steamed all night to rendezvous with the other gunboats.

Early the next day, as Dr. Sandorf and Andrea were having coffee, Dr. Sandorf spoke sadly, "I'm sorry for bringing you so much grief, for losing your home."

Andrea was philosophical. "A fisherman's home is the sea, his bed the waves. I am sorry for Rovigno. It was a nice village. Why did Von Brun have to kill everyone and burn the town?"

Sandorf answered, "Evil has no limits. We should have killed him when we had the chance."

Andrea fought back tears. "This was meant to be. We cannot look back."

Reflecting on his last remark regarding Von Brun, Dr. Sandorf looked back and saw something that aroused his concern. "You have a telescope?"

Luigi fetched the telescope, and Dr. Sandorf looked through it. There in the distance, three German gunboats were gaining fast. Andrea borrowed the scope, gritted his teeth, and said, "I'll bet you Von Brun is on one of those gunboats." He paused.

"It will take more than gunboats to stop us. Luigi, attach the fishing nets to the buoys and wait for my signal."

As the three German gunboats fanned out and closed to within canon distance, Andrea said, "I have sailed these waters since boyhood and even at night. I do not believe the Germans are familiar with these waters. My friends, we will out-sail them. We are entering a very dangerous series of small islands, with rock formations and reefs above and below the waterline." Then, Andrea spun the steering wheel while shouting, "Luigi, trim the jib and drop the buoys, now. They are steam powered, but their very speed will not serve them as we zigzag through these rocks and reefs."

Just then the three gunboats closed in and began firing. The buoys spread out in the only channel available between the underwater reefs. As the shells landed behind them, Luigi exclaimed, "They'll get the range soon, Papa."

At almost that precise moment, the gunboats realized the trap. It was too late. One gunboat's propeller was caught in the fishing nets. A second gunboat was upended and exploded as it smashed into one of the unseen reefs. Only the quick thinking of the third gunboat captain prevented it from being ensnared or wrecked. The captain quickly cut the engine and then threw the craft into reverse. Then, they hoisted sail and began slowly to thread their way through the reefs in pursuit. For the next nine hours, the two vessels glided through the labyrinth of death. Von Brun noted that his captain was sailing adroitly in the wake of the fishing vessel. The fishing boat and stalking shadow gunboat moved inseparably. A suspenseful silence prevailed.

Andrea broke the silence. "We're sailing over the last underwater reef right now." They were so close to this last reef that they could see it clearly as they passed over it with only inches to spare. Unknown to the German captain, his bigger craft would not pass safely. He dropped sail, restarted his engines, and closed in for the kill. Von Brun savored the moment as the soldiers reloaded the canon. They fired just as their bow was torn by the last reef. The craft came to a dead standstill.

Meanwhile, the small fishing boat was embraced by a heavy fog bank. The last round of canon fire struck the rear of the craft. The blast destroyed the rudder and hurled Étienne to the deck. Dr. Sandorf rushed to Étienne, gathered him in his arms, and inspected his mortal wounds. Étienne's last words were, "Give my wife and son, Pierre, my love."

Luigi inspected the rudder shouting to his father, "The rudder is gone, but we can sail her."

Andrea said, "We may yet get to France, my friend."

Back at the reef, completely out of sight, Von Brun boarded a rowboat, shouting at the fog bank. "We'll meet again Dr. Sandorf. We'll meet again." The sound of his fading voice reached those on the fishing boat.

However, fate had other plans for them. With no rudder, they were at the mercy of the turbulent currents.

They solemnly gave Étienne Bathory the traditional burial at sea. Andrea presided, "Ashes to ashes, dust to dust."

Dr. Sandorf closed the ceremony saying, "A true son of Austria."

Within the fog bank, they were almost immediately drawn into a fierce storm that pushed them clear through the Strait of Gibraltar. They were propelled out beyond the Mediterranean Sea by powerful currents. The storm itself was then engulfed by an even greater storm, which lasted eleven days and nights. They were carried far out into the Atlantic Ocean. They were unable to resist the storm's power. The fierce wind and current forced them ever southward. Even after the storm subsided, they were still at the mercy of the swelling waves.

9

The Island

On the deck of the fishing vessel all were gathered on a sun-splashed day. Andrea greeted everyone, "We've been sailing for six days since the storms subsided. Soon we shall see where fate is taking us."

Dr. Sandorf asked curiously, "Any idea where we are?"

"Somewhere in the Atlantic Ocean, well off the coast of Africa, near the Equator," said Andrea. "We've seen no other ships, which leads me to believe we are far from any of the established shipping lanes. Perhaps we'll find land soon."

"Papa, you mention land, and land appears!" cried Luigi. All caught sight of an island on the horizon. It popped up like a small black dot and got bigger fast as they were drawn to it. At first they were delighted since they naturally thought it might be populated. In addition, they could use some fresh fruit and a welcome change from their all-fish diet. As they drew closer, Andrea noticed that as far as he could see, a barrier coral reef stretched between them and the island. There was no way of avoiding the reef. The small craft was about to crash within minutes. The current forced them ever closer to disaster. They could hear the thunderous boom of the waves smashing into the reef. The island that lay peacefully beyond the spray was not a haven but a death trap. Andrea knew from many years of experience that they could not possibly avoid the reef. He thought they might have a slim chance.

"Quick! Throw everything overboard that isn't tied down. We haven't a moment to spare. Luigi, hoist every bit of sail we've got."

They did not understand this abrupt order, but they respected Andrea and knew he was their only hope. After everything was thrown overboard, and the sails caught the wind, Andrea leaned well overboard inspecting how the craft was now much higher in the water and gaining momentum. With all his skill, he maneuvered the craft toward a point where thinner coral appeared between two huge sections.

Andrea said, "The bottom of the boat will be torn to shreds on the reef, but, if we gather enough speed, the boat may hold on the reef for a few seconds. Hold on tight when we hit, then run forward on the deck and jump as far as you can over the jagged coral reef. Leave your shoes on and jump feet first. We'll only have a few seconds at best. The water beyond the reef looks calm and protected by the reef. If we can get past the reef, we'll swim to shore."

The boat continued gathering speed. The waves lifted the craft and slammed her onto the reef with a loud, crackling, and splintering wail. The bottom of the boat was torn out from under, but the deck slid forward onto the reef due to the momentum. After the initial shock, the deck lifted and began to slide back slowly toward the crashing waves.

"Now!" shouted Andrea.

No one hesitated. They quickly scrambled to their feet, darted along the deck, and leapt as far as they could, splashing into the water beyond the reef. As they began swimming for shore, they could see their small craft slip back and crash against the coral. Within seconds the craft was completely gone. They continued the long distance to the shore without any difficulty. When they reached the shore they rested, finding the sand warm and inviting. Occasionally, they looked out to the reef as if expecting to see the boat resurrect herself. From the shore, they could see numerous fish dancing in and out of the waves.

"I built her with my own hands," mused Andrea.

"You built her well and you sailed her magnificently," said Dr. Sandorf.

Luigi broke the sad moment, "From the looks of those fish, at least we won't go hungry,"

Maria chided, "Don't talk to me about fish; let's find some fruit. I've had enough of fish."

They were all in rather good spirits as they set about exploring the island.

Dr. Sandorf reminded them, "Keep a sharp lookout for any signs of life. We may not be alone on this island. If there are any other people here, they may not be friendly."

They entered as a group into the gentle green forest. Immediately, they were welcomed by a host of long- and short-tailed monkeys—macaques with their noisy voices, which seemed to shout "intruders". A host of birds also greeted them with their respective singing voices. These birds seemed eager to out sing each other. Among the identifiable birds were the honeycreepers with their remarkable diversity of bright colors, shapes, and varied bill structures; red-crested cardinals; Chinese doves with their decorative lace-necks; African silverbills; egrets, which look similar to herons; skylarks; and zebra doves. The island teemed with life. Intermingled with these colorful birds were a host of lovely dragonflies and damselflies.

The group strolled through a kaleidoscopic carpet of dazzling flowers: begonias, crotons, hibiscus, and numerous others. They walked under rainbow shower trees, which were in full bloom—a mind-blowing sight. Maria stopped under one of the many orchid trees with their multicolored butterfly leaves. Then, she scooped up a handful of fallen plumeria blossoms for a refreshing whiff. She shared this precious scent with each of her companions. They toured endless pockets of ginger, yams, taro, bananas, bamboo, coconut groves, turmerie, and "ti," which grew everywhere and were useful for wrapping food or to decorate.

They spotted a few animals like pigs, wild chickens, and rats. They knew there were other animals keeping their distance for the moment. Not too far inland they came upon a storybook waterfall and pond. Maria gasped, "It's beyond words. It's beautiful." She plunged in, followed by Luigi.

"The waterfall is fed by the rainfall on the mountaintop. We have a shower," said Andrea.

They spent the next few days exploring the island, which turned out to be completely deserted as regards any human life. However, there were animals in abundance and plenty of fresh water and fruit. In most respects it was a sort of paradise.

They fashioned several lean-tos near the shore, to provide temporary shelter. They fashioned some crude weapons, just in case.

One day after Andrea announced, "I've had my fill of fruit and meat," he extracted a sturdy line from his pocket and from a leather pouch, a fishing hook. "From my point of view, I'm ready for some fried fish."

"Me too," said Luigi.

Dr. Sandorf and Maria stayed behind to fuss over the huts and prepare a fire for dinner. Both watched as the father-and-son pair strolled off together.

Luigi ambled along after his father in search of a good place to fish. They found a deep lagoon running into the island. They could tell from the color of the water that the lagoon was deep and fish could enter easily. They discovered a toppled palm tree that hovered over the lagoon. It was from here that they sat and fished. They cast their lines and waited. They admired the abundant sea species below.

They saw some turquoise herons against the peacock-blue and exuberant purple shades of the lagoon. A small group of Atlantic halibut glided close to their bait. These halibut were each nine feet long with their traditional brownish-to-olive colors. They always looked strange since both eyes were only on their right side. However, the halibut seemed oblivious to the bait.

Some dark-spotted codfish tagged along behind them and they, too, ignored the bait. Some flying fish broke the surface, sailing three feet into the air for twenty seconds, traveling at thirty miles per hour. Several forty-inch, pointed snouts with large mouths signaled the arrival of a pool of bluefish. While these and many other species came by, none took any bait. Andrea knew that patience was a fisherman's greatest virtue. Thus, he made himself comfortable waiting for the inevitable tug on the line that would signal dinner. The afternoon passed by without so much as a nibble. Luigi changed his bait several times. He watched the fish pass by, ignoring it completely. All was quiet but for the regular rise and fall of the waves and the intermittent suck-cluck of thirsty clams. By evening, both Andrea and Luigi were thoroughly perplexed by the fact that they had not caught fish to eat.

That night, as they all gathered by the fire, Andrea shared the unusual fishing experience of the day. "I could see the fish, many of them, but none of them would take the bait. It is incredible and baffling. There is just no way for me to explain it."

"All day I had the feeling we were being watched, and not by the fish," remarked Luigi.

"Me too. I've had that feeling every day since we landed on this island. Papa, will you try to fish again tomorrow?"

"Yes, but I hope we get a bite."

Dr. Sandorf did not give their feelings much importance. "We have plenty to eat, and we've seen no trace of anyone. We'll all go fishing tomorrow. Besides, I'd love to see this lagoon you discovered." With that, the small group went to sleep. Above, the moon shone brightly and the stars winked at them.

The next day at the lagoon, Dr. Sandorf and Maria realized that Andrea and Luigi had not exaggerated the beauty of the place. However, just as the day before, they were all frustrated that not a single fish took any bait.

Andrea was certain that something inexplicable was occurring, "There is absolutely no reason why the fish should not bite."

Each of them tried again and again with no better results. Scores of fish glided beautifully within the mantle of the blue-green water, seeming to dance to their own respective undulating rhythms—their own throbs, the pulse of eternity. The fish approached the bait, then turned away, as if they knew what would happen. One anglerfish peeked over a ledge at the tempting bait, wiggling by coquettishly.

Upon seeing this, Luigi exclaimed, "It's as if they knew, I tell you."

"That's not possible," said Dr. Sandorf.

Andrea made yet another remarkable observation. "You see that large fish, there? That's a kingfish, and just in front of him is a trout, which he would normally eat. Over there, you see the octopus within reach of that young mackerel. Normally, he would eat the mackerel. In fact, the adult mackerel in turn feeds on the octopus. These are mortal enemies, but look how they interact, like friends. If I didn't see this with my own eyes, I would not believe it."

Luigi responded, "You're right, but what does it mean?"

Maria, too, said, "What could cause such behavior changes? It's so strange." Then, as Luigi admired the bizarre shapes—some appearing like dragonflies while others looked like wafer-thin triangles—Maria gently pushed him off the palm tree. They all laughed as Luigi submerged into the vast coral garden: pink grass, heliotrope mushrooms, violet and gold cauliflowers, and rainbow-colored sea foliage greeted him. Luigi surfaced with an amused grin. Everyone enjoyed this moment of humor, and Dr. Sandorf managed a long-overdue chuckle.

On the way back to camp, Dr. Sandorf stayed a little behind the others in order to speak with Andrea. "What do you really think?"

"I can't explain it. The marine life behavior is unnatural and eerie. I have not seen any signs of life, and yet I feel we're being watched."

"I think we had better explore the island thoroughly tomorrow. I plan to climb to the very top of the mountain. We have yet to make observations from there. Who knows? Also, I hope to see a break in the coral reef. It's about time we started to build a ship and return to Austria."

"You'd better keep your eyes open," cautioned Andrea.

Early the next day, Maria watched Dr. Sandorf arm himself and slip away from camp. She decided to follow him up the mountain. It was a rather easy climb up beautiful, grassy slopes. The day was warm with the ever-present sun sweetening the fragrances of the abundant flora. When Dr. Sandorf neared the top, he heard a twig snap behind him and quickly hid in the brush. Maria came ahead, and Dr. Sandorf startled her when he rose from where he had hidden.

"I was just as curious as you to see whatever there is to see from up here."

"Come along, then." He was pleased to have her company.

Soon, they reached the pinnacle and were amazed at the magnificent panoramic view. Maria was spellbound. "I've never seen anything so beautiful. It takes my breath away."

Dr. Sandorf was also initially delighted, saying "Nothing surpasses God's creations." Indeed, stretched out before them was a watery Eden with cobalt tinges mixed with purples and greens.

His admiration of nature was suddenly replaced by a cold reality. Dr. Sandorf's eyes darted everywhere. "Good Lord! The coral reef has no breaks in it. The reef completely surrounds the island." He was shattered with the realization, which his trembling voice betrayed. "We are trapped. We'll never get free of this island. I'll never see my wife and Austria again." It was too much for him after all they had endured. Disheartened, he kneeled down as if all his inner strength had left him. He began to sob unabashedly as the total hopelessness of their situation rocked his spirit to the core. This was the most devastating moment of his life. He wept with the simplicity of a child.

Maria could only follow his gaze, reflect on their being trapped, and also feel his hopelessness. While she too felt miserable, she reflected on her different reality. All those she loved were there with her. She imagined how painful it would be if her father and brother were not there. She understood how lonely and desperate Dr. Sandorf must have been feeling. Then, she knelt and held him in her arms as one would a child.

Only when his sobbing subsided did she dare release her tender embrace to look into his tearful eyes. There she saw true misery and pain. Locked in an embrace, there was no kissing, no passion, yet there was love. They shared more than bodily warmth or passion.

Neither would be the same toward the other from that day forward. Maria knew Dr. Sandorf was married but could not keep from loving him. Dr. Sandorf, in turn, felt no guilt. They each discovered that love transcended all of man's logical rules. Love was beautiful when it sprang from the soul and each cared only for the happiness of the other, selflessly. Their souls became entwined and would never be parted. It was a long while before they recovered enough to descend the mountain together.

On the way down they noted the rest of the island from their vantage point. The island was thick with trees and mint-green vegetation. While they saw no signs of life, they often felt they were being watched. This feeling of being observed stayed with them all the way down to the beach. Yet, whenever they looked behind and around them, there was no one. They descended and reached the campsite. By then Dr. Sandorf had regained his composure. As they did every evening, the group gathered at their makeshift campsite and each recounted the events of the day. Of all the things noted, it was Dr. Sandorf's discovery that the island was completely surrounded that naturally dominated their dinner conversation. As Dr. Sandorf recounted his discovery, his voice almost gave out. Maria stayed close to him so that should he succumb again to despair she would be there for him.

Andrea looked upon his sweet daughter and saw in her the mother, his wife. Maria was a woman in love. She radiated the pure love, which enriched her personality. Andrea smiled, delighted and proud of the transformation he was privileged to witness. He leaned forward and kissed Maria on the forehead as he had done thousands of times.

Andrea said, "We better begin preparations for a long stay."

10

Ten Years Later

To drive away the thought of their island prison, the group threw themselves into building more permanent structures. They toiled, dug, hauled, and hammered. They had lots of wood, gravel, and sand. Mostly, they built in the shade to avoid the sweltering sun. Nonetheless, all were soon sporting suntans. They found the easiest structure to build was a post-and-beam house sitting on wooden poles cemented into the ground. Basically, this is a deck with a roof covered with palm leaves. Even the few timbers from the destroyed fishing boat washed up on shore and were utilized. They called this "driftwood architecture."

The marooned group had used their time wisely. Notwithstanding that most days became somewhat routine, there was danger and adventure. If one were to compare before and after, one would have been amazed at the difference. Little by little, they had built far more sophisticated dwellings. Their tables, chairs, water-kegs from coconut shells, windows, thatched roofs, and beds all combined for a rustic yet well-created environment. So, too, they had fashioned, thanks to Maria, a wardrobe that was unpretentious and highly serviceable. Yet, the most dramatic difference was in the men, who had decided to give up shaving. Now they sported beards. They fashioned bows and arrows and improved on their spears in addition to the other weapons they always kept at the ready. Once the dwellings were complete, Dr. Sandorf began to accept his fate as a prisoner on an island. Some plain fishing boat plans served Luigi and Maria as surf boards.

With respect to adventures and close calls, three were quite notable.

Luigi's Mermaid

Out near the coral reef, Luigi was submerged with his spear. As the son of a fisherman, he was an exceptionally strong swimmer. Comfortable underwater, he could submerge for nearly five minutes at a time. Having given up on fishing, Luigi would nonetheless spear an occasional fish for their lunch or dinner.

One day, Luigi entered and exited a series of underwater caves. Unknown to him, a hulking figure watched his every move. After surfacing for a breath, he descended into one of the caves in search of a prize. Instead, all of a sudden, he was held in a vise-like grip at the ankle. Swiftly, a giant octopus wrapped another tentacle around his midriff and then about his spear arm. There was no escape from a giant octopus, whose eight tentacles grasped and sucked simultaneously.

Luigi knew he was facing certain death as he watched the beak-like mouth of the creature closing in. The mouth of the octopus was like that of a parrot. However, it was far larger and able to rip an adversary to shreds within seconds. His struggles were in vain, and his lungs gave out.

Amidst churning sand, the last of his air bubbles, and the dim but penetrating light of the sun, he lost consciousness. His last movements were his blinking eyes swollen with the need for oxygen. In this last delirious state, a swift-swimming mermaid approached. At least, the form appeared to be a mermaid to Luigi. The mermaid had an incredibly beautiful face and slowly kissed him. Luigi thought he had died and gone to heaven.

One could hardly imagine the absolute surprise on Luigi's face when he found himself alive on the beach with gentle waves caressing his ankles. He stirred and then his eyes blinked open. He found he was not spitting up any water, yet he had drowned. Upon close examination, he surveyed the telltale marks of the tentacles on his torso. Then, he sat bolt upright and scanned the beach, expecting to see footprints. He was perplexed by the absence of any footprints and the presence of his spear. He thought out loud, "So it was a mermaid."

At the campsite that evening, Luigi recounted his ordeal and rescue to an astonished group. Andrea asked, "A mermaid saved you?"

"How else did I get on the beach? There were no footprints." While none of them could offer any explanation, they were indeed grateful to God for having intervened. With time the memory of this adventure passed. More adventures lay before them. Every night Luigi dreamed of his mermaid.

The Great White Shark

For months after the close call with the octopus, Maria and Luigi would swim together. It was Maria who teasingly challenged Luigi, "I'll race you to the shore." Luigi took the challenge, sprinting shoreward. Actually, Maria took only one or two strokes, having decided to fool Luigi into racing, while she floated and swam out near the reef. The next few minutes were humorous, drawing the attention of both Andrea and Dr. Sandorf. They were up the slope of the mountain and could easily see the two. Luigi was swimming furiously, intent on winning the race. Maria hung back playfully. It was a lovely sight and disarmingly peaceful. Andrea's peripheral vision, however, noted a dark shadow moving swiftly toward Maria. He gasped in horror as the recognizable dorsal fin surfaced. Dr. Sandorf followed Andrea's eyes and also noticed the dark, gray form of the great white shark as it streaked toward Maria.

Maria was oblivious to the danger, enjoying her little joke on Luigi. When she finally looked shoreward she saw Luigi on the beach and her father and Dr. Sandorf running and waving. It took her several seconds to realize that their waving was actually a frantic signal to her. She glanced about, noticing the dark, sleek form coming straight for her. Maria knew at once that she could not swim to shore in time. From the dorsal fin, which now broke the surface again, she knew it was a great white. Sharks are notoriously attracted to coral reefs, and this one was no exception. There was no possibility of escape. Moreover, she was not armed.

On the shore, the three were desperate. There was nothing they could do for Maria. "It is a great white. Maria, my baby," said Andrea.

The great white shark reached Maria, and she was swallowed up from sight. The three on shore stared at the huge dorsal fin as it continued on. Andrea fell to his knees horrified as Dr. Sandorf came to his side. The three of them were in total shock, breathing heavily as if they had run a race. They huddled together, trying to console one another. Long moments of anguish engulfed them. Suddenly, their heads snapped up as one when they heard Maria's clear voice, "I'm all right! I'm all right!"

Maria had listened to her father's wise counsel over the years. As the shark had approached, she submerged, facing the creature. That is why, as the shark passed, she appeared to have been eaten. The shark was not hunting and simply passed by.

Within seconds they saw Maria swimming strongly over the remaining distance. They all ran into the water to greet her joyously. They also looked out where they could yet see the dorsal fin of the great white. Now, the dorsal fin broke the surface as if in a friendly wave. They were all too happy to express themselves in words. They all laughed hysterically, hugging each other.

Dr. Sandorf ventured an opinion, "For whatever reason, there are no killer instincts in the fish of these waters. Not only are the fish incapable of attacking one another, they are not capable of killing anyone."

"I shall spear fish no more," promised Luigi.

Andrea noted that Dr. Sandorf and Maria needed to be alone as they held each other. "Come, Luigi." Luigi understood and they left the two alone in an embrace. Quietly, Andrea prayed, "Thank you, Lord, for sparing my children."

The Giant Boar

Yet another great danger would befall them, testing their courage. Of all the creatures on the island, the deadliest by far were the boars. Luckily, these boars stayed deep in the brush on the far side of the island where the stranded group seldom traveled. So it was that Dr. Sandorf and Luigi normally skirted the deep underbrush. However, one day they spotted the footprints of a giant boar. When Luigi first spotted the tracks, he could hardly believe his eyes. He signaled for Dr. Sandorf who, upon examining the tracks, quietly gestured for them to leave the area. A giant boar was not at all an interesting hunt.

Luigi said, "A boar with tracks that big must be half the size of a large horse at least. Let's get out of this area before we find out the hard way."

They were keenly not interested in following the tracks and decided jointly to make a quick retreat from the area. Fate had another agenda, as is often the case. They distinctly heard the loud grunt, which was unmistakably the giant boar deep in the brush. The giant boar had been circling the area for some time on the scent of game. Both froze, listening carefully. They could hear the creature grunting, snorting, and forcing its way through the underbrush. The birds that fled their perches gave both of them a very good idea of just where the boar was. It appeared that the boar was not after them, and they sighed in relief and continued their retreat. Then, they heard the boar crash through a thicket after its intended prey. They knew the boar was seconds away from whatever it was attacking. They were not eager to know what the wild pig was hunting.

They were well on their way out of the underbrush when the sounds of a struggle reached them. The two animals were engaged in combat; the sounds were unmistakable. That's when both froze in their tracks at the distinct sound of a human voice. It was more like a sharp shrill yell, yet it was unmistakably human.

Dr. Sandorf responded, "That's a human cry. Quick! We must try to help."

Actually, both thought it might be Andrea looking for them. Thus, they both ran headlong toward the struggle, readying their spears. As they reached a small clearing, they were amazed at the sight before them.

A giant boar was indeed readying for another charge. A huge spear protruded from its side. Yet, even more surprising was its intended target. Waiting for the charge was a man about seven feet tall holding a curved sword. The man was an oriental in simple, loose-fitting garb. He looked as if he were wearing a camouflaged cassock with a seaweed sash at the middle. He wore elevated sandals with one thong separating his big toe from the others. A turban-like cover on his head made him appear even taller. The man was wounded and bleeding from a gash on his right leg. He stood fearlessly waiting.

Then the great beast lunged forward. Both Dr. Sandorf and Luigi did not hesitate for a second. They hurled their spears, which penetrated the boar. Yet, even wounded, the boar was far from dead. The creature continued its charge, and it appeared he would surely get his intended victim. Just as the boar reached the tall oriental, the man deftly leapt high in the air over the creature. While sailing over the creature, he swiftly slashed at the back of the boar's neck. It was a maneuver Dr. Sandorf had seen only once in an exhibition of martial arts. Having completed the move, the man landed smoothly on his feet facing the boar. Along the neck and side of the boar, they could both see blood as it oozed from the gash. The boar never turned around. It fell heavily. With a last gasp for breath, the boar died at the man's feet. Calmly, the tall oriental placed his foot on the boar and extracted his spear.

Dr. Sandorf and Luigi could not quite believe that the creature was dead. They approached with great caution and set about retrieving their own spears. Within seconds they turned to speak with the stranger. The tall oriental had disappeared without a sound or a word into the brush. They were perplexed since they had only lost sight of him briefly.

"Where did he go?" inquired Dr. Sandorf.

"Was he ever really here?"

Dr. Sandorf inspected the human blood and they both wondered why he left without a word.

Later, at the camp, they discussed the tall oriental man and his obvious preference to remain aloof. While they cooked a portion of the boar, they described the oriental man to Andrea and Maria. They had deliberately left most of the boar for the oriental hunter who might return to claim his prize.

"From your description, he might be Chinese, probably from the north of China," reflected Andrea.

"What troubles me is did he recently arrive on the island, or has he been here all the time?"

Dr. Sandorf said, "The man knows we tried to help and we left him food. His wounds may get infected. If the man has been here all along, then he might not be alone. However, I don't believe that's possible since one of us would surely have noticed some sign of human life by now. We will search for him tomorrow."

The next day, the remains of the boar were gone. They kept an eye out for the stranger for weeks but never found a trace. They finally decided to respect his privacy and gave up the intriguing search.

11

The Seaquake

Nearly three years had passed since seeing the Chinaman, when the island was shaken by a powerful earth tremor. The first indication that something was wrong was in the glass of water Luigi was about to drink. As he reached for it, the cup moved, with its contents vibrating. Then, there was a noisy fluttering as all the birds took off into the sky at once. Within seconds, the group was violently tossed to the ground. Luckily, the sand made for a soft landing.

Maria asked, "Papa, what's happening? What was that?"

"Somewhere far off, there must have been a seaquake."

"We're lucky it's not here," Luigi added.

Andrea concluded, "Yes, but will there be more and bigger?"

"There is no way to know," said Dr. Sandorf. "If there are more, but not any stronger than this one, we should be all right."

"A little luck we can use," said Luigi. They began to go about their usual routines. However, Dr. Sandorf said to Andrea, "The shore birds, hawks, and gulls are not returning to the island. Instead, they are hovering."

Suddenly, they were all completely taken by surprise when the tall Chinaman of a few years before appeared in their camp without any warning. They had not seen him approach and initially reacted fearfully. The tall man said and did nothing so as not to alarm them further. Slowly, they realized he meant them no harm. He waited until they all approached him.

Luigi was the first to speak, "I wonder if he speaks any of our languages?"

Then, Dr. Sandorf tried the international language of diplomacy, French, "Parlez-vous français?"

They were all taken aback when the tall man spoke their language, "You must trust me and follow me quickly. I am Confucius, and there is great danger." Confucius turned and strode quickly toward the foot of the tall mountain path. The others followed, although they were quite perplexed. To keep up with Confucius's steady pace, the others had to jog. It took time for the entire group to reach the highest point on the island. There, as they broke through the forest into a clearing, they were met by roughly fifty Chinese men, women, and children. They each carried strong ropes made of seaweed curled about their necks and shoulders. At first, they thought the Chinese meant to tie them up. However, the Chinese set about fastening one another to the tall trees and rocks. When it came their turn, they were not fearful. Still, Confucius cautioned, "I shall answer your questions later. For now, keep your eyes on the eastern horizon." There, barely discernable, was the unmistakable formation of a one-hundred-foot tidal wave. Now things made sense. Had they remained on the shore, they would have been killed. Their only chance was atop the island, fastened as they were.

At the edge of the mountaintop, Confucius was joined by his father, Chang, and sister, Kumiko. All three had yet to be secured. All three began a series of synchronized patterned movements. Their hands were clasped above their heads and then, lowered to their midsections. They expelled air using their abdominal muscles but in rapid succession. They inhaled and appeared to be in a trance. However, their eyes did not glaze. Instead, their eyes were clear like crystalline pools. The trio was in the process of deep meditation, breath control, and oxygenating their systems.

"What are they doing?" asked Andrea.

"I think they are pumping more blood into their brain cavity. Their craniums are actually expanding just above their eyes and ears." Dr. Sandorf could see their temples vibrating with the powerful surges of blood. He knew they were sending enormous amounts of blood into the brain cavity. The why became self-evident. "Look, Dr. Sandorf! Look at the fish," said Andrea. Far below, all the large fish could be seen enveloped in an electrical energy pulse emanating from the trio. They were simultaneously moving toward the coral reef on the western side of the island. The fish took shelter in the thousands of caves and crevices of the coral reef with the island between them and the tidal wave.

Dr. Sandorf and the others now realized that, somehow, these Chinese were able to communicate with the fish. Suddenly, the mystery of the fish that would never take their bait became clear. Also, they realized that these Chinese were already on the island when they arrived. Indeed, they had been observed since the day they arrived. Yet, how these Chinese managed for so many years to avoid being detected befuddled them all.

The tidal wave continued closing in on the island. They knew that because they had risked their own lives to save Confucius during the attack by the giant boar, as a matter of honor, they in turn were deemed deserving of being rescued. Confucius was returning a favor. As the tidal wave drew dangerously nearer, they realized that, had they remained on the beach with their dwellings, they would have been engulfed.

The trio came out of the trancelike state and moved quickly to a great tree. At the tree, Chang and Kumiko stood against it while

Confucius took one of the strong seaweed ropes and quickly twirled it with a powerful snap. The rope curled around Chang and Kumiko, fastening them to the tree. With incredible speed, Confucius darted to the tree, enfolding himself in the rope just as it finished its twirling.

The tidal wave drove hard and fast at the island. The day was beautifully clear and sunny, and the great one-hundred-foot wave seemed completely out of place as it hurtled furiously toward them with a rising crescendo of sound. They watched in wide-eyed wonder as the tidal wave cleared the outer coral reef. Then, the island shook with its impact. The wave tore at everything in its path. The homes they had built were squashed flat and then carried away forever. The lower hills and valleys were completely submerged. There was a shattering, deafening roar. On the high mountain, the wave broke furiously, the water behind climbed over the water and spray in front. Although they initially thought they would be safe here, they were now worried and held frantically to the trees and rocks. Only a small portion of the wave reached them. Had they not been securely tied, they would have been swept away. As it was, the tidal wave made a great effort to snatch them away but could not. They watched through soaked eyeballs as the wave cleared the reef on the western side of the island. Then, the wave cleared the outer reef, which had served as a refuge for the sea creatures. All on the mountaintop were drenched but alive, thanks to Confucius. As if celebrating a great occasion, the thousands of fish below emerged from the reef refuge dancing, splashing, and darting about joyfully. All the Chinese were far more restrained in their happiness, and they quickly set about untying one another as well as the new group of friends. Then, to complete the happy turn of events, even the birds returned chirping and singing their respective melodies.

12

New Friends

Following the tidal wave, there was no reason for secrecy. Confucius knew that the group would not be satisfied until they knew why and how they had managed to conceal themselves for so long. The Chinese gathered around the new group, eager to make their acquaintance. It was their leader who presided over introductions. He wore a blue Shaolin warrior monk robe, patterned-stitched top, full cut pants, thick oversocks, and plain sandals. "I am Chang. My son, Confucius, was right to save you. Thank you for helping him kill the boar. This is my daughter, Kumiko."

Luigi had been staring at the trio, fascinated with the Chinese group and riveted on the tidal wave and the mystery of the fish. Now, as Kumiko warmly met them, he was dumbfounded and could barely speak. He whispered to Maria, "She's my mermaid." Kumiko wore a demure, gray-colored, loose-fitting garment with traditional yellow trim. Her outfit accentuated her natural endowments. She had a regal bearing with large, round eyes and arched eyebrows like a child. She had a smooth oval face, fine forehead, full cheeks, small nose, pointed chin, and fine neck. Her mouth was generous, and most males would call her lips sensuous. Clearly, Luigi was bedazzled remembering her lips during the embrace of the giant octopus. One Shaolin named Nato did not welcome Luigi's attention. However, he greeted everyone cordially. The entire community was introduced for quite a while. There were ten incredibly lovely children of varying ages, about nineteen gorgeous women, and the remaining Shaolin.

With a follow-me gesture, Chang led the entire entourage to the far side of the mountaintop. There, only a slim crack in the rock surface permitted entry. One actually had to walk straight up to the sheer rock surface before seeing the slim opening. It permitted entry only one at a time. Inside they entered a vast underground cave. The ancient volcano was hollowed out. The group was at a loss for words as they entered the strange cavernous dwelling. They were surprised that the interior wasn't dark like a cave. Instead, it was illuminated by a strange form of light, encased in glass panels. Behind the glass, they perceived tiny lightning flashes sort of zigzagging.

Further on, the passageway opened into a large compartment with small chambers cut into the rock formations. Each of these proved to be private living quarters, illuminated by the same light source. Now they could see more clearly into the main chamber below. Here, there was an assortment of furniture formed by smooth cut stones with varied colors. The shock of the tidal wave had jarred a few lightweight items loose. They soon reached a corner where the floor seemed to be cut in an oval fashion about twenty feet across and ten feet wide. A huge ball of illuminated glass hovered above this section.

Chang motioned for a few of the Chinese to mount this cut section of floor with him. He gestured for his four guests to join him. Then, Chang pushed a section of rock and the slab of stone began to move slowly downward as if suspended by air. They were descending into the very heart of the cavern.

Maria reflexively clasped Dr. Sandorf's hand, fearing they would all fall off. Andrea, too, was apprehensive. Luigi was terrified. He moved to get off the stone slab. Kumiko deftly leapt onto the slab and restrained him. She smiled at his discomfort. Her presence on the slab reassured them that there was nothing to fear. Luigi calmed down in a hurry as they descended. Nato was unimpressed as he looked on.

Chang said, "It will take us harmlessly to the lower level. We call it a 'drop' when we take it down, and a 'lift' on the way up."

"A what?" asked Andrea.

"You do not have drops where you come from?"

"No. And we don't have the strange light behind the glass," said Dr. Sandorf.

Chang was pensive, "Ahh, so; then I will explain everything. The chamber below will prove very instructive."

As the great stone slowed to a stop, they were more puzzled and amazed than ever. The chamber into which they had descended was stunning and awesome. Looking upward, Dr. Sandorf said, "It resembles the great cathedrals of Europe." The lights played with the complex stone layers, highlighting and accentuating their multifaceted contours.

Chang proceeded toward two pits filled with water and some strange machinery.

"What are they?" inquired Dr. Sandorf.

"Those are part of the explanation I promised, as well as the beginning of some new questions. For the present, we call them fans, for they turn with the pressure of the water. My father, Moti, and his father, Chao K'uang-Yin, discovered many years ago that it is possible to harness the power of the ocean in many ways. By attaching the fans to several specially built batteries, we can make an endless supply of electricity. It is this force that powers the 'drop' and 'lift,' supplies us with light, and enables us to do other things."

"That's fantastic; there is nothing like it in Europe," noted Andrea.

The entire group moved on to where there was a special rack of what appeared to be gadgets or some kind of weapons. Here, Luigi was curious and reached for one, "Are these some sort of tools or weapons?"

"Do not touch them, for they can be dangerous," advised Kumiko. They exited this chamber.

All of a sudden, where there should have been a rock wall, there was a huge sheet of glass through which they could see into the deep lagoon of their early attempts at fishing. "The glass serves as a one-way prism through which we can observe the marine life beyond," said Chang. They were spellbound as they watched the abundant varieties of multicolored species playfully maneuvering in their enchanted underwater garden.

Luigi was first to break the nostalgia of the moment. "How is it possible that I never noticed this? I have been swimming here for years."

Once again it was Chang who explained to everyone, "It is a naturally formed one-way prism. You could not see in, but we could see you. We've seen you swimming often." Luigi's face turned beet-red with embarrassment as his eyes darted toward Kumiko.

Maria understood at once and piped teasingly behind Chang's inflection, "You're blushing, you're blushing."

"Even as a child, I cautioned you to swim with your shorts on. Someday, you'll learn to listen to your father." He had caught the drift of Chang's admonition and Maria's chiding.

Chang enjoyed his joke too, saying, "The child that obeys, never regrets." Poor Luigi—swimming nude had finally caught up with him. Nato did not find this amusing and left the group.

The remaining entourage passed on to a small underground lake that looked like an enormous swimming pool. It was alive with sea species of all kinds. "We can reach the coral reef via this underground pool and cave," explained Chang. "As you can see, our aquatic friends enter our dwelling whenever they like." At this moment, the lagoon began to rapidly fill with species eager to also get acquainted formally. Meanwhile, Kumiko entered the pool and was immediately surrounded by hundreds of friendly sea species.

As if a signal had been given, a team of dolphins pulled up. Kumiko introduced them as Ying and Yang. These dolphins had special harnesses into which several Chinese placed broken furniture and other debris caused by the tidal wave.

"The dolphins will take the material out past the reef," explained Confucius. The group watched in amazement as the dolphins came and went with their cargo.

Suddenly, Luigi stepped back from the pool's edge. Emerging from the pool was the giant octopus that had nearly killed him. It approached Kumiko, and Luigi regained his composure, realizing the octopus meant them no harm. The octopus nestled close to Kumiko. Its giant tentacles gently caressed and hugged her. Then, Kumiko signaled for Luigi, coaxing him into the water.

"Come on over here. Hands is her name, and she will not harm you. She is sorry she attacked you." Hands shook a tentacle in the direction of Luigi's hand while cuddling another tentacle warmly around Kumiko's waist. Luigi treated the tentacle as a handshake. To each in turn, Hands, the friendly octopus, offered tentacles. "She winked at me!" exclaimed Luigi in amazement.

"See? She likes you. She hopes you will forgive her. She was only protecting her young. You were hunting too close to her children." Then, four younger, smaller octopi arrived, squirming and equally friendly. Nato had returned and was staring. For many years he had felt Kumiko and he would eventually wed.

Another surprising guest arrived. The great white shark surfaced, also drawing near to Kumiko and Maria. Kumiko said, "I think Maria has already met Tooth."

Maria smiled. "Hi, Tooth! Talk about a big smile!" Sure enough, although it was difficult to imagine, Tooth was indeed smiling. Some time was spent meeting numerous new friends.

Upon leaving the lagoon, Luigi spoke to Kumiko, "You saved my life."

"Yes, you were unconscious and never saw me."

"I did see you. I thought you were a mermaid. I've seen your face in all my dreams ever since that day." His candor made Kumiko blush. It was definitely time to change the subject.

"Why don't we save some questions for dinner?" suggested Chang. "You are welcome to stay in our chambers and whenever you like we can help you rebuild your own homes. Perhaps you will decide to stay with us?"

Luigi broke free of his enchanted state. "Food sounds good. Let's eat."

Table Talk

The tables were arranged in an upper chamber and were low to the floor. At the center of each table was a circular tray that could be turned so as to place within easy reach the scrumptious assorted delicacies that had been assembled. The new arrivals found the offerings to be absolutely delectable.

"This is great salad," said Luigi with his mouth full.

"It is an assortment of marine foliage that is highly nutritional," said Confucius.

Surprisingly, the main course consisted of fish. This prompted Andrea, "We thought you would not kill fish, and we haven't tasted fish in quite a while."

Confucius explained, "You are right and wrong. We do not destroy or kill the fish we eat. Nature has her own way of creating a delicate balance in all things. The fish we eat die of natural causes. The high protein is most beneficial and essential to good health. Outside the reef, all species follow their preordained roles. Some are brought to us wounded, and we care for them in our laboratory. Others are too far gone to help. Our friends bring us a variety, and some die of old age."

Chang wore a tunic buttoned up to the neck. It was one solid color, almost gray. A bright disc hung around his neck on a chain as an adornment.

Dr. Sandorf queried, "Am I correct that you are wearing the Lo-king magic disc?"

A smiling Chang asked, "How do you come to know it?"

"The six circles suggested that it was the famous Chinese horoscope. It was brought back to Europe by the Venetian merchant, Marco Polo, in thirteen hundred."

"Precisely."

Then quite inquisitively, Dr. Sandorf picked up on an earlier statement. "You say you care for sick fish?"

"We have time. Tomorrow, you and I will spend some time together in our laboratory. If you do not mind, I too have many medical questions I would like to ask you." The two intellectuals had already formed a bond of sorts, based on mutual respect and inquisitiveness.

Over the leisurely dinner, Dr. Sandorf offered a brief account of how they came to be marooned on the island. All listened intently. He concluded with, "The conflicts in Europe pitted the French and Austrians against Germany on repeated occasions. Essentially, the eighteenth century was one of continuing conflict and aggression." He continued, "China has had its difficulties as well. In 1641 the troops of anti-Ming rebel Li Zicheng sacked the Shaolin temple. In 1674 under Kangxi Emperor the same occurred. It was reported that five fugitive Shaolin monks escaped and spread the Shaolin way all over China and beyond." This came as welcome news to all in the dining chamber.

It seemed natural for Chang to flow easily into their story of arrival. Here, however, was a five-hundred-year-old saga that began in the Sung dynasty in China. Chang said, "Our story is quite long. I suggest I share with you over the next few weeks."

The Shaolin enjoyed their dinner since they knew their historical journey very well.

As time passed, the new arrivals learned that in the Emperor Sung dynasty of China their great-grandfather, Chao K'uang-Yin, became a trusted minister to the emperor. He was the only man in China's history to have scored a perfect one hundred on the civil service examinations given periodically. Only the finest minds were even permitted to take the examinations.

Chao K'uang-Yin spoke most of the languages of the world, knew the series of annals that are China's glory, and knew the secrets of history, agriculture, mathematics, and astronomy. He was intimately well-versed in the Confucian philosophical volumes, the countless Buddhist scrolls, and could recite from memory all the glowing verses of the Tao-te Ching. Additionally, he was the most skilled surgeon and medical practitioner in China. As the story unfolded, they learned that Chao K'uang-Yin's first calling was that of the way of the Shaolin. Undisputedly a genius, he chose the monastery. In fact, he presided over the most famous Shaolin Kung Fu Temple of China.

Located in the Songsham mountain range, this temple meant "monastery in the woods"—"Shao" means temple, and "Li" forest. The temple was built on the north side of Mt. Shaoshi, the western peak of Mt. Song—one of four sacred mountains of China.

Dr. Sandorf and the others recalled Chang's explanation since he was an excellent storyteller, "He was a great Sifu. In Japan, they use the word Sensei. In your world he was a revered teacher. Out of respect, then and now, we most often refer to him as Sifu."

The newcomers could picture the Shaolin monastery and Sifu surrounded by pupils as they performed their patterns of dance-like movements. Sifu wore an orange warrior tunic with baggy brown pants. He wore oversocks bound up to the knees with elastic leg bindings. He stood on slightly raised sandals. The front of his scalp was bald, while in the back he had long, braided queue. He often wore this queue curled up on his head. When he unwrapped it, he could insert a blade or stone at its tip. Thus with a head movement, the queue was quickly converted into a formidable weapon.

Chang recounted some of the lessons taught by Sifu. "Once when a pupil smiled for having caught an arrow in flight, aimed, by the way, directly at his heart, Sifu admonished, 'No! Smiling is not permitted at any stage of learning. You have a long way to go. Let me demonstrate.' At a signal, six pupils lined up, three with spears and the others with bows and arrows. Sifu, blindfolded, caught all three arrows while dodging the three spears. Sifu then handed the three arrows to the student who had smiled, thus demonstrating just how far the student needed to go. However, to encourage the pupil, Sifu confided, 'I, too, have smiled a few times.'"

They also were informed, "Sifu would demonstrate how, in close-quarter combat, one might not have room to prepare a blow. In this lesson, ten students stood against a wall facing ten others. The object of the lesson was to note that the striking arm could only move forward, being blocked from behind by the wall. Most often, the students would bruise their elbows against the wall and strike with very little force. Sifu was always patient and encouraging. His point was to enable them to rely on their chi, or inner power. This required much patience, training, and focus.

"When Sifu demonstrated the technique from the same position flat against the wall, no one could discern any movement. Yet, the pupil in front of him was propelled backward into the air roughly fifteen feet.

"Another lesson involved the tolling of a great bell. Students would first push a great log, held in a wooden harness, against an ancient bell. The bell would respond with a bright, clear sound throughout the valley. However, when students tried with their hands and feet, barely a whisper of a sound was heard. Then, Sifu would demonstrate that with one finger, he could make the bell ring clearly. Here, too, it was a matter of focusing one's chi."

There were many feats extolled by Chang as his reverent reflections on Sifu's extraordinary genius and martial arts skills continued. Yet, deliberately, the salient characteristic that always came through was that of teacher. Chang noted, "The example of students striking hanging bags filled with sand, beans, pebbles, and rocks made this point well. Depending on a student's advancement, he would select one bag and strike at it with hands or feet. This enabled pupils both to harden their hands and feet and to learn how to deliver ever more powerful blows. In the instruction that Sifu gave, none of the students selected the weighty bags filled with rocks. On rare occasions, Sifu would demonstrate counseling that '*when a student knows a thing can be done, then he will study harder, and eventually rejects all doubt.*'" Chang added, "This is the reason a teacher teaches. For this reason, rejecting all vanity, Sifu would strike the rock bags in a series of swift strikes with hands and feet, tearing the bags from their perches and pulverizing the stones into a cloud of dust. However, Sifu's teaching days were put on hold."

Chang explained how six emissaries from Emperor Sung rode into the courtyard of the monastery to deliver a sealed parchment. The message in Chinese read: *Please come to Peking. I need your advice.*

The note was signed by Sung, and it had the imperial seal of authentication.

Upon reading the message, Sifu interrupted his class, leaving one of his top students in charge. Within minutes he accompanied the six horsemen and rode off to Peking. There was no way to know that he would spend the next five years as an advisor to the imperial court dealing with affairs of the nation. From the very first, Sifu rejected all the royal garments and evaded pomp and ceremonies unless commanded by the emperor. He alone wore the humble Shaolin garb. While in appearance he seemed out of place, the emperor kept him very close and clearly appreciated his wise counsel.

The real reason the emperor had sent for him was not revealed during the five years. Then at last, the time came when the emperor invited Sifu into his private chamber confiding that he desired to discuss several items that were on his mind.

Emperor Sung confided that he had sought the wise counsel of each of his advisors one at a time over the years. The first question dealt with a thousand-year-old issue. Sung asked, "What would you say to opening a dialogue with the West, Europe? How would Europe, with its warring independent nations, receive China? Is it to our advantage? Should we wait? These matters and questions have arisen for thousands of years. Well?"

As was his fashion, Sifu pondered the questions considerably, and then he answered each question in sequence. "Yes, it is an important dialogue. China should initiate it. Each nation of Europe will respond differently. It is to our advantage even if we uncover enemies within these nations. Our advantage is to know our enemies as well as our friends. Waiting is no longer wise; the thousands of years in which we have waited have given us no answers to these very questions."

When Sifu's response became known to the imperial court, some ministers reacted with rage at even the suggestion, so caught up were they in tradition. Others decided cunningly to eliminate the emperor and his chief advisor, Sifu. The latter course of action proved much more difficult than anyone could have imagined. Indeed, there were attempts on their lives.

Sung confided in Sifu that he alone had advised opening a dialogue with Europe. Then, the emperor asked yet another question, "How did you know which antidote to administer in the most recent attempt on my life?"

Sifu's response was, "I had no idea which poison would be used. Such is the nature of poisons. Each must carry a separate antidote."

He noted the questioning look on the emperor's face and continued, "For the past five years, we have both taken antidotes for every known poison, usually in our food."

Now Emperor Sung knew. He asked his next question. "The recent attack on you makes the fifteenth?"

"Yes," was Sifu's simple reply.

Chang related that the emperor was tired of the intrigues of the court. Also, it had become obvious that many at the court were jealous of the unique friendship between Sung and Sifu. So it came as no surprise that soon afterward Sung sent Sifu as his royal representative to Europe.

One day Luigi interjected himself into the narrative begun by Chang at their first dinner, with this, "So Sifu was sent to Europe to keep him alive?"

"No, to the contrary. It was to keep the other advisors alive. Emperor Sung knew firsthand that they would fail in their attempts to assassinate Sifu in any covert or overt attempt. So, too, since only Sifu had advised an opening with Europe, the only person Sung could trust with so vital a mission was Sifu. He knew that upon his return, Sifu would give him an honest report. Likewise, Sung reasoned that if the Europeans were foolish enough to try to harm his emissary, they would regret it just as many of his counselors had."

Chang's tale continued over many weeks. He recounted how Sifu sailed from China in a sturdy craft called a sampan. The sampan had a single Chinese lugsail adorned with the imperial emblem and carried forty people. The craft was severely damaged as it fought the gales while rounding the southern tip of Africa. Here, the Indian and Atlantic Oceans meet and the currents are known to be among the most dangerous on the planet. Their rudder, like that of Andrea's craft, was damaged. However, their rudder was struck by a lightning bolt. They too were at the mercy of the tides, which delivered them to the island. They tried to use what was left of their sail to steer clear of the coral reef. Unknown to them, the coral reef surrounded the island. They were driven by the currents onto the reef. When they struck the reef, a few managed to jump clear. The others drowned, and some were eaten by sharks.

Marooned as they were, they tried to signal a ship some five years later by lighting a great fire. However, the ship that came to rescue them ventured too close to the reef and was wrecked. All hands were lost, just out of reach of the safety of the island. Sifu decided after witnessing the shark feeding frenzy that they would never signal for help again. So it was that they abandoned the shore for the inner sanctum of the mountain, venturing forth for food and recreation.

As a matter of honor, Sifu turned his brilliant mind to the fish kingdom and the marine food chain. He believed that with enough knowledge of the sea, the problems of lack of food which plagued China for centuries might be solved. China, as they knew, had one-third of the world's population. Sifu was also committed to finding a way to communicate with the fish of the sea so as to prevent a similar unfortunate tragedy for others. Daily, he thought of the victims of the sharks. The sea represented a unique challenge for the advanced mind of Sifu. The coral reef became his laboratory for a lifetime of devoted study.

Chang also shared, "Many years later, Sifu took a wife, and my father, Moti K'uang-Yin, was born. It was immediately apparent that he was born with the unique mental gifts of his father. So it has been now for four generations. Collectively, in three hundred years we have progressed beyond what we believe other civilizations have even imagined was possible. However, there is great danger in what we know. Our ability to communicate with fish must never be divulged."

Finally, Dr. Sandorf had asked his first question. "Why hide such a wonderful ability?"

"With time you will accept that there are strong reasons that will require you to share our silence. It was for this reason we did not make ourselves known to you for so long. We were not at first certain that searchers would not come for you."

Andrea asked, "You mean there is a way to escape the island?"

"If a ship were handled properly, it could stay a mile or two off shore, and if one could communicate with the captain, then perhaps one could swim the distance. However, outside the reef the sharks go about their business as usual. Given these obstacles, the situation would be hopeless," said Chang.

"If that were the case, you would not have wanted your secret known, right?" noted Dr. Sandorf.

Chang looked deeply into Dr. Sandorf's eyes and for a moment, it seemed the conversation had come to an end. Then Chang said, "Dr. Sandorf, you seem unduly concerned about our desire to keep our secret. Suppose there are other secrets of the mind that are equally dangerous? Why do you think that the ability to communicate with fish is the only skill that four generations of highly intelligent persons would want to keep secret?"

Even after many weeks, Dr. Sandorf and the others were stunned and bewildered. They had not given any thought to the possibility of other abilities. After a long pause, Dr. Sandorf replied, "We are, of course, limited in our appreciation of the problems and burdens of the responsibilities that you have. Perhaps, with time, you will find it wise in your judgment to share more with us, as the best means of ensuring they remain a secret. After all, we shall be curious, and I am a scientist. As people whose appetites for knowing may be less than yours, we nevertheless share the same basic human nature to be inquisitive. Thus, we shall inquire one way or another since it is natural to do so. However, if we could be taught why there is danger in your abilities, we would be more likely to share in the sense of responsibility you have. The secrets are yours; they do not belong to us. We owe you our lives, and as honorable persons, we pledge not to give away that which is not ours to give."

Chang was very pleased with Dr. Sandorf's reply and began again, "After a lifetime of study, Sifu was able to ascertain certain basic truths. For example, the basic food supply of all fish is plant life. However, the rooted vegetation is usually small in aquatic environments. Here in the coral reef kingdom there is abundance. So, too, there is large variety of microscopic plankton whose mass and size enable fish to utilize them directly as a food source. No one species is dominant. Here at the coral reef, fish are abundant and almost every species can be found. Sifu studied in great depth the behavior of almost all known species. Thus, he ascertained that there were indeed certain common denominators, as it were. The fish were always intelligent enough to communicate adequately with one another within the same species. More interestingly, most could also understand numerous other species."

Andrea asked, "You mean that whatever any one fish communicates is understood by all?"

Chang needed to clarify. "Some species are mute while many are quite vocal. Others use electrical impulses. The range of sounds includes grunting, tooting, chirping, clicking, rattling, humming, and drumming. Each species differs from one another. Some make croaking or pumping sounds by rapidly contracting and expanding their air bladders. This causes the walls of their bladders to vibrate while the organ itself serves as a sounding board. Whales emit a considerable range of sounds, from that of a low, creaking gate to high-pitched whistles that are easily associated with various activities such as feeding, breeding, and aggression. Their range indicates a higher level of communication choices with more subtleties than a human expresses. While most people learn a language, they use only a small fraction of its choices in a lifetime. For example, most people get by using only ten thousand words of the English language, which offers a couple of million choices. The whale would never limit itself so foolishly. The dolphin calf emits high-pitched whistles at birth, which serve as directional guides."

Andrea was fascinated and nodded affirmatively on many occasions during the weeks needed to relate Chang's story. One day he remarked, "True, true, but there is no way to translate these sounds into conversation that is intelligible to us. I have heard these creatures communicating when fishing. When there is a general condition of danger, they often make a lot of noise."

Kumiko interjected, "Noise to you, but it is speech to them. While humans are not capable of duplicating their numerous sounds, there is a basic requirement for all such systems to rely on. As Chang said, the common denominator is intelligence—all fish species must possess intelligence if they are to communicate. It is only the system that changes between the species, just as it changes in human languages."

"It all makes sense; I just don't understand," said Luigi.

"All wisdom is approached by taking a first step. In this case, the first step is realizing that which one does not know."

Maria held herself in check for many weeks. Then at one of their many dinners, she said, "I still have difficulty understanding how Sifu could defeat so many of Emperor Sung's advisors."

"Enough is enough when it comes to storytelling. Maria, perhaps if you were to join us for exercise tomorrow morning, you might better understand," said Chang.

"I think I'd enjoy it very much; thank you."

Chang sipped his wine and asked, "How do you like this wine?"

Andrea perked up, "Since I seem to be the only one enjoying a third glass, may I say that it is excellent? I have been fortunate to have cultivated and indulged myself in many fine wines." Andrea was feeling the wine and continued, "Austria has four thousand years of wine making. I particularly like Steinfeder, Federspiel, and Smaragd. All are made one hundred percent from the Wachau grape. The Wacho valley climatically marks the transition from the Alps to the Hungarian plains but is located in southern Austria. With the beautiful Danube River moderating the effects of the cold Alpine winds, there is no better grape in all the world."

Chang's response ignored that Andrea was tipsy. It came with a paternal proud smile as he explained, "This wine was cured from undersea berries and mixed with pure spring water and herbs. It is very nutritional. My daughter, Kumiko, is to be congratulated, for it took her many weeks to prepare."

Dr. Sandorf picked up on the inflection in the word nutritional. "I notice that everything you eat or do has a relationship with maintaining good health."

"Every person owes it to himself to become all that he or she can be. Our bodies and our minds, like our muscles, thrive on use. Therefore, everything we do or eat is directed at improving ourselves. Man lives in a rhythmic universe; all about us are pulsating cycles. These can be seen in plants, animals, our own bodies, and the stellar constellations. All creatures sleep and wake, experience hunger and weariness. The universe is full of rhythms—night follows day, tides ebb and flow, and each season follows the one before. One of the great joys of living is to do that which ought to be done at the precise time when it is best to do it. As a doctor, have you noticed or studied the changing consciousness of sleep, the vivid dreaming accompanied by physiological changes every ninety to one hundred ten minutes?"

"Why, yes."

Chang elaborated, "Then you know that a normal, healthy person will secrete more than 50 percent of his daily quota of adrenocortical hormones into his blood in the last three hours of sleep. A sick person does not."

Dr. Sandorf continued, "At low and high tides, depending on the amounts of these important hormones available to the tissues and nervous system, there can be important implications for a person's reaction to stress, a quarrel, or fatigue."

Chang picked up, and for a moment, he and Dr. Sandorf left the others far behind in their conversation. "Precisely, and an inverse relationship exists between sensory keenness and the amounts of steroid hormones."

Andrea finally interrupted, "Well, now, that's all fine, whatever it means. You two have lost me again."

Dr. Sandorf smiled at the rebuke and explained, "In simple terms, our sensitivity to things like taste, smell, or sound will vary according to these hormones and the time of day. Thus, the wine you just had is especially pleasing in the evening when the hormone level is low.

Later, when the hormone level drops, you will experience fatigue. When people consume their heaviest meals in the morning rather than after sunset, they will be considerably less obese."

Chang was obviously delighted with the level of conversation while the others were lost. "We are driven passionately with the synchronization of our bodies and minds, with that of the universe around us. Doing the right thing at the right time is to strive for perfection. It is also to find the balance and harmony in all things. It is the essence of happiness, for it is the fulfillment of one's reason for existence. These are all part of the truth as we know it, passed on to us by Sifu and my father, Moti. Dr. Sandorf, in what do you find the meaning of life?"

Dr. Sandorf responded without hesitation, "The meaning of life for me is not as noble nor fulfilling. For me there can only be escape from this island. Then, I must return to Austria and learn who the traitor was. The meaning of my life and that which moves my soul is revenge."

Chang and the others listened respectfully. Then Chang said, "From what you have told us, it would appear that Germany would impose an unnatural influence on Austria. Such a condition will test the Austrians, and they will win their cause if it is meant to be. It is interesting to note a parallel spanning the ages. Sifu was most attracted to one particular form of government taught by the legendary Moti for whom he named my father, his son. Moti lived between the times of Confucius and Mencius, teaching that, universally, all government institutions should be submitted to the ultimate test—were they of benefit to society? Moti was deeply religious, believing that T'ien—what you call heaven—loved men and that all men should love one another."

"You are a fascinating and most gracious host," noted Dr. Sandorf.

Chang paused for a moment as he and the others sipped their wine, "I believe we have arrived at many things in our brief discussions. Let us not further delay the answer to your unstated question. We have no name for the system of communication we use with the fish."

"It sounds to me like telepathy," ventured Luigi.

"Let us explore that, Luigi. What do we know of telepathy? Well, the distance between two people in telepathic contact appears to be immaterial—it can take place over thousands of miles or over just a few feet. Another important characteristic is that telepathy appears at times to be independent of time. There are numerous examples of people seeing events that were to take place at some future time. Neither future visions nor contact over thousands of miles is at all involved with our method. Also, there is no evidence of telepathy being used to control the behavior of one person or animal by another."

"Then it's not telepathy," concluded Luigi.

"No, it's definitely not telepathy, although that was a very good guess."

Dr. Sandorf decided to join in. "I sincerely hope you are not going to explain what it is by telling us that which it is not. I had an experience with this approach to sage-knowledge that was not the most rewarding."

Once again, Chang was obviously delighted and commented, "Sage-knowledge or no-knowledge is an even more excellent way of describing our method of communicating. Dr. Sandorf, you are indeed most sagacious. I never would have guessed that you had any idea of no-knowledge."

Dr. Sandorf rejoined, "I only know how much I do not know. I am aware, however, that the way to comprehend no-knowledge rests in testing that which we think we know, and examining the limitations of such knowledge. Beyond this, there is a big gap in my grasping what is meant by no-knowledge."

Chang suggested, "Perhaps you had the wrong teacher, for it seems you stopped precisely where you should have begun. We men of science all realize that there is much more to know than we have at any one time mastered. If we did not accept that we are always asking more questions than delivering answers, there would be no advancement of science. Thus, science—as man has cultivated it—is always an imprecise tool since it usually explains that which has occurred. It is always dependent on further inquiry, which, at times, totally refutes previous beliefs, and which uses the ability to reason as its highest virtue. Reasoning and perceptions themselves are again imperfect tools. One does not always perceive what one thinks is perceived. For instance, there was a time when people believed that placing a long pole in deep water bent the pole. Obviously, the light refracted through the water was a new phenomenon for the eye, and considerable adjustment was required before man realized that his perception of the world and reasoning skills were both not the most reliable of tools. For a very long period of history, man also believed that the earth was flat. As a man of science, Dr. Sandorf, you realize that, thus far, we have no controversy."

Chang continued, "We are likely in agreement that science, reason, and perception are all subject to considerable error, either jointly or independently. Andrea, Luigi, and Maria should also find this acceptable. Now, to simplify the rest, I believe I should first explain that the term no-knowledge does not imply any lack of knowledge nor ignorance. It is rather knowledge that is neither acquired nor dependent on science, reason, and perception solely. You all can readily accept that there is such a thing as intuitive knowledge not governed by the above. In fact, in most cases, intuitive knowledge will master the direction in which these three will be used for the furtherance of additional knowledge.

"The Taoist Chuangtzu, who lived in the fourth century before Christ, suggested that sooner or later when man hesitates at the outer limits of rational and intuitive knowledge, then there is yet more. While our minds realize there is more, our usual scientific approaches are not equal to the task of comprehending the how or why of it. In fact, the greatest obstacle—and I believe the place at which you stopped, Dr. Sandorf—was here: the place where the mind must seek comfort, resolution, and security in what it cannot know. May I suggest that just as we can all recognize that none of us possesses all knowledge, the human mind can accept that there is more to know. The quest for knowledge need not stop just because our usual tools are not up to the task. We need merely to search for newer and better tools. There is, in fact, more knowledge in the universe than any mind can hold. Because we are not there to witness through our senses the sound of a falling tree or stone does not warrant that we conclude there is no stone or tree. We ought never to deny the existence of anything based on our own limitations or observations. The universe must be taken far more seriously than that. "At this higher level of cognizance, one must transcend events and qualities, for the knowledge one becomes one with has no shape and no time. One gains humility and harmony with knowledge at this level by widening one's awareness of the vastness of nature through ungrudging communion with her. With rational knowledge, the scientist is but a spectator of nature. With no-knowledge, one becomes a participant in nature. As a participant in nature one understands beauty through being beauty. One finds one's place in all things and shares in the beauty of all things. One enjoys the balance and harmony of the universe. I do not think you need to be able to do it in order to understand that we do it. There are forces in the universe that are good and evil. Even we dare not tamper with all things. We are privileged to communicate with the fish of the deep through no-knowledge. Simply put, some of us have been blessed with the ability to utilize a far greater portion of our brain capacity. There are those in the world who would want to put this ability to their own wicked use. There are those who, knowing of this force, would try to become masters of the sea to become masters of the world. We, and now you, have an obligation to use that which has been entrusted to us wisely and well. Will you then give me your word that you will never divulge our secret?"

13

Another Secret

As was promised, the very next morning the entire community met in another large space called the Shaolin chamber. The Chinese lined up while Chang offered the others a seat by his side. Normally, Chang would lead the group. However, today he was the gracious host, and Confucius officiated. Just prior to starting, Dr. Sandorf took the opportunity of asking Confucius, "According to the dates your father gave us last night, Chang would have to be roughly one hundred forty or fifty years old."

"Chang is precisely one hundred fifty years old in June," replied Confucius.

Dr. Sandorf managed a response, "Chang looks like a man of fifty."

Confucius said, "He takes good care of himself."

"That is the understatement of the century."

Clearly, Dr. Sandorf was not going to be told how this was possible. Dr. Sandorf said, "Man has wanted to know the secret of longevity for thousands of years, and I guess I can wait a few more days."

If there was a command, Dr. Sandorf and the others did not see it, yet, everyone else took up positions in three rows facing Confucius.

As they began to move, the entire group seemed intent and yet at rest.

"It looks like a dance," said Luigi.

Chang overheard and explained, "It's not a dance but a system of exercise and defense movements known as fighting patterns. The end result is excellent health, fortitude, and great skill in self-defense."

Maria said, "The movements are graceful like those of a ballet. Why do they move so slowly?"

Luigi asked, "Why do they use those funny outfits, and why are their movements not athletic if they are preparing for combat?"

Chang was patient and informative, saying, "The clothes allow for the maximum freedom of movement. The women wear black because the astrological Yin is dark and static. On the other hand, the Yang is male—bright and mobile—so they wear white. We do have days in which we concentrate on strength and speed. However, the roots of Shaolin martial arts and their unique teachings go far deeper than the body—they are nourished more by the spirit. A correct attitude and not athletics is the key to progress. For today, there will be no quick power punches, no snap kicks, no fighting. Observe."

There was total silence during their slow-motion movements, and Chang spoke reverently, "The body hieroglyphics of 'Tai Chi Shuan.'"

"The patterns are beautiful," whispered Maria.

Luigi asked, "What's a fighting pattern?"

Chang explained, "Every possible blow with foot, hand, or any other part of the body must eventually be able to be executed while the body is in motion. There are numerous set practice exercises designed especially to enable you to do this. Since each practice technique has its own form, we call them fighting patterns or forms. I believe, Dr. Sandorf, that you mentioned seeing an exhibition of martial arts. Well, you probably saw a version of Karate or open-hand combat. The origins of karate go far back to the Ryukyu Islands lying between China and Japan but not as far back as the Shaolin way of China."

Chang continued, "In the fifth century AD, Bodhidharma, an Indian Buddhist philosopher and missionary, brought this belief to China. He entered the Shaolin-ssu temple but found that the priests there were not up to the rigorous training of both mind and body. Thus, he set about developing their physical and mental abilities so as to make them strong enough to withstand his severe training. He began with a system of mind-body self-control that he himself had learned in India. One of the cardinal teachings is that Shaolin martial arts must never be used in unprovoked aggression against an opponent. The Shaolin way is to develop spirit and body into a unified personality against which evil is powerless."

Luigi temporarily broke the discourse with another observation, "Some of the movements resemble those of animals."

Chang summarized, "As in all things, the Chinese created variations and introduced combat methods based on the movements of animals. Even oriental fencing became part of the system. All systems spring from mankind's need for discipline and growth. As originally intended, the Shaolin way is to be dedicated to the building of a better society and world. There is simplicity in the concept, for what good is a strong body with a wicked heart? Conversely, what good is a weak body with a pure heart in any confrontation? Evil wins out, and society must bear the consequences. Thus, to be of real value to society, a strong body must be allied with a deep sense of justice, humility, wisdom, and honor."

"In the exhibition I saw, a fighter would invariably pull one fist back toward his body as the opposite fist moved toward the opponent," recounted Dr. Sandorf.

"A keen observation. In Karate, the action-reaction motion of both limbs adds to the blow's impact. Tai Chi Chuan is considerably more complex. It flows from what many believe to be a mere oracle or fortune-telling. I can assure you that *The Book of Changes*—called the *I Ching*—is more revelation, more philosophy, and a door to wisdom unlike any other. The Shaolin universe begins with what you would call a two-sided coin—a positive and a negative, or Yang and Yin. If you can visualize a single line turning upon itself to form a circle, you will be able to contrast it with the single line of Karate. Also, in order to be a true Shaolin, one must cultivate one's Chi."

"Chee," repeated Luigi.

"No, the correct pronunciation is either Chi pronounced 'Ki' or as in a 'key' for a door. For three thousand years, long before Karate, there was the chi. Literally, the word chi means any of the following: atmosphere, climate, vapor, and air. Anyone in the martial arts would associate it with breathing and concentration. Actually it is much more than these. If you recall that reason fails to define many things, then you can again see that air and breathing are terms that define things in such a way as to make them appealing to the senses or understandable through reason. The chi is a force in the universe that permeates all things and makes them the way they are. In humans, it might be described as the inner being. Thus, to cultivate one's chi, concentration in a receptive state is essential, rather than the exertion of physical energy in breaking boards or bricks. The chi must flow within the entire body so that spontaneity of reaction is stressed continuously."

Chang continued to explain. "Unlike Karate, which means open hand, the Shaolin must be a master of all weapons, including the open hand. In the example last night of Sifu ringing the great bell with just his finger, he drew on his chi. In the art of fencing, to cite another example, the counter movements must be made without slow logic or hesitant reasoning. If one trusted to reason, one would perish. The counter movements in fencing must spring forth as wordless and even thoughtless messages translated into integrated and immediate action.

In the Sumiye school of painting, the chi is expressed by painting on paper so thin that the slightest hesitancy will cause the paper to tear. Each stroke must be swift, decisive, final, and irrevocable. For the Shaolin, there is no question of fame, reward, titles, or honors. Rather, there is only participation and oneness with nature. Confucius taught that throughout the universe one finds centrality, which he called Chung, and harmony, called Ho. He taught that these are inescapable laws of existence. In practice, all things must be measured, and extremes must be avoided."

Chang proceeded to illustrate his points, "The bow that is pulled just a bit too far is useless. The knife edge honed beyond its sharpest is equally flawed. To truly be a Shaolin is to be all one was meant to be without reserve. In combat, the Shaolin uses his chi as an infinite well from which to draw strength. Only this enables him to focus the mind and muscles in combination to produce the greatest amount of strength that the human body is capable of."

All the time that Chang spoke, the entire group flowed gracefully through one pattern after another. They never seemed to get tired. Maria was grateful to Chang. "Thank you for your patient explanations. I still wonder how Sifu could defeat so many warriors."

Luigi asked, "Will we be permitted to try the exercises, I mean the fighting patterns?"

"It would give us great pleasure to teach all of you."

The group found the way of life of their new friends to be fascinating. They accepted the invitation to remain with them and enjoyed the endless interaction with so wise and interesting a community. Every morning the entire community worked out together, and Luigi tried in vain to impress Kumiko. These efforts were not lost on Nato, who was ever-present.

Some afternoons found them out at the safer coral reefs. From the chamber of unused weapons, they were outfitted with special head masks that incorporated very small tanks of compressed air. They soon discovered that these breathing head masks enabled them to remain submerged for hours.

Like their Chinese friends, they entered the reefs through the interior lagoon, surfacing through great water holes. One of their greatest joys was the friendly reception they always got from all the fish. They found that many of the species had distinct personalities. Hands would keep close to Luigi as if to keep him from any harm. Tooth would swim along as Maria hitched a ride on her favorite giant turtle. They would visit a deep nest of tridences—mollusks—of five hundred pounds. They were always accompanied by curious dolphins, manta rays, remoras, swordfish, carp, kingfish, and hundreds of smaller species that often appeared to be fascinated with Kumiko's and Maria's toes. They gathered around the two in great bunches.

Chang enjoyed his endless conversations with Dr. Sandorf, especially the intricacies of medicine. They all listened intently to the endless stories and enlightening conversations of Chang, Confucius, and Kumiko. They learned how easily the Shaolin could hide in the shadows in open daylight by flattening their bodies and pressing against the foliage. They found they had no need for weapons except for an occasional hunt. Yet, the Shaolin training included proficiency in the use of numerous weapons. They learned that the original set of weapons that Luigi had noticed on the first day turned out to be unique underwater weapons developed especially by Sifu during the initial fifty years of study. Then, when Sifu mastered communication with the fish, he no longer needed these weapons. These weapons fired pellets under extreme pressure, which could give sharks a nasty jolt while not harming them permanently. They learned that if used on a human, they would knock him out easily, but one would recover.

In his well-equipped laboratory, Chang shared with Dr. Sandorf his advanced studies of cellular rejuvenation. Many species of fish had the ability to re-grow limbs that were lost. These studies fascinated Dr. Sandorf, who saw the implications for cripples. Chang understood that people with serious accidents who lost the use of their limbs were not able to acquire movement because the nerve cells were damaged. This damage was usually somewhere between the affected limb and the brain. Chang shared with Dr. Sandorf that administering certain hormones immediately after limbs had been severed in fish enabled the fish to rebuild the nerves and obtain the use of otherwise crippled appendages. Essentially, he learned from species that had the ability to re-grow limbs and applied this knowledge successfully to species without the ability. These successes could theoretically be applicable to man. Dr. Sandorf found that in almost every imaginable arena of science, medicine, and associated study, Chang, Confucius, and Kumiko were astoundingly advanced for people marooned on an island. They were fascinated by Dr. Sandorf's exceptional capabilities as well. Over time they came to realize that if they left the island, they would make a formidable medical team. Very likely, they would open a hospital in order to carry on the work that so intrigued them.

Dr. Sandorf was exposed to the age-old practice of acupuncture in which needles are inserted into the body in order to combat illness and pain. He learned that there are hundreds of vital points in man and considerably fewer in fish. In fact, there was absolutely no formal study of acupuncture in medicine in Europe, and any application to sea creatures was unimaginable. The differences between man and fish were astonishing. Man had twelve channels or meridians, which serve as pathways for the body's vital energies. When Chang and Confucius demonstrated their power to hypnotize, Dr. Sandorf was even more astonished. They could hypnotize a person by merely touching the person. So powerful was their mental energy that it could tap into any place on a person's body. The knowledge and wisdom that Chang and Confucius possessed turned every passing month into an adventure of the mind.

After several months, Maria's question about Sifu's Shaolin abilities was answered. One day, the exercise chamber was prepared for an exhibition of martial arts. All were present.

Unlike the previous days, the Shaolin were warming up with fast-paced patterns, jumps, gymnastic summersaults, knuckle pushups, finger pushups, and other physically demanding exercises.

Suddenly, at a signal from Confucius, the fighting patterns ended. At four sets of double-rounded beams placed four feet above the ground on two special racks, two students per beam mounted the apparatus. Two other students immediately began to turn the beams. This reminded Dr. Sandorf of the Canadian logrolling competition whereby loggers tried to knock one another off a log in the water. Then, as soon as one combatant lost footing, the pair was replaced by another team. However, the Shaolin would strike at one another with furious series of blows with feet and hands. It was not the turning beam that caused someone to fall, but rather the blows. Some Shaolin mounted the beams from the floor with uncanny gymnastic ability. Finally, after ten teams had all taken their turn, only one of the original pairs continued. It appeared that neither could take advantage of the other. It ended only when Confucius clapped his hands. Miko and Chuan were satisfied with a draw as usual. Nato was declared the overall winner. Kumiko smiled.

Speaking about the pair who fought to a draw, Confucius explained, "Miko and Chuan have been known to go at it for hours. They are equally expert in almost any encounter."

Dr. Sandorf, Andrea, Luigi, and Maria applauded enthusiastically. Luigi shouted, "Wow! I've never seen anything like it."

"Excellent! More!" cried Maria.

Her wish was to be granted. The Shaolin upended the balance beams and set them close to the guests for another demonstration. Confucius gave the signal, and ten of the Shaolin lined up in front of the beams. Then, Confucius clapped his hands. At this signal, the ten Shaolin, in a lightning-fast blur, released what appeared to be eighteen metal flying stars.

Luigi burst out, "What are those?"

"Flying stars are small throwing knives. An expert can throw eighteen from each hand in rapid succession," explained Confucius.

Once again, the flying stars landed with resounding thuds and the beams bristled with starred knives. The four guests broke out once again with excited applause.

"Kumiko will now demonstrate a dangerous technique," said Confucius. At that, Kumiko took center stage, sitting with crossed legs. She blindfolded herself. Nato, the Shaolin warrior, volunteered to be clad with a breastplate and armed with a sword within its sheath. This warrior knelt in front of Kumiko.

There was absolute silence in the chamber but for Luigi's distracting whisper to Chang, "Why is she unarmed? That's not fair; he wears a breastplate and gets the sword."

Chang raised a patient hand, "Shhhh! Observe!"

The chamber was silent when without warning, Nato's hand darted for his sword. In a flash Nato's sword was unsheathed. Even faster, Kumiko leapt into the air, arched backward, and kicked at Nato's chest. A very loud crack was heard as Nato flew backward, recoiling from Kumiko's kick. His sword sliced through thin air as he landed nearly ten feet away. He seemed unconscious as Kumiko and the others rushed to his side. However, within seconds, he recovered and bowed to Kumiko and Chang.

Luigi exhaled, "Good God!" Maria gasped.

"How did she know when he would draw the sword?" asked Luigi.

Chang clarified, "She felt the air move as soon as his hand moved. Without the protective breastplate, she would have crushed his ribs."

The martial arts demonstration continued with mock duels with various weapons: swords, flails, sickles, and fighting sticks. Then, to the further delight of the guests, they also broke piles of stones and hard wood in a spectacular display of focused energy.

Confucius demonstrated a particularly sensational feat. He placed a long spear against the base of one of the beams with the pointed blade squarely at his throat. Then, he leaned forward, bending the spear incredibly, and this, without penetrating his skin. It appeared that at any second, the spear would go through his throat. When Confucius concluded, the four guests applauded spontaneously. Confucius bowed to Chang, and all the Shaolin bowed as one.

Confucius was not finished. He went to Chang and whispered. Chang nodded affirmatively. Confucius indicated, "There will be one more demonstration, and Chang will perform it."

Chang was soon surrounded by his Shaolin warriors and signaled for Luigi to join him. Luigi was willing thanks to a smile from Kumiko, saying, "Just so I don't have to wear a metal vest. What do I do?"

Nato handed Luigi a spear, and Chang invited, "Attack whenever you like." Luigi began to circle, always looking at Chang's eyes as if he were spellbound, as indeed he was. For just at the moment he was going to strike, Chang's eyes became the eyes of a Bengal tiger. Chang had disappeared before Luigi's eyes. Only the Bengal tiger remained, circled, and then attacked. Luigi fainted. Nato was first at his side. Within seconds, Luigi recovered and asked, "What in heaven's name happened? A tiger, no less!"

Confucius answered, "The technique is called the 'tiger's eyes,' which freezes an untrained attacker. Actually, it is a powerful hypnotic projection."

"It was real to me," sighed Luigi.

"The first time I saw the tiger's eyes I was scared, too. I was seven years old. You'll get used to it," said Kumiko.

It was at this moment that Luigi decided he would study the Shaolin way.

However, for Luigi things did not go well at first. Nato was assigned as his primary Sifu. Also, from the very beginning, he tried too hard during the Shaolin exercises. To learn that which can only be learned through patience takes time. It was also evident that he was attracted and frustrated by Kumiko. Simply put, she was superior to him in all things, and he was foolishly trying to establish what he perceived to be a normal male-to-female dominant and subservient relationship. He quickly got nowhere. While he did strengthen his body, his mind just wasn't in the right place.

If Luigi's initial attempts were compared to his achievements after five years, the difference could only be described as remarkable. In great measure this was due to Nato's constant supervision. For example, at the start, he exhibited zero proficiency in everything: in knuckle push-ups, Luigi could not lift himself an inch from the floor; in sit-ups, he was exhausted after just twenty; in chin-ups, he barely made it to ten; in board-breaking, he almost broke his hand instead; in fighting patterns, he stumbled around awkwardly; in running, he was exhausted after the first mile; while kicking a dummy, he hurt his foot; when blocking a midsection blow, he was painfully too slow; when blocking a blow to the head, he received another headache; when anticipating a blow blindfolded, he might as well have been an immovable rock. Finally, there was Luigi ungracefully falling off a balance beam. Nato was unimpressed.

The Chinese never failed to politely cover their mouths with their fingers, but the laughter from their eyes resounded throughout the training chamber.

However, Luigi's perseverance would prevail. It was no surprise that after the first five years, no one could recognize Luigi as the same inept and clumsy student. He had improved dramatically in all exercises, techniques, and skills.

Reflecting on his progress one day, Dr. Sandorf indicated, as an aside to Chang, "Luigi is persistent. I give him credit."

"He has improved much over the last five years. He does not quit. This is a good sign."

"He likes Kumiko a lot."

Chang chuckled. "She is superior to him in all the ways of the Shaolin."

"Does he stand a ghost of a chance?"

Chang's reply actually surprised him, "Yes, when he gives up foolish notions. This may take a while. Luigi has a true and noble heart. As in his exercises, he is likely to persevere and succeed. More importantly, while she never shows it, Kumiko likes him."

"What about the other women?"

"Many like Luigi and would be quite willing. He is what we call a one-woman man."

"I don't ever see anyone even holding hands."

Chang said, "Our women are exceedingly liberated. They are treated as equals in the Shaolin way, which was not the case historically. They are free to indulge themselves sexually with any of the available men. Nato is a favorite."

"I never noticed."

"They have been rather obvious by our standards relative to Luigi. In our culture, we are not demonstrative in public."

"Does Luigi know?"

"Yes, but his heart is committed."

On overhearing this exchange, Andrea remarked, "I was just like him when I first met his mother."

A few weeks later, Kumiko led a group of women and children on an outside excursion to the waterfall. Luigi followed out of sheer curiosity. At the falls, several of the women climbed up the rock surface to dive from various heights. The children gathered at the other end of the pond where the water was shallow. Below the falls, the water was very deep.

Luigi was astonished to see the aerial diving capabilities of these Shaolin woman warriors. He knew they were graceful but never imagined the level of competence they were capable of as they dove and performed aerial acrobatic movements. He was in total shock when he watched Kumiko climb to the very top of the falls and without flinching launch herself into a dive that left no splash—such was the accuracy of her skills.

Her perch atop the falls gave her unlimited view of all the children. However, as soon as she dove, one of the ten-year-old kids swam to the rocks and began to climb up. The ladies ordered him in Chinese to descend, but he kept going. Luigi sensed danger and climbed after him. Sure enough, when the child looked down, he froze. Within seconds, Luigi was with him with a reassuring smile. He whispered something into the child's ear. The child nodded affirmatively.

Kumiko surfaced in time to see the child jump feet-first with Luigi. The child had overcome his fear of heights that day. All the ladies were impressed with Luigi. The child never indicated what Luigi had said to him.

Luigi undertook the building of a tree house at the site of the waterfall so that everyone could be assured of shade and a safe place to rest. The tree house became a favorite of everyone.

In the evenings, Luigi took to storytelling of the great science fiction and adventure stories that he could recall. The children and the ladies enjoyed his choices, which included: *Twenty Thousand Leagues Under the Sea*, *A Floating City*, and *Around the World in Eighty Days*, all three by Jules Verne. They loved Alexander Dumas Sr.'s *The Count of Monte Cristo* and *The Three Musketeers*. They were especially intrigued by Daniel Defoe's *Robinson Crusoe*, which was about a man marooned on an island. Luigi's stories told at the tree house in the early evenings became the most popular recreation. All the ladies and particularly the children came to enjoy them. Luigi became a highly esteemed member of the Shaolin community.

14

Time Was Running Out

One day Dr. Sandorf was summoned to the laboratory. Once there, he could easily ascertain that there was tension in the air. Chang, Confucius, and Andrea were already there gathered around the drawing of a yacht. Actually, it was a multidimensional blueprint of a yacht. Dr. Sandorf, sensing that something was not right, offered, "Whatever it is, I would like very much to be of assistance."

"During the last four hundred years, the shock waves of a great underground movement of one of the earth's rock layers have brought periodic tidal waves to our island. As you may know, the highest mountains in the world are actually below sea level here in the Atlantic Ocean," said Chang.

"At first, the tidal waves came roughly every fifty years apart, one more violent than the one before. This is another reason why we built no above-ground structures. However, in my own lifetime, the tidal waves have come almost every fifteen years. According to my calculations and the astrological signs—including a full moon—the next one will come ten years from the date of the last one," noted Confucius.

Dr. Sandorf did not fully understand. Chang saw his perplexity. "We believe the next tidal wave will be so large as to completely cover the island forever. It is the inevitable sequence of an atoll such as this. I decided to make my own independent observations and concur with my son."

"We have been discussing several ways to escape the island, of which none are to our liking. I have offered to swim until I enter the shipping lanes," said Confucius.

"I believe that given his unique physical and mental capabilities, Confucius might well swim five to six hundred miles. However, should he encounter any bad weather, this distance would be drastically reduced," said Chang.

Dr. Sandorf nodded in agreement.

Chang slowly moved to the large rendering of a yacht, as he explained, "We have had many very enjoyable discussions with Andrea who, as you know, is both a ship builder and a fine captain. It is his opinion that we are well out of reach of any major shipping lanes. Otherwise, we would certainly have seen at least one or two ships in so long a time. Therefore, I believe it would be certain death for my son to try to swim for help. However, I recollect stories of fishermen in China, which Andrea confirms, in which men have survived tidal waves in ships. Some have dropped anchor and others have sailed straight for the wave, being picked up and tossed like a matchbox."

Chang crossed to a twenty-by-eight-foot glass enclosure filled with water. At the middle of this tank was a miniature replica of the island and a small-scale model of the yacht from the drawing.

Chang dropped two large bags of sand into the water tank at one end, displacing the water. This caused a large wave to move across the tank. When the wave struck the island and model boat, the craft was lifted like a matchstick. Chang underscored, "It floats away every time."

"As a fisherman, whenever there is a major storm, we sail out from the harbor. To be trapped near shore, we would lose our boats. I have heard of fishermen surviving even a great tidal wave by sailing straight for it."

Then Chang reminded the group, "The greatest of all floods as described in the Western Bible clearly indicates that a ship can be constructed that can withstand the greatest tempest. With Andrea's practical experience and our new design for a ship, we believe we can ride the next tidal wave across the coral reef in our own Noah's ark."

From the enthusiasm in his voice, one could feel the optimism in Confucius. "We can build a ship. We have Andrea's basic principles, a tireless group of Shaolin, unlimited trees, parts from sunken ships, and we've incorporated chambers for our batteries and electric fans. We even have the valuable assistance of our sea friends."

Dr. Sandorf moved closer to the chart and pointed questioningly to a section drawn parallel to the ship's keel. Chang explained, "Andrea drew us a picture several months ago of a small fishing vessel used in Hawaii. The main body of the craft is in the middle with two side portions that make it veritably unsinkable. Here, let me show you." He flipped the chart to another detailed sketch. In this drawing, one could more readily make out the configuration. "Our ship will have two huge ballasts that, after clearing the reef, will be cut free.

"What would we do for sails?"

Confucius flipped the chart to yet another drawing of two inner chambers reflecting the use of electric fans. "We shall actually have the best of two methods, electric energy from our reconfigured power, and we shall obtain sails from sunken ships."

Dr. Sandorf placed the toy ship on the island in the tank, dropped a large bag of sand as Chang had done, and peered closely at the ship. Sure enough, it bobbed on the wave. He smiled.

During the next four years, all efforts of the entire community were mobilized around building the ship that was to be their salvation. They built large pulleys on top of the mountain in order to lift the huge trees once they were cut down. They spun rope from the huge seaweed deposits. Since the Chinese were the inventors of gunpowder, they blasted the small opening to their dwelling, making room for the electric fans and batteries. These were carried by their lift—their elevator.

As predicted, they found usable sails at the site of wrecked ships. Most captains had reserve sails in storage bins. These were in excellent condition and retrieved by the Shaolin along with their dolphin friends. Little by little, the great craft took shape on the mountaintop.

Furthering their strategy, they began arrangements to be independently wealthy once their escape was achieved. Confucius said, "To this end, we'll enlist the giant mollusks. It was the Chinese as long ago as 2000 BC who used pearls in the collection of tribute and taxes. In the thirteenth century AD, Ye-Yin-Yang, a native of Hoochow, discovered how to introduce foreign objects into the shells of mollusks. Thus, in China, pearling has been an ancient industry. Thanks to the friendly mollusks, no deforming pressure will ensure that the current crop of pearls will be ball-shaped, iridescent, and translucent. As I recollect from our discussions, Dr. Sandorf, cultured pearls continue to be the most sovereign commodity in the world."

Then, too, many of the ships that had sunk on the reef over the centuries carried treasures beyond belief. The Shaolin, with the assistance of their fish friends, were able to locate a vast number of treasure chests. Overall, their spirits were high and the work progressed on schedule. Moreover, Dr. Sandorf and Chang resolved that if the fates permitted, they would form a partnership and set up a hospital dedicated to international patients and not just for one nation.

When the ship was completed, she had the fine look of a two-masted sports yacht although she was larger and weighed 350 tons. It would be difficult to describe adequately in words the magnificent impression the ship gave. One would have to see her. Every inch of her had been fashioned with loving care. All the wood had been polished to a high gleam. All the metal trimmings were in gold. Each room was designed to be comfortable. Without their knowing it at the time, they had built a ship more beautiful than the international cup winners of the day—*The Boadica, The Gaetana,* and *The Mordon* of the United Kingdom.

The two side braces of the ship were locked in place in such a way as to enable them to be unfastened once they had served their purpose. As a surprise for Andrea, they had left the name of the ship for last. Confucius put the gold letters in place one night, and everyone gathered the following morning as usual. When they unveiled the nameplate, Andrea could not keep the tears of joy from bursting forth. They had named the ship *The Andrea Ferrato.* Chang announced ceremoniously that Andrea was to be her captain. So it was that *The Andrea Ferrato* was the most beautiful and elegantly ship built up to that time. With the inserted electric fans, the ship would be the fastest to ever sail the seas. It would be this electric power that would be harnessed at the time of the next tidal wave.

Fate decided to intrude once again. One morning the fish scrambled into the inner lagoon to report a major disturbance at the reef. A pod of killer whales was fast approaching the coral reef. Their sea friends indicated that the pod was led by a rogue killer whale named Oden. Most of the pod had been hunted and wounded severely. They would kill anything they found in the reef shelter.

Alarmed, Confucius noted, "Kumiko is there at the reef with the children and our sea friends."

Indeed, Kumiko had spotted the approaching pod and alerted all. Tooth and his family, the dolphins, hammerhead sharks, manta rays, swordfish, tuna, Hands and her family, and even the tiny remora were all hastily retreating for cover.

All the children and their escorts returned safely to the shelter of their habitat. Prudently, Confucius led the Shaolin armed with the weapons of yesteryear out through the inner lagoon to meet the pod. He rebuked Luigi for wanting to come along, saying, "You'll only be in the way."

Dr. Sandorf placed a comforting hand on Luigi's shoulder. "Confucius is right; he just doesn't want to worry about you, too." However, as they left, Luigi would not be deterred. He shook off Dr. Sandorf's hand, grabbed a spear, and quickly followed the group.

Meanwhile, Chang, Dr. Sandorf, Andrea, and Maria took the lift up for a view from the mountaintop. From there, they witnessed the pod as it crashed into the reef, deliberately dislodging portions so as to get to the hidden fish.

Kumiko had tried to reason with the leader of this pod of killer whales—Oden. Oden was battle-scarred from encounters with man. He had a ragged scar over one eye and fragmented harpoons in his side. Others in his pod bore the telltale marks of having been hunted. There was no reasoning with Oden and his team. Within seconds, they were slamming into the sharks and dolphins. Their mighty tails would stun the fish with powerful blows. Then, as they sank helplessly, they would devour them mercilessly. Hands was a formidable opponent. Her giant tentacles could hold a killer whale and inflict damage rapidly. The dolphins would strike the whales at their sides. While these blows would distract the whales, they could not halt the onslaught.

As Confucius and the other Shaolin broke the surface of the water, they were met by the charging whales. Oden was not in a rush to destroy them and dove under the group. Then, Oden's whiplash tail hurled Confucius and the others into the air. However, Confucius took the impact in stride, sailing into the air and converting it to a shallow dive.

Kumiko was joined by Nato and two Shaolin. They faced yet another attacking whale. No matter which way this whale would turn, one of them was sure to land a strike with their special tipped spears. As the whale dove, Kumiko and another Shaolin dove after it. They reached it and drove their spears into the creature. The whale went limp. Oden and a companion whale had seen this situation and closed in on Kumiko and the others quickly. The companion whale left Oden when two Shaolin used electrical stun guns. These weapons could not kill a whale but played havoc with its delicate nervous system. For minutes, this whale would be out of the fight, in what appeared to be a nervous seizure. Even the tiny remora would affix themselves to the whales, trying to slow them down.

Kumiko and Nato took refuge in one of the lower caves of the reef, just as Oden was joined by two other whales. The fierce trio dislodged the reef above Kumiko and Nato, imprisoning them in an avalanche of coral. Then, they turned savagely upon the Shaolin. One whale snapped off a Shaolin's spear-arm at the elbow. Quickly, Confucius reached the wounded warrior, fastening a tourniquet to the wound. Two other Shaolin escorted the wounded man as they withdrew from the heat of battle.

Oden had now identified Confucius as the leader of the remaining Shaolin. He gathered three whales and they all charged. Two of these whales were met by a group of Shaolin. One whale got through to Confucius, while Oden supervised this attack. Confucius managed to avoid the gaping mouth of the killer whale by adroitly arching and spearing the delicate underbelly. Confucius held firmly onto his spear, thus hitching a ride with the whale. From the position of Oden, it appeared Confucius had been eaten. The powerful drug on Confucius's spear would put this whale to sleep.

Oden then turned his attention to something that had distracted him. Now, he looked straight at Luigi, who was just above the position at the reef where Kumiko was trapped. Luigi planted his spear nearby, dove, and began to remove the coral covering Kumiko and Nato. He knew precisely where they were from the deliberate, sporadic air bubbles they were releasing. Luigi worked feverishly, dislodging the coral. Soon the coral bloodied his hands, for it was sharp as razors. Luigi ignored the pain, intent on freeing Kumiko and Nato.

Above this scenario, Oden supervised the carnage. To his surprise, once again Confucius had evaded his partners. Oden circled sharply. His already sour disposition turned uglier as he made straight for Confucius. Confucius dove deep into the caves, thus avoiding Oden once again.

Meanwhile, Luigi had managed to free Kumiko and Nato. Nato was able to swim to the surface. Kumiko was unconscious. Luigi brought her to the surface. He carried her up quickly to a ledge roughly fifteen feet above the waterline. His feet and knees were bloodied from the jagged coral, but he kept her safe. Upon reaching the ledge, he immediately administered mouth-to-mouth resuscitation, and due to her remarkable training, she recovered quickly. Only then did he check on Nato, who had recovered. Then, Luigi ventured a quick look out over the water. He did not see Oden. Then, as he peered over the edge of the ledge, the gaping jaws of Oden flew up at him and nearly snapped his head off. He was quick and lucky to avoid the beast's attack. Oden submerged and began circling. Once again, Confucius's head bobbed above the water, baiting Oden. Confucius started swimming for the reef. Oden instinctively realized that Confucius could not out swim him. Thus, Oden circled and closed in for the kill. This was precisely what Confucius wanted. In order to cut Confucius off from the safety of the reef, Oden needed to swim a path directly under the ledge where Luigi was perched. In a flash, Oden, intent on finally getting Confucius, was directly under Luigi. Without hesitation, Luigi picked up his spear from where he had planted it and leapt from the ledge. He landed on the head of the whale, driving his spear into the brain of the creature. Oden reacted with a last jerk of his entire body, sending Luigi thirty-five feet into the air. The years of training paid off for Luigi, who never panicked.

He converted his aerial flight into a neat, clean dive. Nato smiled approvingly. After all, this was his student.

With Oden out of commission, the other whales turned docile, especially when they were informed by Confucius that Oden had not been killed. The special spear contained a powerful drug that put Oden and several of the pod to sleep. Then, the other whales bore witness to the amazing sight of the assorted sea creatures actually assisting in moving Oden and the wounded whales to the shoreline. Left alone, they would have sunk and drowned.

Chang lost no time in treating the Shaolin who had lost his arm. The remarkable medicines and techniques developed over the years were brought to bear. Where the Shaolin had lost an arm, they encased it in a special elongated cast filled with a special radiant enzyme. They planned successfully to re-grow the arm over the next few weeks. While they had numerous successes with fish, this was the first regeneration of a limb on a human. Its implications for medicine were astonishing.

Meanwhile, from the very first day, Chang, Confucius, Dr. Sandorf, and the others administered to the wounded whales. They surgically removed the harpoons, cleaned all open wounds, and almost magically treated the vicious scar over Oden's eye. As the whales recovered, they finally realized that they had no enemies and nothing to fear from these humans. Upon realizing this, Oden and the other whales decided to join the community.

Oden relinquished his role of master of the sea. He regained his strength and enjoyed the peaceful days and months that followed. Oden, who had only known bitterness and hate, learned that peace and tranquility are priceless treasures. The friendship was evident every time Confucius and Kumiko swam with the pod.

Luigi, too, was treated and on the way to recovery. Between Maria and Kumiko, he was babied night and day. In fact, from the first night after the battle with the whales, Luigi slept with a faint smile on his lips. On that night, Kumiko had crept silently into Luigi's chamber and ever so gently placed a soft kiss on his bandaged hands. She looked up as Luigi opened his eyes. Then, Kumiko whispered, "This time you're not dreaming. I've never been kissed before." The ensuing kiss was not passionate. It was sweet, loving, tender, and enduring, as their love would prove to be.

15

Riding the Tidal Wave

In spite of all their careful preparations, there was a tremendous feeling of apprehension and anxiety when the actual moment came to escape the island. As they approached the full moon, they knew the conditions were ripe. Like the tremor of ten years before, the ground shook mightily without warning for several seconds. The group was prepared and immediately boarded the ship on top of the mountain. Once there, they waited for the inevitable tidal wave. Unlike the former wave, which broke on a clear and beautiful day, this wave came in the midst of a severe storm. The winds were not predictable, and the tidal wave picked up tons of additional water because of the full moon and the storm. When it first appeared over the dark horizon, it looked like a great black cloud of death.

Andrea manned the helm while everyone else fastened themselves securely to the vessel. Within minutes, the crackling, deafening roar of the wave blasted their ears. The tidal wave broke as expected, only much more intensely than anticipated. To Dr. Sandorf, it seemed that only a miracle would save them. Within seconds, the ship was snatched up by the wave. She was lifted from her perch on the mountaintop like a bobbing toy. Andrea's sense of timing was uncanny. He turned on the electric power at precisely the right moment. A moment too soon and they would have been in front of the wave, sliding down the mountain of water to be crushed. As it was, their position relative to the wave was ideal. They were able to rise and fall to the rhythm of the waves that followed while the first great wave drove on before them. They were clear of the reef, and Dr. Sandorf was on his way home.

Soon, all were on deck looking back for some trace of the island. From the sea, the island had arisen. Now, back into the sea it had sunk. Dr. Sandorf was the first to turn away from the island prison and look forward to their future. His anxiety would grow with every passing day. Maria would join him on deck every evening, placing her hand in his. They had shared so much together. She was not afraid of the future. Yet, she could sense Dr. Sandorf's apprehension.

If anyone could have seen the ship, they would have been shocked. Here was a ship sailing faster than any other vessel in history. Also, this was the only ship in the world with its own special aquatic escort. All the fish of the coral reef had decided to stay with their friends. Their multivaried forms broke the surface of the waves on each side of *The Andrea Ferrato,* making this one of the most unusual sights ever. Out in front of the beautiful craft was Oden and his pod leading the way to who knew what. When Chang joined Dr. Sandorf and Maria on the deck, Dr. Sandorf said, "To Austria and our new adventure."

16

The Return

They reduced speed as they entered the Mediterranean Sea through the Pillars of Hercules. As planned, they entered Gibraltar to stock up on provisions and inquire as to current events. It was in the harbor master's office that Dr. Sandorf posed the question that had haunted him for twenty years, "What flag flies over Austria?"

"The Austrian flag has flown for nearly twenty years. Where have you been?" The harbor master was perplexed.

Dr. Sandorf was wearing the broadest grin. His efforts and those of his companions from twenty years before had resulted in a free Austria.

Even in Gibraltar, where all the people of the world meet, there were incredulous stares at the new arrivals. Their Chinese garments and manner were astonishing. So, too, was their magnificent vessel. However, upon entering and leaving port, they only navigated with their sails, never revealing the true power of the ship.

Within a few days, they sailed between Malta and Sicily, then past the heel of Italy and on up the Adriatic Sea. On the day they were to sight Trieste, all were on deck, curious and apprehensive. Dr. Sandorf spoke, "I feel like a child on his birthday." Indeed, all anticipated the view of the city and their first glimpse of the Austrian flag.

"We are all delighted that your countrymen are free. We hope we can make our own new home here. The matter is well out of our hands. It has been said that if you can do nothing about a situation, then do nothing," said Chang.

"There is the port of Trieste now," shouted Andrea.

The old and the new Trieste came more and more clearly into view. They could see the Cathedral of Trieste perched high above the city, reminding all the world of the strong religious convictions of the Austrians. Andrea wiped his tearful eyes, and all regarded the beautiful city in wonderment.

Chang put their thoughts into words. "The buildings are strangely shaped. They are very beautiful." Indeed, under the twenty years of freedom, Trieste had transformed itself greatly. The city had all the signs of prosperity as the number one seaport of the Adriatic.

Almost without warning, the pilot boat came to lead them to an appropriate pier. They would need to undergo the formality of registering the ship and obtaining the necessary papers authorizing visitation to the city. Here, also, as they disembarked, people gathered, gazing keenly at the new arrivals. Dr. Sandorf had secured a wardrobe at Gibraltar. Upon arrival, he had shaven his beard and put on the traditional clothes of an Austrian gentleman. As he and the others descended the gangplank, they made quite an unusual sight. An official of the harbor master's office was waiting with the official log. This official asked, "By what name will your ship be registered? What country and ownership?"

"The name of the ship is *The Andrea Ferrato*, my country is Austria, and my name is Dr. Mathias Sandorf."

The official, startled, stared at Dr. Sandorf in disbelief, then proceeded to double-check. "Dr. Mathias Sandorf?" As Dr. Sandorf nodded affirmatively, the official said, "Wait right here. I'll get the harbor master." Then, as he darted down the pier, others who had listened in on the conversation began spreading the news with warm smiles on their faces. The group could hear the repeated whispers of many voices, "It is Dr. Mathias Sandorf."

Within minutes the pier was mobbed by hundreds of patriotic citizens. The harbor master broke through the crowd, beaming and declaring in a loud voice, "Welcome back to Austria, Dr. Sandorf. Welcome. I've sent word to King Ferdinand of your arrival." It took only a few minutes for the king's platoon to arrive, welcome Dr. Sandorf, and bid the entire group to follow them to the court of King Ferdinand.

As Dr. Sandorf and the others entered the court, they were stared at by everyone. It seemed that no Austrian was unaware of Dr. Mathias Sandorf and the liberating role he had played in securing Austrian freedom. Even the king descended from his throne to greet Dr. Sandorf in a far more unofficial manner than customary. The king would not have greeted royalty with the warmth with which he greeted Dr. Sandorf. In fact, he was beside himself with delight and hugged Dr. Sandorf like a long-lost son returning from abroad. The king's first words were, "God bless the mysterious fortunes that have guided you back to us. Welcome home. The affairs of state can be considerably tedious, but do you know what I like most? The day after tomorrow will be declared a royal holiday in honor of your return. Tonight, I insist you dine with me, you and all your friends."

The evening's dinner was replete with the best of foods and entertainment. The royal band played typical folkloric music, while dancers moved gracefully in typical Austrian dance steps. Dr. Sandorf was visibly moved by the occasion and warm attention. Without divulging any secrets, he narrated their adventure and that of his new friends during the prolonged evening.

The king was fascinated. "An amazing story, Dr. Sandorf. Riding a tidal wave! Astonishing! What would you like to do first?"

Dr. Sandorf was ready with his answer, "I have a message for Madame Étienne Bathory, if she still lives."

The king was immediately responsive, "Yes! Yes! Of course. I will arrange for safe passage anywhere you and your friends desire to go. The entire country is open to you all. I'll expedite the paperwork as well." At a signal from the king, a captain was at his side. The king whispered his orders, and the captain left to make the necessary arrangements. Then the king continued addressing Dr. Sandorf, "Your home was confiscated by the Germans and repossessed by the Austrian government after the war. We have treated it like a national monument. You are welcome to move in at once."

Dr. Sandorf was grateful. "Thank you, but for tonight, we'll stay aboard *The Andrea Ferrato*."

Earlier in the evening, King Ferdinand had inquired as to any plans or desires Dr. Sandorf might have. Dr. Sandorf had taken the opportunity to indicate briefly his desire to resume his medical practice, establish an international hospital, and secure an autonomous island on which to set up his institution. King Ferdinand was delighted to be of service, and the idea of an international hospital appealed to him. The king offered to organize a strategic planning group to analyze both the feasibility and any obstacles that might exist.

The very next day, a platoon escorted Dr. Sandorf to the home of Madame Étienne Bathory. On this visit he went alone. He had an important twenty-year-old message to deliver. Upon his arrival, he was delighted to be greeted at the door by his old servant, Borik. The reunion with Madame Bathory was a warm and tearful one. It did not take Dr. Sandorf long to recount Étienne Bathory's dying words of love for her and their son, Pierre. As soon as he had entered her parlor, Madame Bathory knew Étienne had died. Otherwise, both Dr. Sandorf and Étienne would most certainly have come together. She in turn related the tragic news that his own wife, Savarena, had died in a German prison.

Madame Bathory was a very ill woman, and Borik had moved in to care for her. Within minutes, the sadness and the happiness proved too much for her. She felt faint and needed to sit quietly. After regaining her composure, she informed Dr. Sandorf that her son, Pierre, was a captain in the military and not likely to appear soon. His assignments were secret. She did not fail to mention that Pierre was the exact likeness of his father, Étienne.

It was on the ride back from Madame Bathory's, when he was alone, that the full impact of the news of his wife's death weighed heavy on his heart. His thoughts drifted back to the happy times and the warmth of her. Savarena had shared in all his undertakings, including imprisonment. He knew she would always be with him in his heart. For now, he fought back the tears.

17

The International Hospital

King Ferdinand sent word to Dr. Sandorf and Chang that there was to be a special audience on the matter regarding an international hospital. This audience would take place in one of the chambers of the palace. Dr. Sandorf and Chang made their preparations accordingly. When they arrived at court, they were directed to a large room with a huge table, somewhat like a tribunal. Seated at the table was a cadre of the king's advisors. They were assembled to assist him in expediting Dr. Sandorf's request for permission to build an international hospital on one of the islands that belonged to Austria.

King Ferdinand began the meeting, "Dr. Sandorf and Mr. Chang, we have been examining your request and we have some questions. First, let us congratulate ourselves on having had a wonderful royal holiday in your honor. Permit me to make the introductions."

Dr. Sandorf and Chang were introduced to Doctor Hans Von Kodrick, chief of medicine at the Academy of Trieste. Next to him was Doctor Herman Gooding, chief of hospitals in Trieste. Following him was Doctor Ivan Snelling, president of The Medical College of Terneswar. This doctor had been one of Dr. Sandorf's professors.

In addition to the three doctors, they met the prime minister, Herzog Dietel. Then, they met General Damien Hattersfield, chief of all military troops on land and sea. The last to greet them was the king's chairman of finance and president of the Consortium of Banks of Trieste, Silas Toronthal.

Dr. Sandorf was a bit taken aback by the fact that he did not immediately recognize Silas Toronthal. Silas had gotten considerably heavier, grown a beard, and was very well-dressed even for a banker. Since Dr. Sandorf believed Silas had been used merely for identification purposes during his arrest twenty years before, he greeted all the king's advisors warmly.

King Ferdinand began, "I am most eager to be of assistance with your project. My advisors have assured me that they do not believe your hospital project is feasible for a variety of reasons. In all fairness, the questions they have raised seem to me to be exceedingly valid. However, I thought it would be faster and fairer were you to hear their concerns firsthand and respond or at least know why the request is turned down. Nonetheless, I have informed everyone that the matter remains open until you have had an opportunity to address the issues raised. Doctor Snelling, would you like to begin?"

"Basically, the medical profession is concerned with your competency, having been away from active practice for twenty years. We also have no background on Mr. Chang's credentials. Would you both be willing to take an examination that we have prepared? The test consists of three hundred questions, ranging across various fields of specialization. Roughly one hundred of these deal with new advances in medicine. We hope that given your previous training, you ought to do well. However, we have no idea how Mr. Chang will do. We can give you both roughly six months to prepare, if you like."

Chang whispered to Dr. Sandorf, who responded, "Chang and I have discussed and prepared for seven years our desire to build an international hospital. Before that, we shared our knowledge of medicine for ten years. Your request was anticipated and is absolutely reasonable. We appreciate the offer of courses so that we might further our studies. However, we would welcome responding to your three hundred questions immediately. The three distinguished doctors could supervise while Chang and I take opposite corners in the room. Within two hours, we can dispense with your legitimate concerns as to competency."

"It would not be fair to you. Take sixty days. If you fail now, we would not be lenient with you," Dr. Snelling responded.

Chang spoke for the first time, "We understand and appreciate your concern. We will take your test today and accept the consequences."

While the others were surprised and reluctant, King Ferdinand interceded, "Let the test be administered now. To both of you, good luck."

The test was administered, and both passed with outstanding and surprisingly high scores. When the three doctors reported the results to the king, he beamed. It was Dr. Snelling who had the honor of reporting the outcome. "Mr. Chang scored two hundred ninety-six out of a possible three hundred. Dr. Sandorf scored two hundred and ninety-six also. It is my honor to welcome you both to our medical profession. Even as my former student, Dr. Sandorf, I would not have believed it was possible. I am very proud, and the medical community will consider it a great honor that both of you have come to help us with our work on behalf of the afflicted."

King Ferdinand was delighted. "Excellent, Dr. Sandorf and Mr. Chang. Congratulations! Let us, however, move on to two additional areas of concern. General Hattersfield, would you address your reservations?"

The general stood, as was his fashion, "Yes, your Highness. As we understand it, you wish to place your international hospital out in the Adriatic, on an island, and function autonomously? If you were granted autonomy, to whom would you owe allegiance? Do you think the Austrian navy will protect you?"

Dr. Sandorf's response was direct and simple, "My allegiance was, is, and shall always be to Austria. The autonomy of which we speak is to permit patients from any country the care they may need. Thus, I have two allegiances. The first is to Austria, and the second, to the Hippocratic Oath, which is universal. To your second question, I would hope that the Austrian Navy would never be needed to protect a defenseless hospital."

King Ferdinand was satisfied, but asked, "Well, General?"

General Hattersfield replied, "Fine. Who would attack a defenseless hospital, anyway?"

King Ferdinand motioned for Silas Toronthal to raise his concerns. Silas did so in a very level tone so as not to betray his real desire to totally squash the plan, "Dr. Sandorf, welcome back to Austria. You undoubtedly noticed that the city has changed considerably during your absence. We are proud of the steady progress we've been able to make. We have many new homes, schools, churches, ships, businesses, and a host of international trade ventures, all going forward simultaneously. These undertakings require a great deal of prudent investment and the nurturing of scarce capital. As president of the Bank of Trieste, I would be remiss in my duty to allow any of these projects to suffer in any way. While your international hospital is a truly wonderful idea, I have made some calculations that suggest such a hospital could not be constructed for less than two million."

Silas had not had the courtesy of addressing any of his remarks to Chang. It was a clear insult and a diplomatic offense. Yet, Chang responded evenly, "We estimate the cost at three million."

Silas acted as if Chang had made his position even more solid. "The only way our banks could undertake such a venture would be collectively. There is no single bank in the country that could do it." Silas turned to the king and said, "Your Highness, I have not been able to persuade a single bank to participate."

Silas clearly felt that he had successfully supported the concept of such a project while actually emasculating it cleverly. While he hid it, he actually enjoyed the power he felt at this moment. Silas was fearful that Dr. Sandorf might realize that his role twenty years before was more than just pointing him out to General Von Brun. He had betrayed a fellow Austrian. At present, Silas's scheme was to put an end to Dr. Sandorf's plans. Dr. Sandorf's only choices were to go to another country or fade into obscurity. Feeling confident, he pressed the matter even further, betraying his own personal prejudice. "Moreover, your Highness, the banks do not feel that Austrian businessmen have any obligation to foreigners as does Dr. Sandorf."

Both Dr. Sandorf and Chang waited patiently throughout Silas's presentation. Both sensed a veiled hypocrisy. Yet, Silas had handled himself in precisely the way a responsible banker would be expected to. Dr. Sandorf realized that this was not a good time to inject any of his hunches concerning the past. To do so would be to personalize the current situation, jeopardize the king's favor, and not further their cause. Chang intuitively sensed Dr. Sandorf's hesitation. Moreover, Chang knew that Dr. Sandorf took the "foreigner" comment to heart. Thus, at this juncture and upon seeing the king's disappointed face, Chang addressed only the king, "Your Highness, we are delighted with the hospitality shown us by the majority of your subjects. We do not expect to borrow the money for the international hospital from any of the banks of Trieste."

There was complete silence in the room as everyone gave Chang their undivided attention. Chang produced three small sacks and placed them in front of the king, Silas, and General Hattersfield. Everyone's eyes were riveted on the three sacks. Chang elaborated as he poured the contents out onto the table, "Would you be so kind as to examine the contents?" There was really no choice. From each of the sacks poured forth some of the world's most dazzling, perfect pearls. Then, as each pearl was examined critically, Chang continued in an even voice, "Presently, we are depositing into the bank of Trieste four chests filled with pearls and other currency—gold and silver. We estimate the value to be at one hundred sixty million."

One could hear a collective gasp in the room. Silas swallowed hard. By now, Dr. Sandorf had regained his usual composure, adding, "We would like these funds to be invested by the banks of Trieste in order to support the many projects outlined by Silas Toronthal. However, King Ferdinand, if we do not receive permission to proceed with the international hospital under Austrian leadership, we will be forced to try another country."

King Ferdinand resumed control over the proceedings. "We had never for a moment considered that you were in a position to finance such a hospital. As I see it, all the questions have been satisfactorily answered. As for the issue of autonomy, that matter can wait until the Diet has met. You can be assured of my support. As far as I am concerned, the matter is closed and you can begin whenever you like. By the way, have you selected an island?"

"Oh, yes. We'll arrange a visit." Meanwhile, the panel adjourned with handshakes and congratulations to Dr. Sandorf and Chang. Even Silas took some comfort in that his bank was going to obtain a windfall. He had underestimated Dr. Sandorf and harbored a deep resentment.

The island they had selected was not too distant from Trieste. King Ferdinand, General Hattersfield, the three doctors, the prime minister, Dr. Sandorf, Chang, Confucius, Kumiko, Andrea, Luigi, Maria, and all the Shaolin visited their choice of island within the week. It was General Hattersfield who raised the question, "Why you chose a rather remote island is beyond me, Dr. Sandorf. This one has a useless stretch of coral reef over there."

As soon as all the dignitaries had left, their aquatic friends emerged from beneath the coral reef, quite content with their new home. The entire assembly of Shaolin and their friends were happily splashing around close to shore as Dr. Sandorf and Chang strolled together. They stopped on a shallow crest and shared a private moment. As they looked over the deserted island, Dr. Sandorf began articulating their plans. "Over here we'll build a long pier; there, the foundations for a complex of buildings; supply ships coming and going; and an entrance there, which will have a sign—*The International Hospital.*"

They nurtured their dream for the two years it took to completely transform the island into their reality.

While the king and many others visited during the construction, it was upon completion that they returned for a serious tour of the facility. The king commented, "Who would have believed it?"

"You have patients from Spain, Greece, Arabia, Egypt, Tripoli, Tunisia, Algeria, Italy, France, and Morocco," complimented General Hattersfield.

"We hardly see any of you in Trieste. Now I see why. It is superb," said the king.

It was Dr. Snelling who put it best, "They are devoted to their patients."

In all this time, Dr. Sandorf never saw the son of Étienne Bathory, Pierre. He took General Hattersfield aside and inquired, "I'm curious, General. Why have I not seen Pierre Bathory in all this time? I understand he is a captain in our army?"

General Hattersfield, not prone to discussing military matters, had become so friendly with Dr. Sandorf that he confided in a whisper, "Pierre does remarkable work. However, he is in our intelligence corps working on a secret assignment. Pierre is a master of disguise and has volunteered to try to uncover the identity of a spy here in Austria. The spy goes by the name of Regent. He has been supplying the Germans with information." The puzzled look on Dr. Sandorf's face revealed that he believed the threat from the Germans was a matter of past history. The next words from the general would once again transform the doctor into the patriot. "There is a plot afoot to recapture Austria. We must learn the identity of Regent."

18

The Son of Étienne Bathory

The son of Étienne Bathory, Pierre, had grown up with his father's profound love of country. Thus, he had enlisted in the Austrian army and meritoriously progressed through the ranks to become a captain in the intelligence division. Pierre was the exact image of his father in physical characteristics with a strong, young, athletic body. Pierre was very adept at disguising himself and had become a real asset to his division. Because of the dangerous nature of his assignments, he kept his private life a secret. Thus, no one knew that he was in love with Sava Toronthal. They kept their love a secret due to Pierre's work and because they did not believe her father, Silas Toronthal, would approve.

Presently, Pierre was on a very special assignment. Their intelligence unit had learned of a secret plot by Germany to retake Austria. If and when that occurred, the Germans planned to name someone of their own choosing as Regent. For the present, they gave this unnamed person the code name of Regent. It became the special assignment of Captain Pierre Bathory to uncover his identity.

A special and unusual undercover team was set up by Pierre. This team was comprised of two soldiers who were fiercely loyal to Pierre. One was named Pescade and the other Matifou. These names were drawn from two peninsulas in the Adriatic Sea that face one another. One is very large and the other quite small.

Pescade was only five-foot-three, with a very thin frame and angular features. He had steady, clear eyes under straight eyebrows. His nose was fine, and he wore an almost Mona Lisa smile all the time. He was a talented acrobat and a very inventive individual. He was also a very brilliant person.

Matifou was a huge, six-foot-two, muscular giant of a man with enormous strength but very little wisdom. He had a large Samson-like head and hands like shovels—the strength of a tiger but the disposition of a lamb. He even went to great lengths to avoid shaking hands, lest he injure someone.

This unlikely pair met on their way to a military training camp for new inductees. Unknown to each other, they were riding on the same train through the area known as the Camargne Plains when fate brought them together. As they passed by one of the many farms where bulls were raised, they saw a huge bull jump a corral and pursue a young child. Matifou and Pescade were on opposite ends of the same boxcar when they saw the child fall from the fence. They knew at once that the child was stunned and in danger from the bull.

Without hesitation, they leapt from the train to help the child. Pescade, who was nimble and fast, got to the pen first, darting between the bull and the fallen child. As he anticipated, the bull began to chase him. Thus, he drew the bull away from the child. Out of the corner of his eye, he was very much aware that someone else had also jumped from the train and was picking up the child. Pescade literally had his hands full, too. He had reasoned that the safest place to be was in back of the bull. Therefore, Pescade had grabbed hold of the bull's tail and was being dragged about.

Meanwhile, Matifou had lifted the child to safety on the other side of the fence. From this vantage point, he saw Pescade sent sprawling on the grass from his own momentum, as the bull turned. The first charge of the bull was met by Pescade, who kicked the creature on the snout. The bull did not appreciate getting kicked in the nose and retreated for a full charge. Pescade was on his knees when the bull made his move. Pescade knew he could not get away from the bull and gritted his teeth for the impact. It was at that moment that Matifou reached them.

Matifou charged the bull from the side, driving his huge arms under the bull between his front and rear legs. With all his strength, he heaved the bull up and onto its back. This knocked the wind out of the bull. In fact, it was almost comical the way the bull got up staggering on all four legs as if he were drunk. Then, the bull collapsed with his tongue lolling out of his mouth. Pescade could barely believe his eyes.

Both Pescade and Matifou exited the pen just as the farmer arrived to fetch his son. As the father and son embraced, Pescade and Matifou faced one another for the very first time. They each examined one another, noting their contrary physical attributes. Then, both smiled approvingly. They could not know that their friendship and affection, born out of courage, would endure and that they would become the best of friends.

Both Pescade and Matifou arrived late for the military induction. However, the others on the train had already explained their absence. It was Captain Pierre Bathory who decided to keep an eye on them during induction as possible candidates for his own plans. For the present, he remained out of sight and unknown to them. Pierre's interest was sparked by the fact that they were the only two out of three hundred "wannabe" soldiers on the train who took selfless action.

Throughout the induction period, it became evident to Pierre that Pescade and Matifou had bonded since they were inseparable. As part of their induction training, each person was asked to lift progressively heavier weights as an indication of overall physical fitness. They had a huge sergeant in charge of the training who, upon meeting them, decided they were misfits for the military. The sergeant had never seen as skinny and puny a person as Pescade. Thus, he decided to make an example of him. The sergeant placed a two hundred-pound weight on the barbell but said it was only one hundred pounds. Poor Pescade nearly got a hernia trying to lift it. The sergeant laughed uproariously.

There were roughly six hundred pounds of weight, four people, plus the sergeant on the small stage where the weight lifting was done. As the sergeant was enjoying his joke at Pescade's expense, only Captain Pierre Bathory noticed as Matifou slipped under the stage. Within seconds, the sergeant and the other candidates stopped laughing when the entire stage shook. Matifou lifted the stage two feet on his back. Pescade had the last laugh.

Throughout the induction exercises, the sergeant supervised the pair. When they finally posted the results, it came as no surprise that both Pescade and Matifou were classified as rejects. They consoled one another and left the training camp.

Matifou carried both duffel bags as they strolled together. After several miles, they were met by Captain Pierre Bathory. Pierre rode up with two extra horses, dismounted, and explained, "I'm sorry, my friends. We had to convince everyone that you both were truly rejected. I am Captain Pierre Bathory, and I have need of both of you for a special assignment. Come."

Later, at an undisclosed office, the trio made their plans. Pierre filled them in. "As far as anyone knows, you are both officially rejects from the military service. All the paperwork is going through. You will both pretend to be very upset about being rejected. It is part of my plan."

After more discussion, Pescade noted, "So, our only lead to the German spy network is this man named Carpena?"

Pierre elaborated, "We know from the few survivors of the executions and fire at Rovigno that he betrayed my father, Étienne, Dr. Mathias Sandorf, and the Ferrato family. Presently, he surrounds himself with thieves and bandits. We've left him alone, but we believe the Germans are using him. Our plan is to infiltrate." It was Pierre who ended the meeting, saying, "We will be the three phantom musketeers of Austria."

One afternoon after observing Carpena for several weeks, Pescade lifted his wallet. This was done in a bristling marketplace as Carpena strolled along with several of his disreputable companions. Pescade arranged to bump into Carpena adroitly, in such a way as to alert Carpena. Carpena and his henchmen gave chase in and around the marketplace. While Pescade could easily outrun them, he arranged to be captured at a prearranged location. There, both Pierre in disguise, and Matifou were available should Pescade's capture have taken a turn for the worse. As Pierre had anticipated, they did not harm a fellow thief eager to return the wallet. They gave Pescade a few lumps but eagerly recruited him. After all, he had a talent they could use.

Pescade was well received and began a vigil from within, at The Three Lanterns Inn where most of the bandits usually assembled. Within several days, Matifou approached the innkeeper, who hired him to do the heavy lifting. For example, the filled beer barrels were very heavy and needed to be placed in their racks on the bar. For Matifou, this was an easy chore, among other odd jobs he was asked to do. The innkeeper was delighted.

After several weeks, Sarcany, Zirone, and a dazzling beauty named Namir showed up one evening. Immediately, the other bandits cleared a table for their more important dignitaries. Carpena was happy to report to Sarcany, "I got us two military rejects." He pointed them out. "The skinny one is a pickpocket."

Sarcany looked them over with his usual suspicions, "Two military rejects? I'll check it out. Keep an eye on them, anyway."

Within weeks, Pescade was allowed to participate in several stagecoach robberies. This is how he ascertained that the bandits' intelligence was very good. Pescade was able to report that each stagecoach robbery was well planned. However, while they stole the gold shipments, they were actually after important documents as well. While the passengers and driver were searched and generally harassed, one bandit with a photographic memory would read through important papers. Hence, Pierre ascertained that the bandit network was larger than suspected and was very well informed. Indeed, when Pierre learned that the bandits had also forged an alliance with the most vicious band of pirates, he realized that the gold and information being channeled to the Germans far exceeded anyone's expectations. The plan for the newest invasion of Austria was in full swing. Worse, the level of coordination had to have a mastermind. Regent was a very busy fellow.

One Thursday night, Pescade decided to follow Carpena from The Three Lanterns Inn. While this was risky, he knew Carpena was meeting with someone likely to furnish the necessary information for their next job. Pescade pretended to be sleepy and retired to his room early. Using his acrobatic skills, Pescade left through his window up to the roof. It was not difficult to follow Carpena across the rooftops since, in the old section of Trieste, the streets were narrow. This proved to be a wise decision since Carpena backtracked and assured himself several times that he was not being followed. Once reassured, Carpena made straight for the rendezvous alley. There, he lit a cigar which was barely visible.

Soon another shadowy figure joined him. This man was Zirone, the partner of Sarcany. "What news, Zirone?"

"Sarcany has spoken with Regent and wants a very special job done in two days."

"What kind of special job?"

"Dr. Mathias Sandorf will be sailing into the harbor on Saturday to pick up supplies for the International Hospital. You know his yacht, *The Andrea Ferrato*?"

"Who doesn't?"

"You know the new ship *Trabaculo* that is to be launched?"

Carpena nodded affirmatively. Then, Zirone spelled out the orders, "Well, we need an accident. An early launching would do it. It must appear to be an accident. Regent was very specific on this."

"I understand."

They departed the alley one at a time, again ensuring neither was followed. However, neither one of them saw the small frame of Pescade hanging upside down from the rooftop drain. From this vantage point, Pescade had heard most but not all of what had been said.

Back at The Three Lanterns, acting on the suspicions of Sarcany, the bandits had decided to check in on Pescade almost as soon as he had entered his room. They discovered the open window and knew he had not descended through the inn. They prepared a warm welcome for Pescade but waited for Carpena's return. However, Matifou, always on the alert, had observed the whispering and furtive glances up the stairs. He knew they were planning to surprise Pescade upon his return. It was time for Matifou to signal Pescade that his cover was blown. So it was that, as soon as Pescade returned and exited his room, Matifou winked at him with his left eye. This was their prearranged signal for danger. At that moment, Carpena entered The Three Lanterns Inn and huddled with the others. This gave Pescade just enough time to return to his room and permanently exit via the window. The cutthroats, armed with knives and swords, climbed the stairs quietly. They burst into his room, which was empty. Pescade had made it to the roof, and they could only watch as he nimbly sped away across the rooftops. Below, Matifou went about his business, prepared to help Pescade, if he needed it. However, the disappointed expressions of the bandits told Matifou that Pescade had made good his escape. Now, Matifou calmly took out one of the empty beer barrels and strolled away from The Three Lanterns Inn, never to return.

At their prearranged meeting place, Pierre, Matifou, and Pescade discussed the entire affair. Pescade explained what he had found out. "Dr. Mathias Sandorf is to be killed on Saturday in what is supposed to appear as an accident. I could not hear clearly, but it sounded to me that someone named Trabaculo would be involved. I never heard of anyone with that nickname. This so-called accident is being arranged by Regent."

Pierre was very interested. "I wonder what connection exists between Dr. Sandorf and Regent and what's the link between the organized bandits, pirates, and Regent? What were the names of the other two?"

Pescade responded, "Zirone was the man Carpena met. Zirone mentioned another person named Sarcany. Sarcany seems to get his orders directly from Regent."

Then Pierre said, "We must warn Dr. Sandorf as soon as he arrives at the pier. I want you both to stay very close to him. He must not be harmed. He was a dear, close friend of my father, and if Regent wants him killed, we may soon have the key to the identity of Regent."

"No one will harm the doctor," said Matifou.

19

The Launching of *Trabaculo*

The pier was like a circus. Everyone was crowded around the impromptu tables and kiosks where all sorts of merchandise were being sold. There were a variety of games of chance, and a large band was playing. Thousands of people were milling about, darting in and out of the numerous tents and small shops. The occasion was the launching of a newly commissioned ship, a fifteen-ton, two-masted merchant ship. This huge ship was to be launched at noon. This was the reason for the grand festivity, demonstrating once again that Trieste was the great Austrian center of commerce. Everything had been prepared, including the untying of all the mooring lines. Only the key-wedge needed to be lifted. Then the huge ship would go sliding down the wooden ramp into the Adriatic Sea.

Many dignitaries were already crowded on the launching platform, and the traditional champagne bottle hung at the ready. At these launchings, almost all of the aristocracy turned out. King Ferdinand and his entire entourage were present, including Silas Toronthal and his wife and daughter. Everyone was jubilant, and obviously, no one anticipated any danger.

Pierre took up a position at the very end of the pier where *The Andrea Ferrato*, carrying Dr. Sandorf, would berth. Pierre's plan was to board the ship and alert Dr. Sandorf. Meanwhile, Pescade and Matifou mingled in the crowd, alert for any sign of trouble. This was very risky for Pescade because all the cutthroats had gotten the word that he was a spy. Matifou strolled a few feet behind his friend protecting his rear. Their eyes scanned the crowd carefully.

Unknown to Pierre, one of the bandits stood only a few feet from him at the same end of the pier. Both watched as Dr. Sandorf's ship quietly entered the channel, heading directly for the dock. Each pretended not to be particularly interested in the approaching ship, yet each one had his own focus and intent. The bandit would be the one to give the signal.

In the thick of the crowd, Pescade thought he caught a glimpse of Carpena and Zirone. He could not be absolutely sure. Pescade quickened his pace, his eyes darting through the maze of heads. Every so often Pescade thought he caught a fleeting glimpse of them as they headed for the rear of the ship about to be launched. When Pescade reached the end of the pier at the side of the rear of the huge ship, he broke through the crowd, his hands on his hips in a somewhat frustrated gesture.

Unknown to him, one of the bandits had observed him following Carpena and Zirone and now slipped neatly behind him at the edge of the crowd. However, the bandit could not step into the small opening—as Pescade had done—without betraying his presence. He waited in the crowd for Pescade to eventually step back. Just then, Pescade caught sight of the bandit at the far end of the pier who seemed to be looking directly at him, signaling with a hand gesture across his forehead. From Pescade's previous experience with the bandits, he knew that the gesture meant "now." However, the bandit could not possibly be gesturing to him. Pescade became very apprehensive.

Just then, a large drape was cut loose, revealing the name of the ship, *Trabaculo*. Pescade stared at the huge letters and suddenly realized what kind of accident was intended for Dr. Sandorf. His eyes darted to the left and down under the pier among the piling. He saw a blur of color behind one of the piles. It was Carpena, he was sure of it now. A hand reached out from the pier piles and in a second the key-wedge holding the ship *Trabaculo* was lifted. The bandit's signal had precisely informed Carpena when to pull the restraining pin. Only the key-wedge held the great merchant ship from plunging down the wooden ramp into the sea. Pescade noted with horror that *The Andrea Ferrato's* starboard bow had just aligned with the launching area.

Pescade stepped back into the crowd hoping to get below and somehow replace the key-wedge. However, it was too late. The *Trabaculo*—with white smoke curling up from the friction of the ramp—had begun its deadly descent. The crowd hushed, realizing collectively that an accident was about to occur. They gasped as one, followed by silence.

The gang member behind Pescade slipped a dagger from his sleeve and pretended to bump into Pescade. The bandit drove the dagger with all his force at Pescade's side. However, his wrist was held in a vise-like grip and he could not budge. Matifou held his arm firmly. Almost casually, Matifou's free arm circled the man's waist and kept him from breathing. Within seconds, the man slumped unconsciously to the floor.

Pescade turned and said, "Thanks. We don't have a second to lose. It's the ship. The ship is named *Trabaculo.* They've pulled the key-wedge and launched her ahead of schedule. She'll smash Dr. Sandorf's yacht like a twig."

Indeed, the *Trabaculo* began to totter and shake. The great vessel began to slide further down the ramp. The rear of the ship was already almost entering the water. Pescade dashed for one of the mooring ropes, which was curled on the pier next to where it had been tied. He shouted to Matifou, "The rope, hold the rope."

Without hesitation, Matifou seized the mooring rope and held it fast. His feet slid on the wooden pier as he was dragged toward the edge. Pescade saw at once that his friend would be dragged and crushed. He shouted again to Matifou, "The iron cannon, the cannon!"

At the very edge of the pier was an old iron cannon mounted on the pier itself. Matifou quickly slipped the mooring rope around the cannon and hauled again with all his strength. Matifou's face became a mask of pain while his hands bled freely from the cutting rope. He breathed in agony as his great biceps bulged beyond belief. His shirt tore right down the back. He braced his feet against the pier boards and stubbornly refused to give up his hold on the ship.

The silent crowd looked on in wide-eyed amazement as the great ship began to slow. For nearly ten seconds the *Trabaculo* barely moved. One man stood against the great weight, drawing on reserves of strength that seemed superhuman. The crowd backed away, fearing that at any moment Matifou would be dragged to his death. Finally, Matifou could not hold on any longer. He slumped in absolute exhaustion on the pier with one arm on the cannon. Pescade dashed to his side and called on two of the bystanders to help him with Matifou. As the crowd helped Matifou to his feet, the old cannon squealed loudly as it was torn from the pier and dragged below. The *Trabaculo* plunged heavily into the sea and then bobbed up, pitching. Her captain immediately dropped anchor, bringing her to a stop. Thanks to the great strength of Matifou, the collision was avoided by only a few feet. Moments afterward, the crowd roared and applauded the hero of the day, Matifou. Unaccustomed to being the center of attention, Matifou relied on Pescade, who ushered him through the smiling throng toward Pierre. During the commotion, Zirone and several of the other bandits made good their escape. In fact, everyone thought that what had occurred was merely a chance accident.

From the dignitaries' reviewing stand, Sava Toronthal saw Pescade and Matifou as they joined Pierre. Pierre hugged them both, acknowledging their heroic actions. Sava smiled lovingly at seeing Pierre. Silas masked his disappointment at having his deadly plan thwarted. Moreover, he hid his disgust when he noticed Sava gazing at Pierre. No one would have guessed that he was Regent, but this was small comfort at that moment.

Within minutes, Pierre, Pescade, and Matifou were allowed to board *The Andrea Ferrato* and were quickly escorted into Dr. Sandorf's private cabin. Pescade and Matifou entered first and both Dr. Sandorf and Confucius immediately attended to the bleeding hands of Matifou. They washed his hands gently and sterilized them afterward. They never revealed the special ointment they applied to Matifou's hands before bandaging them.

Confucius stated warmly to Dr. Sandorf, "This man has cultivated great chi. It was remarkable how he held that ship back with just his hands." It was then that Dr. Sandorf asked, "What are your names?"

"I am Pescade, and this is Matifou. This is our Captain, Pierre Bathory."

At the sound of this last name, Dr. Sandorf snapped his head around, for he now noticed the third man entering the cabin. While Dr. Sandorf had heard from Madame Bathory that Pierre was the spitting image of his father, Étienne, he was not prepared for the reincarnation of his beloved friend. Dr. Sandorf expressed both his shock and joy, "My God, you are Étienne, and Étienne lives in you, my son." There was no containing the spontaneity of the moment. Pierre and Dr. Sandorf embraced and each looked deeply into the other's eyes. The rest of the company seemed to vanish for several precious moments as they each regarded one another with profound esteem.

Pierre said, "It wasn't an accident, Dr. Sandorf. The *Trabaculo* was deliberately launched ahead of schedule because a man named Regent ordered it."

Dr. Sandorf replied, "Regent? I do not know the name or the man."

Pierre, "Regent is the code name of a spy who is conspiring with the Germans to retake Austria. No one knows the identity of Regent, but there must be some connection between the two of you for him to want you dead."

While Dr. Sandorf recalled the words of General Hattersfield regarding Pierre's special assignment, he did not betray the general's confidence. "My son, I am at a loss to even begin to venture who this Regent might be. I'm sorry."

Pierre said, "We hoped you could shed some light on his identity so that we could put him out of business. Now I'm afraid we've tipped our hand and the fox will get away."

Pescade said, "All is not lost. Regent's plan has failed, and that's enough of a reason to celebrate, is it not?"

"You're right, and we shall celebrate. Pierre, can you stay for a while? I want to know more about this plot against Austria and how the pirates and bandits operate."

"Yes, we can stay. I don't think they will try anything overt since they went to lengths to make it look like an accident. I think we are safe for the present."

In the meantime, along the waterfront, the crowd lingered, insisting on seeing Matifou again. Pescade took Matifou up on deck where another great cheer greeted them.

As Dr. Sandorf and Pierre emerged on deck, Silas peered out through the mass of people. He was furious that Dr. Sandorf and Pierre were now together and that his band had been so easily penetrated. Silas had been fearful that Dr. Sandorf might detect him at any time. If the two of them had not already pinpointed him as Regent, he did not believe it was far off. Only his firm grip on Sava and his wife's arm betrayed that something was wrong.

Dr. Sandorf noticed Silas with his family in the crowd. He recalled Silas's move to block the creation of the International Hospital. His thoughts also flashed back to the moment when, many years ago, Von Brun asked Silas to identify him. Now, looking at him and his family—for some inexplicable reason—Dr. Sandorf's eyes fell heavily on the face of Sava. She in turn, found an eerie fascination in Dr. Sandorf's face. However, she did not dwell on it and quickly fixed her gaze on Pierre, standing at Dr. Sandorf's side.

Dr. Sandorf watched as they disappeared into the crowd. No one on board the ship noticed that from deep in the crowd two eyes burned intensely as they fixed upon the face of Maria when she joined the others on deck. The fierce eyes were those of Carpena. His hand unconsciously traveled to his face, and there his fingers traced the old scar.

Carpena spotted Maria and softly uttered these words to himself, "She is like a flower in full bloom." Maria saw Carpena, who had withered.

20

A New Alliance

By the time Pierre Bathory reported to General Hattersfield, the Inn of Three Lanterns had been totally vacated. Not a single one of the bandits could be found. Also, they were not any closer to the identity of Regent than before. Only one major change in their favor had occurred.

Dr. Sandorf and Confucius had decided to join forces with Pierre, Pescade, and Matifou. While they did not know the identity of Regent, they now knew his weakness. If they could cripple his bandit and pirate network, they could slow Regent down. If they got enough information from captured bandits, then little by little they might piece the mystery together. This led to a bold plan designed to drive the pirates and the bandits wild.

With the help of the Austrian Army, all stage coaches began to carry flares supplied by Confucius. The Chinese had used rockets, flares, and firecrackers for centuries. At any sign of trouble, both stagecoaches and sea captains would set off rockets which could climb more than a half mile up into the sky and erupt with such brilliance that they could be seen for several miles around.

On land, the Austrian Army supplied watchers along the major stagecoach routes. This enabled the new alliance to thwart numerous robberies. Even when the highwaymen were successful, it turned out to be a temporary situation for they in turn would be trapped. Early on, they captured the bandit with the photographic memory, which also gave them a tremendous advantage.

At sea, *The Andrea Feratto* was armed with cannon and Gatling guns. At night, they patrolled the Adriatic Sea under a new name emblazoned on cloth that glowed at night. The new name of this surprisingly fast-moving ship was *Vengeance*. In addition to these undertakings, the new alliance armed itself with the water weapons developed by the Chinese. In this way, they ensured themselves of capturing more pirates and bandits unharmed. They avoided killing whenever possible.

Every prisoner was interrogated by Dr. Sandorf, Pierre, and Confucius without exception. Under hypnosis, the pirates and bandits revealed whatever they knew. Thus, the new alliance secured information on how they were organized and the organization's next operations. Slowly, this strategy had an impact on both the pirates and the bandits. Within six months, the major shipping lanes and stagecoach routes became safe for travel. The pirates were forced to move further and further away from Trieste. On land, the bandits retreated into the mountains, striking only on secondary roads.

As was expected, the situation became unbearable for Silas, Sarcany, Zirone, and Carpena. Moreover, Von Brun was beginning to have serious doubts as to Silas's ability to aid the Germans in an invasion of Austria. Regent was thwarted at every turn. The critical information that Von Brun needed dried up.

The last straw, as it were, came when the new alliance almost captured the head of all the pirates, Dragon. As the *Vengeance* closed in on Dragon's ship, Dragon inflicted a full broadside on a merchant vessel. He knew he could effect a getaway because the *Vengeance* would have to stop and help the passengers.

Finally, Silas decided on a daring plan to rid himself of his enemies and regain his esteem in the eyes of the Germans. He selected a group of his own bandits and informed them through Sarcany of an important meeting between Regent and Von Brun. This meeting was to take place within several months high in the border Alps between Germany and Austria. They then sent this group of bandits after a large shipment of gold, knowing they would be captured. Although Silas did not know how information was being extracted from his men, he knew that Dr. Sandorf had his ways. When Dr. Sandorf interrogated these bandits, he realized they were hiding something important. Under hypnosis, they revealed what they believed to be true. Coupled with the news of increased German ski patrols in the border Alps, the new alliance had to believe that a meeting between Von Brun and Regent might actually be scheduled. In fact, they were delighted with the prospect of finally identifying Regent.

At first Dr. Sandorf hoped they could launch an all-out assault on the Triglav Mountain where the meeting was to be held. Pierre explained why this was not possible. "The Triglav is an impregnable military objective for several reasons. First, it has hundreds of depressions and wide hollows separated by rounded, snow-capped peaks. There are a number of glaciers that commit climbers to one slope at a time. Some of these glaciers run as low as thirty-two hundred feet while others break the top at eight thousand feet. Our alliance troops would be useless because any movement on a major scale would be noticed long before they could even reach the foothills. The Germans would see us coming and simply ski away to the far side of the Alps."

Dr. Sandorf asked, "What's the alternative, then?"

It was Pescade who shrewdly offered a workable plan. "Suppose only a small group of mountain climbers were to scale the Triglav. Certainly the Germans would not panic. There are always climbers going to the top of the mountain."

Dr. Sandorf asked, "Could we capture Regent with so small a group?"

"Our objective would be to ascertain the identity of Regent. When we spot him, we would have to let him go and deal with him back here in Trieste. Once we know who Regent is, we can successfully neutralize him," said Pescade.

"A small group would be exposed to dangers and almost defenseless should this prove to be a trap," said Confucius.

Dr. Sandorf asked, "What makes you think it's a trap?"

"I feel it."

The group had come to respect Confucius's fighting and analytical abilities and recognized that he was probably right. Pierre answered for all of them, "We really don't have a choice. That in itself might suggest a trap."

Dr. Sandorf arranged for the great mountain climber François Lumeaux to help prepare the group. François immediately set up a training regimen. As François put it, "The easiest part will be the fifteen-mile daily run."

Climbing up a mountain is a science of its own that requires considerable advance preparation. They found they were lucky to have François Lumeaux leading the expedition. There was nothing that François did not know or that he failed to take into account.

They also decided upon who would comprise the mountain-climbing force. Included were Dr. Sandorf, Pierre, Pescade, Matifou, Confucius, Kumiko, Miko, Chuan, Nato, and two Austrian soldiers. Four Alpine citizens would handle the base camp setup and supplies.

Over the next few weeks, the group started their day with a fifteen-mile run. As expected, Matifou was always the last to finish. But he always finished, to the joy of the others. They took turns learning to handle climbing shoes, ropes, ice hooks, and skiing. They practiced on particularly rough terrain. They took turns squatting with heavy weights on their shoulders. In this exercise, Matifou excelled. They spent long periods of time hanging upside down and crossing ravines with just ropes. For Pescade this was a piece of cake. They also practiced on sheer ice surfaces. For some, the plunges into ice-cold water were a nuisance of an exercise. However, Confucius, Kumiko, Miko, Chuan, and Nato made this seem like a comfortable bath. The others nearly froze to death. Yet, little by little they all acclimated to the freezing temperature and were able to function under these harsh conditions.

Five weeks later, they were all at base camp number one on the Triglav. François said, "We will climb for two days just to get above the timberline and snowline. Our destination is Casa Inglese, which is seventy-five hundred feet up in the deep snows of the Triglav. Early in the century, the Franciscan monks built a chapel high on the mountain as a refuge for stranded climbers. Roughly fifty years ago, a large portion of the cliff overlooking the chapel had broken off. The ensuing avalanche demolished the church, leaving only one small wing intact. Travelers now use the one wing very infrequently. However, Casa Inglese provides one of the best views of a major portion of the Triglav and the surrounding mountain range. From there, any movement of troops or other climbers can easily be seen. We plan to use Casa Inglese as a base until the rendezvous point for Regent and Von Brun can be ascertained."

Unknown to the group, they had done everything according to the master plan of Silas Toronthal. He had made his plans meticulously, knowing that the Austrian army would prove useless while gambling that the new alliance could not afford to pass up the opportunity even if it were a trap. So, the new alliance advanced through the deeply incised valleys and basins blanketed with heavy fog.

Higher, they emerged to a temperature comparable to that of summer with plenty of sunshine. This was due to the fact that normally the temperature decreases with every one thousand feet in elevation. However, during the winter, air circulation causes a temperature inversion. This has a ripple effect on all life on the mountain. The group was treated to the scenic wonders of Austria. The Alpine flora surrounded the group with dwarf pines, certain willow species, and various low shrubs. They traversed meadows where the Alpine roses were in full bloom. Dr. Sandorf stopped at the crest where he discovered the rare species of edelweiss—Austria's national flower. It had been nearly a quarter of a century since his eyes had reveled in the unique beauty of this flower. His nostrils filled with the sweet scent, and he felt warm and fulfilled as an Austrian. From this bed of delight, he watched the ibex, chamois, marmot, red deer, and roe deer. Even an eagle drifted by as if saluting them.

Their second campsite was at roughly five thousand feet. Here, they reviewed their strategy. François said, "The Germans must know by now of our excursion and destination. Yet, not a single patrol has come close to check us out."

"It smells more and more like a trap to me, too," said Dr. Sandorf. "However, we must go into the trap and watch it snap shut if we are to know for certain."

It was Confucius who offered a deviation from their original plan. "Have you ever seen a wise mouse? He does not put his head in until he has examined the situation very carefully. He'll even try to get the cheese with only his feet."

Pescade was curious, "So?"

Confucius expanded, "I think a few of us should go ahead and reconnoiter. We ought to move ahead while the others slip back down the mountain under cover of the cloud bank, which is moving in. Once we reach Casa Inglese, we will light three fires, which ought to convince the Germans that we are all together in camp, and settling down. I suggest we keep our skis on for a fast getaway should we be attacked. Agreed?"

So it was that under cover of the cloud bank, the group split up. Kumiko, Dr. Sandorf, Matifou, Luigi, Miko, Chuan, and the two Austrian soldiers descended to the four-thousand-foot mark. Once there, they avoided lighting any fires, which would reveal their position from afar. Meanwhile, Pierre, Françoise, Confucius, Nato, and Pescade ascended to Casa Inglese. There, the three fires were seen for miles around. From a very far safe distance, Von Brun peered through his telescope and sneered because his prey had entered the trap. In turn, the new alliance looked out over the black night but saw no fires at all. Von Brun had ordered his forces to keep their camps shrouded in darkness.

With the use of mirrors, the Germans flashed a signal on the following morning after sunrise that indicated it was time to set off the dynamite. High above Casa Inglese the blast erupted and a slow but steady portion of the snowcap began to slide down, creating an avalanche. The new alliance had anticipated well. Nonetheless, Pescade tersely noted, "The fiends! It was a trap all the time."

François said, "The trap is sprung, and we are in it. They know there is no way to outrun an avalanche. Thank God the others are safe."

Confucius sprang into action. He, along with Kumiko, Miko, and Chuan, unpacked several water weapons, which they had placed by the fires during the night. Confucius had studied the terrain maps and had envisioned a way out of even a manmade avalanche. He said to François, "At this altitude the water weapons will work for a brief period. Am I correct that the glacier there on our right is covered with snow, which further down becomes sheer ice?"

"Yes, but there is a large break in the glacier three thousand feet below that will plunge us into a one-mile ravine and certain death. Besides, no one has ever skied down a glacier."

"Follow me. As I fire water pellets in front of us, the water will freeze instantly, creating a slick of ice on the snow. Further on, when we reach the glacier ice, we will not need the pellets. As for the ravine, Kumiko, Miko, and Chuan will take care of this. We must gather as much speed as possible on the glacier."

There was no time for additional explanation. They were off as the avalanche approached. Their angle of descent was very steep. It required all their skill to maintain their balance as they quickly surpassed all record-breaking speeds.

Above, the avalanche broke mostly to the left, sweeping away what was left of Casa Inglese. The Germans had anticipated that at best the group might retreat down the normal slope and thus the principal portion of the blast was set to maximize the avalanche in that direction. However, there was more than enough snow crashing down behind the skiers to crush them. They needed to keep going, even though it was impossible to stop.

Meanwhile, at the sound of the first blast of dynamite, Dr. Sandorf and the others sped toward the glacier from below. It was a tough trek, but they made it without a moment to spare. As soon as they arrived, they broke out their water weapons and javelins. Miko and Chuan hurled the javelins across the ravine and into the ice. Then, they alternated their shots of water in order to maximize the freezing potential. Within seconds, an ice ramp began to form, extending well out from the far wall of the glacier. This artificially created ice ramp was to be the exit for the fast oncoming skiers. The only remaining question was whether they would gain enough speed to clear three hundred feet, a record distance never before accomplished by anyone.

The skiers plummeted down the glacier at fantastic speed. For a moment, they were on the glacier, then the ramp, and finally, in rapid succession, they were airborne. Everyone held their breath as the skiers shot skyward. They hung in the air like birds in flight. They leaned forward, the tips of their skies just in front of their noses and their arms tight against their sides to reduce any air friction. François cleared the three hundred feet with room to spare. The others landed closer to the ravine. All plowed into the safety of the snow on the other side. A second later, the avalanche roared into the ravine behind them harmlessly.

The new alliance was overjoyed by their narrow escape. They were far from safe yet. Von Brun had witnessed their gallant and bold escape from the avalanche. Immediately, his ski patrol flashed mirror signals to other forces placed strategically around the mountain. These forces now converged below just in front of the tree line. From where the new alliance was, with their backs to the ravine, there was no way down the mountain except through the converging German ski patrols. Von Brun and his forces were violating the Austrian borders on the Triglav in a last effort to destroy the new alliance. The new alliance took refuge in the rocks as the Germans formed a line between them and the safety of the trees below. Once in the rocks, the alliance fired a flare so that the Austrian troops would know they were in trouble. It was doubtful that they would be reached in time. Once the flares were spotted, the Austrian ski patrols were on the move.

Huddled as they were among the rocks, the members of the new alliance were able to avoid the Germans who had begun firing upon them. The Germans had to ascend the clear slope without any cover. While clearly outnumbered, Matifou and the others began to create their own mini avalanches by loosening boulders that gathered snow as they were rolled down at the Germans. The Germans fell like bowling pins. They broke their ranks, avoiding the stones as best they could. Those Germans who got closer were frozen by the water pellets. These weapons also formed a slick coat of ice, which prevented the Germans from climbing the slope. For every step forward, many were sliding back with no progress in sight. Von Brun was furious. He had the new alliance within his grasp, yet he could not close his fist to finally crush them.

Soon the Germans realized that the newly formed slick ice could be broken with a hard downward kick, and they began to advance on the helpless position. Von Brun also had some of his key forces outflank the new alliance. These troops were in the rocks just to the left of the new alliance along the ravine. In a minute or two the Germans would have them completely at their mercy. Under the circumstances, surrender was out of the question, for they knew they would be killed. Thus, a life-and-death struggle was at hand.

All of a sudden, there was a tremendous volley of shots from below. The Austrian troops were breaking through the tree line. Now, it was Von Brun and his forces that were caught in a crossfire. The Germans decided their position was no longer tenable and broke ranks. They split, heading for the German border.

The Germans, who had outflanked the new alliance, were still in the rocks and advancing. They were led by Zirone, who was not going to give up just when they were so close. These forces continued to make their way through the rocks, firing as they advanced. Zirone fired a shot that caught Pescade in the chest. As he fell, Matifou rose like a giant and charged the Germans. He was joined by Confucius, Kumiko, Miko, Nato, and Chuan. The Chinese hurled their flying stars in a barrage of blades that demoralized this last group of Germans. The Germans retreated while their rear guard fired a hail of bullets. This barrage caught Matifou. Somehow, Matifou kept going, ignoring his wounds and his pain. Zirone kept firing, not believing that anyone could not be stopped by bullets. Finally, Matifou caught up to Zirone high in the rocks. He lifted Zirone over his head and tossed him into the ravine. His death cry echoed as he fell to the valley floor. It was a fitting end for the villainous Zirone.

Dr. Sandorf and Confucius treated Pescade and Matifou on the spot. Nato, Miko, and Chuan brought firewood and started a blaze with which to heat knives.

With respect to Pescade, Dr. Sandorf said, "The bullet went straight through without hitting any vital organs or shattering any bones. We'll seal the wound and he'll be all right in a couple of weeks."

Matifou was another matter. He was riddled with bullets. Dr. Sandorf indicated, "The bullets must come out if he is to have any chance."

Confucius nodded in agreement. To Matifou, Dr. Sandorf said, "I wish we had something for your pain."

It was then that Confucius placed an affectionate hand to Matifou's head, instantly hypnotizing him. Confucius reassured Dr. Sandorf, "Matifou will not feel any pain."

With that, both Confucius and Dr. Sandorf began to remove all the bullets. Within the hour, they had Pescade and Matifou on stretchers being taken down the mountain to the nearest Alpine village.

The group stayed together for the next week, enjoying a much-deserved vacation. While they were disappointed that they had not uncovered Regent's identity, they were nonetheless happy that they had once again foiled Regent's plans.

In the Tirolian village, they enjoyed the hospitality of the community. The villagers appreciated that, once again, the Germans had been handed a defeat. This was cause for much celebration and an overall festive mood. The Austrian men wore their traditional gray coats and trousers decorated with wide green stripes. Some wore grey leather shorts and bright vests, coats, stockings, and hats. The Austrian women wore colorful regional costumes with embroidered blouses and bodices and full skirts gathered at the waist. There were dances and songs, and the patients recuperated very nicely.

The house where Pescade and Matifou were welcomed was a typical peasant home with balconies and a gabled roof with overhanging eaves. The lower part of this house was of light stucco. There was a brightly painted doorway and the usual flower boxes so common in Austria. The interior was warm and inviting like the area residents.

When the new alliance members left, Pescade and Matifou were doing fine. Still, Dr. Sandorf insisted they remain behind for another week. They were out of danger but needed rest and relaxation. Dr. Sandorf reflected on the fact that he could not have found a more ideal place for them to stay.

21

A Deadly Vengeance

Silas Toronthal waited for word of what had transpired. When the coded telegraph came, he turned beet-red. The news included the loss of Zirone, which meant he needed to communicate with Sarcany. He wrote a message on a small piece of paper. Then, he went down to the lobby as if to inquire at the main desk. Once there, he slipped the note under the sign-in register. He had ascertained on his walk through the lobby that Namir was there. She was loyal only to money and spent a considerable amount of time with Sarcany. Since the abandonment of The Three Lanterns, she and many others were being sought by the army. However, it was very easy for a woman to disguise herself—a change of color for her hair, a less provocative dress, and she passed for just one more housecleaner.

Even as Silas ascended the stairs, she had scooped up the note and exited the hotel. Secretly, she loved Sarcany and hoped someday to marry him. Since he never brought up the subject, she did whatever she could whenever she was asked. Presently, she was eager to see Sarcany. She knew where to locate him and lost no time bringing him Silas's note. The note was in French and read: *"S. Viens."* It meant come at once.

Later that night, Sarcany slipped into Silas's suite and was greeted by the news of Zirone's death and the failure of their plot. Silas said, "I know you lost a friend, but he will still be avenged. I have a new plan." A steely-eyed Sarcany listened eagerly. Silas spelled out his new plot: "When the *Trabaculo* venture failed, I noticed Sava's loving glances at Pierre Bathory. I am convinced that they have been seeing each other for years. Now, what would Pierre do if we started a rumor that Sava was going to marry someone?"

Sarcany caught his drift and answered, "He would make every effort possible to contact her. Either he would venture to come here or he might try to get his mother to make contact."

Silas outlined his plan. "Place guards outside the hotel, and by all means watch for him at his mother's house. We can't have any incident in the hotel."

"Of course I understand. Consider it done. With Pescade and Matifou recuperating, Pierre will be quite vulnerable. This is one assignment I am going to enjoy personally."

"Meanwhile, I'll alert Carpena that we must get Dr. Sandorf at any price."

As expected, all the members of the new alliance returned to Trieste except for Pescade and Matifou. Within hours of his return, Pierre learned of the impending wedding. This shocked him beyond anything else. Since Silas Toronthal was such an influential figure, the news of his daughter's wedding became the talk of Trieste. While Pierre did not believe the rumor, he was compelled by his heart to find a way to clarify what was transpiring. He never anticipated a plot aimed directly at him. He believed his romance was yet a secret. Moreover, he had not put Silas and Regent together as the same man. After agonizing about this development for several days, he decided to call upon his mother for advice. Perhaps she could see Sava and make some sense of it all.

Madame Bathory lived at 17 Marinella Street in the old part of Trieste. This area was drastically different from the Stradone. Marinella Street was an endless staircase rising up the side of the hill. It was a narrow street with houses clustered one on top of the other. At night, it looked like a dark cavern. Like many of the old streets, it was also poorly lit. Thus, Pierre never noticed the bandits who hid in the shadows. Three slid silently behind him, blocking any retreat. Three others walked calmly toward him as if to continue down Marinella Street. All of a sudden, Pierre realized that he was trapped.

Pierre was unafraid. He was a very experienced soldier and a very capable fighter. As soon as the initial three made their move, he went directly at them, holding his own. He knocked one out while kicking another in the groin. He sidestepped another and elbowed him in the face. He drew his sword and a battle ensued with the remaining cutthroats. Just when it looked like he might slip through the six attackers, four more joined in, including Sarcany. The outcome against ten opponents was inevitable. Pierre was subdued and held against one of the buildings. In an exceedingly cold-blooded manner, Sarcany placed a pistol in Pierre's hand and slowly forced it to his temple. Pierre's struggles were to no avail.

Suddenly, the pistol discharged and a bursting pain seared Pierre's eyes and head just before all went dark. The shot rang loudly in the narrow street. Then, a sprinkling of lights sprayed the scene. The bandits had faded away into the black night of shadows, leaving Pierre lying seconds away from the safety of his mother's home. It was old Borik who responded to the shot, venturing forth to discover Pierre. All Borik saw was a lifeless form on the steps under the dim lights. Borik quickly identified Pierre and rushed him into the house. There, his mother burst into tears while Borik bound the head wound tightly. To Madame Bathory he said, "It's a miracle he is still alive. Keep the bandage tight while I go fetch Dr. Sandorf."

Riding hard in the night, it did not take Borik long to reach the home of Dr. Sandorf. Within minutes of the shooting, both Dr. Sandorf and Confucius entered the Bathory home and tended to Pierre. They labored all through the night in a desperate effort to save Pierre. It seemed a hopeless situation—a shot in the brain. They tried nonetheless. At 5:00 AM, they pronounced Pierre dead.

At the military headquarters, an official pronouncement of suicide was made. Pierre was believed to have become despondent upon hearing the news that Sava was to be married. For the present, this story was designed to keep the bandits off guard and buy valuable time for the new alliance. As was customary, the military took over the funeral arrangements and telegraphed Pescade and Matifou, who jumped on the very next train for Trieste.

By late the next day, there was a short street procession from the Church of the Franciscans down the Stradone. From there they would travel by coach to the cemetery, which overlooked the Adriatic Sea. As the funeral procession made its way down the Stradone, Madame Toronthal and Sava were leaving their residence to go shopping. No news of Pierre's death had reached them since no one knew of their romance. For some time now, Madame Toronthal had been gravely ill, and a brief carriage ride to the shopping district might cheer her up. So it was that Sava and her mother were just mounting a fine coach in front of the Stradone when the funeral convoy left Marinella Street and turned toward them. Since their coach intended to travel in the opposite direction, they were required to wait until the procession had passed.

As the coffin passed, Sava noticed Dr. Sandorf and a strange feeling of apprehension came over her. Moments later, she noticed Pescade and Matifou and others from Pierre's regiment. She stood up in the coach hoping to catch a glimpse of Pierre, oblivious to the fact that he was in the coffin. It was when she saw the weeping face of Madame Bathory that Sava's eyes darted from Pierre's mother to the coffin. In turn, Madame Toronthal also realized for whom the funeral dirge was being held.

The realization that Madame Bathory was on her way to bury Pierre was the most shocking moment in young Sava's life. She was overcome with such horrific grief that she could not endure it. She fainted into her mother's arms. Madame Toronthal loved Sava dearly. She was very much aware of her husband's earlier betrayal of the patriots but could say nothing for fear of losing her position in society. She also knew of Sava's love for Pierre. In her heart, she felt it was unsavory since her husband was responsible for the death of Pierre's father, Étienne. Madame Toronthal hoped in her heart that Sava and Pierre would never marry. Yet, she never betrayed Sava's secret love. Now, she noted the pain in Sava's face, realized how her daughter must be suffering, and her ailing heart suffered the worst heart attack yet. She, too, fell backward in the coach, hanging on to life by a thread.

Dr. Sandorf witnessed the double collapse of the women and dashed from the procession to their carriage. He immediately ordered the concierge to arrange for them both to be taken to their suite, where he tended to both of them. Since Sava's situation was not life threatening, he concentrated on Madame Toronthal.

When Sava regained consciousness, she was startled to see Dr. Sandorf tending to her mother. It grieved Dr. Sandorf to inform Sava, "It is not likely she will live out the day."

"My mother and Pierre. Oh my God!" Sava rushed to her mother's side and wept over her double sorrow. Now Dr. Sandorf realized that Sava and Pierre had been secret lovers.

The scene in the Toronthal residence changed abruptly when Silas and Sarcany entered. They had learned of Madame Toronthal's relapse upon entering the hotel. However, they did not expect to see Dr. Sandorf comforting Sava, his arm warmly over her shoulder.

Sarcany donned a disguise. He and Silas froze in the doorway, shocked to see Dr. Sandorf and Sava together. Suddenly, a combination of thoughts and feelings surged through Silas and Sarcany. They each felt awkward under the circumstances. Sarcany actually put his hand on his pistol. Silas thought that perhaps his wife had divulged his secret betrayal of Dr. Sandorf. Their own guilty consciences and furtive glances at one another were telltale.

Dr. Sandorf recalled their encounter at the time of his arrest by Von Brun. He now realized that here—in his presence—were his past and current enemies. Now he knew the secret of Regent's identity. In turn, Silas knew he knew. Silas lost his composure. His voice was menacing and quavering as he ordered, "Get out of my house." If he was remotely aware of the assistance Dr. Sandorf had given his wife and daughter, he did not show it. He never associated the doctor's presence with his wife's condition. Silas stood, shaking, trying to control his rage.

As Dr. Sandorf left, Sarcany reluctantly stood aside to let him pass. All the while, Sarcany's hand rested firmly on his pistol. Sarcany would have shot him there if he thought he could get away with it. He averted Dr. Sandorf's eyes by looking into the fish tank where Silas kept his pets. Sava could not understand their behavior but sensed the danger for Dr. Sandorf. She placed herself between Dr. Sandorf and the pair and escorted him out of the residence.

In spite of her sorrow, Sava was furious at her father's behavior. She knew none of the motivations that prompted his behavior. She only knew that he was wrong. In the foyer, Sava placed a grateful hand on Dr. Sandorf's arm. She found it easy to look up into his clear, strong eyes as she said, "I am grateful for your help. I know my mother would want you to know. Please accept my apology for my father."

Dr. Sandorf tried to make things easier for Sava by gently reassuring her, "He must have been upset with worry."

Sava appreciated Dr. Sandorf's graciousness, but neither one of them believed for a second that Silas's behavior was prompted by any concern for Madame Toronthal. At that moment, Sava and Dr. Sandorf shared a deep affection for one another. How different this meeting might have been if each had known all that had transpired. Somehow, nature touched each of these tragic figures and permitted a genuine warmth and respect to be shared. Neither could understand it. Each was happier in these few preciously shared moments. As they parted, their respective momentary happiness evaporated.

Dr. Sandorf was relieved. He now knew the basis for the rumor of a wedding and the real cause of the attack on Pierre. He realized that Pierre and Sava could never marry—not with the legacy of betrayal as an endowment from Silas. Then, too, he naturally reflected upon the fact that Pierre would have become the son-in-law of Regent. No marriage could be built on such a foundation. Sava was an innocent victim of circumstances, but that did not change anything.

These thoughts faded as he left to catch up to the funeral. He had pressing matters to attend to.

22

Cheating Death

At the cemetery, it did not take long to carefully place Pierre in the family crypt. The soldiers fired a salvo in salute to their dead comrade. The funeral ended as General Hattersfield handed a distraught Madame Bathory the Austrian flag that had draped the coffin. As everyone cleared the area, Dr. Sandorf remained briefly with Pescade and Matifou for a word. "How are you both feeling? Matifou, can you handle some heavy lifting tonight?" Both nodded affirmatively, although they found this brief exchange very strange.

That night, *The Andrea Ferrato* weighed anchor and sped for a nearby cove. Once at anchor, Pescade and Matifou joined Dr. Sandorf in a small skiff. Dr. Sandorf quietly rowed it to shore. For the present, only Dr. Sandorf knew the nature of this night adventure. Since Pescade and Matifou held Dr. Sandorf in the highest esteem, they loyally offered their assistance. They put their personal grief aside and were ready to serve him in whatever lay ahead. Dr. Sandorf shared with them his belief as to the identity of Regent. However, he also noted that they had no proof.

Pescade and Matifou were naturally curious and glanced questioningly at each other as they left the shore. The group climbed a low embankment. They had not come far from the port of Trieste. The lights from the city touched the sky with a soft tinge. They quickly passed a large row of trees and climbed over a low fence. Suddenly, Pescade and Matifou realized they were back in the cemetery. They stood facing rows of tombstones. Within seconds, they were at the Bathory crypt. At night it looked like a small monument—a small chapel. The iron gate was not locked. The trio entered.

There was no light inside the crypt. It was cold and damp because nothing blocked the constant ocean spray from reaching the cemetery. Dr. Sandorf lit a candle, which illuminated the face of a wall on which three marble plaques were encrusted. Their attention was drawn to the middle plaque, which bore the inscription:

Pierre Bathory
1857–1888

"Remove the plaque," said Dr. Sandorf.

It came off with ease since the tomb had not yet been permanently sealed. It was set aside and they could now see the coffin deep within the wall cavity. Dr. Sandorf said, "Help me pull out the coffin." Between Matifou and Dr. Sandorf, the coffin slid out easily. They placed it gently on the floor. The casket was nailed down, and Dr. Sandorf asked Matifou, "Can you open it, or do we need a lever?"

Matifou grasped the edge of the coffin top and applied a slow, steady pressure. In a moment, it popped open as easily as one would a cardboard box. "Matifou, lift Pierre gently." Pescade replaced the empty coffin and plaque. They left the cemetery, retracing their steps to the skiff. Once aboard the Ferrato, they sped for the island hospital.

As soon as the yacht docked, Confucius and Chang met them with two attendants and a stretcher. The attendants took Pierre into the hospital. Dr. Sandorf explained briefly to Pescade and Matifou, "Pierre is in a deep hypnotic trance. We have already partially treated him. We can revive him, but his wound is extremely dangerous. Only in the deep hypnotic state where he is in now can the body's needs be minimized for a long period of time. We must operate on Pierre's damaged brain and extract the bullet that is inflicting pressure. There is much damaged tissue, and we are not certain we can save him. I will assist both Chang and Confucius, who are the only ones who believe there is a chance."

The three doctors labored for twenty-seven hours. It was one of the most puzzling and perplexing operations Dr. Sandorf had ever participated in. Chang and Confucius combined acupuncture and hypnosis. They applied the glowing enzymes they had developed for tissue rejuvenation. They retrieved the bullet. They continually maintained the lowest possible level of bodily functions in order to focus the body's own healing energies on just the brain. At the conclusion, Dr. Sandorf said, "At no time in the history of man has there been such an operation."

"Quite true. We've done all we can. The rest is in the hands of Providence," said Chang.

Pierre did not regain consciousness for five days. Twenty times they thought they would lose him. He was so close to death that he did not even recognize Pescade and Matifou, who never left his side. Dr. Sandorf never ceased to be attentive to him. He treated Pierre constantly with caring devotion. There was no doubt that, in his heart, Dr. Sandorf had adopted Pierre. From this time forward, he would always call him son.

Pescade and Matifou easily arranged for unsuspicious sick leave since they both had wounds in need of attention. That they stayed at the hospital was not considered out of the ordinary. They anticipated that, with Pierre's ability to disguise himself, they would soon be back in action.

On the fifth day Pierre finally regained consciousness and said, "I'm hungry."

While under hypnosis, they informed Pierre that Sava was not really going to be married. They also briefed him as to the identity of Regent. Pierre was young and strong. However, he had two of the most powerful forces in the world working for him—love and revenge.

23

Catania: Stronghold of the Pirates

The pirates had moved their operations to the province of Etna in Sicily just on the outskirts of the provincial capital of Catania. Almost five thousand cutthroats were assembled in this region. They had a fleet of ships always ready for their misdeeds. The port of Catania had evolved into a stronghold. The pirates had commandeered the old Roman fortress on its outskirts and to date, no country had dared attack them. Only a well-armed flotilla would successfully attack Catania. However, this would be a costly invasion in terms of men and money. In spite of the pirates' raids, no country wanted to commit themselves to so costly an invasion. Since most of the countries along the Mediterranean did not talk to one another, they never thought about a joint venture to clean up the area. It was in this citadel that Carpena and the pirates—led by the ruthless leader named Dragon—made their home.

Operating from the safety of Catania, Carpena developed a sense of overconfidence. Since the day he saw Maria on the pier, he plotted his own revenge. He had always indulged himself in his weakness for women. Now, with the death of Zirone and Silas's orders to eliminate Dr. Sandorf at any cost, his devilish mind devised a sinister plan. He would kidnap Maria.

Carpena knew that Maria and her brother, Luigi, would often supervise the supply ship used frequently by the International Hospital. This was one of the few ships that traveled freely without flares. No one thought that a hospital supply ship would ever be attacked. So it was that Maria and Luigi fell victim to Carpena when he commandeered a pirate ship, intercepting them on the short run from Trieste. One shot across the bow forced the supply ship to heave to. They boarded her easily over the protestations of the small crew. When Maria and Luigi were face to face with Carpena, they realized that the supplies were not at all what the pirates were after. They were taken for ransom to Catania.

Carpena sought to ingratiate himself with Silas, especially since he believed the German invasion was imminent. In addition, with Zirone out of the picture, he sought to improve his own position. Therefore, he sent a message with the released crew of the supply ship, indicating that Dr. Sandorf was to come alone to Catania with a million in pearls. Otherwise, both Luigi and Maria would be killed. Carpena had absolutely no intention of letting them go. Once Dr. Sandorf arrived, Carpena intended to turn him over to Silas and Von Brun, pocket the pearls, and have his way with Maria at last. While Luigi was useless to Carpena, he took him along because he happened to be on the supply ship. He also reasoned that Andrea Ferrato would be more vexed that both his children were captured. Carpena savored his revenge at long last. Indeed, Andrea was devastated.

Carpena was delighted with his fiendish plan. Once the ransom was paid, he would feed Luigi and Maria to the sharks that infested and protected the subterranean waters of the Roman fortress. Under the draconian leadership of Dragon, disobedient pirates and captives were regularly tossed from the fortress to be eaten by sharks.

Upon Carpena's arrival, Dragon was just in the process of administering his own brand of justice. Carpena enjoyed exposing Maria and Luigi to this demonstration. Dragon was over six feet tall, weighed 160 pounds, and was built like a battering ram. He was ruthless and wore many battle scars proudly. As Carpena entered the large mess hall outfitted with an arena, he was greeted with a smile from Dragon, who looked the captives over. Two of the usual prostitutes who pleased Carpena sauntered over to him, brushing their bodies up against him suggestively. Once he had seen to his captives, he planned to have a good time with them. Dragon entered the ring. Four prisoner pirates were brought in. Dragon had a unique way of administering his own brand of justice. He stood perfectly still with his hands on his hips. "You are permitted to strike me full force while I offer no resistance. If you knock me out, you will not be fed to the sharks. If you defeat me in combat, your lives will be spared."

The four opponents struck Dragon simultaneously. He staggered but did not fall. He shook off their blows and immediately kicked out at two of his challengers. His kicks were powerful, and both went down in pain. He quickly defeated the remaining two. His adroit foot technique was known by the French term *savate*.

Dragon then shouted, "Discipline! Discipline or death! You all saw. I gave them a chance. Feed them to the sharks. Shit! I can't get a decent fight these days." With these closing remarks, Dragon stared at Luigi, who knew his turn would come. Then, the entire band—along with the new prisoners—exited the mess hall and headed for the top of the fortress rampart. As they ascended, the entire mob took up the chant, "Discipline or death! Discipline or death!" It was obvious to the two prisoners that this chant was frequently used. At the top of the fortification, the four rebellious pirates were hurled to the waiting sharks below. Carpena ensured that both Luigi and Maria got a good view as the sharks ripped the four in a feeding frenzy. They died screaming.

Carpena did not hesitate to offer Luigi to Dragon for sport. Dragon was grateful, and the mob took Luigi off to the arena. Dragon asked, "What about the little missy?"

"She's mine."

When Luigi was forced into the ring, his hands were untied. Unlike the previous fight, Luigi was not offered the first blow. Dragon's plan was to beat him half to death. However, no one told Luigi what the plan was. He believed he would be thrown to the sharks. He resolved to die bravely. Of course, only Maria knew that Luigi had trained for years with the Shaolin. He was more than a match for Dragon.

Dragon came straight for him and tried to connect with a straight fist to the face. Luigi saw him telegraph the blow and was not there to receive it. Dragon immediately closed the distance between them and tried to kick Luigi in the head. Luigi anticipated this, having seen how Dragon favored his feet as weapons. Luigi decided on a strategy of his own. As Dragon's foot sailed up toward his head, Luigi side-stepped the blow and moved in close to Dragon, catching his leg on the upswing. From this position, he was able to force the leg up easily beyond its intended range. This caused Dragon to lose his balance completely and fall heavily on his back. At this moment, Luigi pretended to fall awkwardly. However, he deliberately dropped both knees directly on the inside of Dragon's right leg just above the knee. This is a very delicate area. Essentially, Luigi masked the move so that it would appear to everyone that the injury was accidental. However, Luigi was actually inflicting the most painful "Charlie-horse" of Dragon's life. The idea was to test whether, once injured, Dragon would continue. Screaming in agony, Dragon held his leg in both hands. Everything had happened so quickly that only Maria realized it had been done intentionally. Meanwhile, the pirates took up a chant: "The sharks! The sharks! The sharks!"

Dragon intervened, "No! No! No sharks for this one, yet. Lock him up. I want another crack at him." The fun period was over, and they led Luigi to a room where he was held captive. Carpena took Maria to a separate lockup.

After a secret meeting with Von Brun, it was decided to launch the offensive against Austria. The plan was for a large naval invasion of Trieste with a simultaneous land assault across the border. Sarcany spread a large map on one of the tables and went over the details with his band of thieves.

Silas's role was to finance a major portion of the invasion. A considerable amount of money was needed within five days. Supplies were needed, and the pirates were to be given large bonuses. The German fleet would set sail and join them in Catania. The pirate forces would join the fleet with their own ships, making the invasion force unbeatable. The key to their success lay in forcing the Austrian army to commit most of their forces to protecting Trieste. In this way, they anticipated being able to bombard Trieste until the German border troops were victorious. The pirates were to be given all they could carry from Trieste as a reward for their participation. The wealth of an entire city was a prize they could not refuse.

After Silas and Sarcany finished describing the plan, they left the meeting, sharing a secret that caused them some worry. Just a few days before, Silas had gone to Monte Carlo and as usual, had gambled heavily. Silas was on a lucky streak and believed he could not lose. He began to play carelessly and lost a considerable fortune.

Silas said, "We were wise not to have mentioned our financial situation to Von Brun. It is impossible to raise the necessary funds for our part of the invasion unless we're able to get hold of funds put aside in Sava's name. However, the only way to obtain this money will be for you to actually marry Sava."

Sarcany added, "Since we begun the rumor that Sava would marry, the wedding between us would be an expected event."

24

Madame Toronthal's Death

Madame Toronthal lingered on for several days after her heart attack, thanks to the expert care Dr. Sandorf provided. Perhaps she refused to die because she had some unfinished business that tormented her. There was no doubt that Mme. Toronthal loved Sava as if she were her own daughter. On her deathbed, she fervently desired to confess the identity of Sava's real father. She had always been sickly and could not bear children. For twenty-two years, everyone had believed Sava's real father was Silas, and Mme. Toronthal saw no need to inform Sava to the contrary. With Sava's real father alive, Mme. Toronthal's conscience was extremely perturbed at the hour of her death. She faded in and out of consciousness. Only by a supreme effort was she able to pull herself from her sick bed to write a letter.

Mme. Toronthal wrote to Pierre Bathory's mother because she wanted to express her condolence at Pierre's death and because she could not go in person to Sava's real father. She was sensitive enough to want the news to be delivered in person. It was with great effort and pain that she managed to write this letter. Perspiration beaded on her forehead and her hand trembled as she wrote. When she finished the letter, she slid it into an envelope and addressed it to Mme. Bathory, 17 Rue Marinella, the Stradone, Trieste.

Somehow, Mme. Toronthal found the strength to open the door, descend the stairs, cross the hotel lobby, and with much difficulty, managed to reach the postal box where she deposited the letter. Then, she retraced her steps to the foot of the stairs. There, her strength gave out and she fell down heavily. Had she left the letter upstairs, it might never have gone out. Later they found her and carried her back to her quarters.

Sava was asleep, although she had been attentive. She had not heard her mother leave. When they returned with her, Sava blamed herself for what had happened. Mme. Toronthal said, "I feel as if an ice-cold blanket has been placed over my entire body. I know this is the end." She paused, "My child, listen. I'm so sorry. I know I was wrong not to have told you. Please forgive me."

"You ask me to forgive you? What is it, Mama?" Sava asked. Realizing it was difficult for her mother to speak at all, she gestured for her mother to be still.

The dying woman continued, "One last kiss, Sava! Yes, the last, a kiss to show me you forgive me."

At these words, Sava's first reaction was to suppose her mother was delirious and gently placed her lips to her mother's forehead.

Her mother's last words were, "Sava, we adopted you. Silas is not your father, you are not my real daughter, your real father ..." She never finished. A last convulsion seized her and she expired in her daughter's arms. Sava, trying in vain to revive her, wept painfully for the loss of the only mother she had known.

The very next morning Silas and Sarcany returned to Trieste. Silas made the necessary funeral arrangements, and Mme. Toronthal was interred late in the day. It was an ostentatious funeral that many of the aristocracy felt obliged to attend. After the funeral, Sava returned home with Silas and Sarcany, not having said a word to either.

Upon entering their quarters, Sava headed for her room. Sarcany had other plans and nudged Silas's arm as a reminder.

"Sava," barked Silas. "I respect the sorrow your mother's death is causing you. In spite of your grief, we have to think of the living and certain, ah, affairs; since you're of age, it's good for you to know about your inheritance."

Sava did not want to be in the presence of the two men and hurriedly said, "If it's only a question of money, it should not take long. I don't want any inheritance."

Silas said impatiently, "You no doubt forget that your situation will change. The death of your mother doesn't change our plans at all."

"What plans?" asked Sava in a challenging tone.

Silas gulped and said, "The plan to make Sarcany a member of the family, my son-in-law."

As if on cue, Sarcany stepped proudly forward and was about to say something. Sava, ignoring his presence, said, "Listen, father, because this is the last time I shall call you father. Sarcany has no interest in me except for the money he hopes to get, which I want no part of. If you wish to enrich him, give him your fortune. That's all he really wants." Visibly bothered with the presence of the two men, Sava headed for her room.

"Sava!" cried Silas, following after her. "You don't make any sense. I don't understand. Do you know what you're saying? I wonder if your mother's death ..."

Sava cut him off, "My mother? Yes, she was my mother. My mother because of her unconditional love."

"If your mourning has not affected your mind, what I've planned for you will come to pass. You will marry Sarcany. I must insist on this."

"By what right?"

"The right which is given to paternal authority."

"You, sir, are not my father, and my name is not Toronthal!" With that, Sava hastily exited the room.

Silas and Sarcany stood dumbfounded. Silas paled and could not think of any reply. Only after she had gone did Sarcany realize that he had to take control of the situation, "How much she knows is not important," he said. "Our entire plan will be jeopardized if she has her way. She must be prevented from speaking to anyone. Here is what we must do and as quickly as possible." An assertive Sarcany laid out his Machiavellian plan. "We must leave Trieste, you and I, taking Sava with us. We should return to Trieste only after the wedding unless we can arrange for the funds to be transferred from one bank to another. We should only return for the invasion. As far as her consenting to the marriage, that's my business. I'll be damned if I don't succeed."

Silas saw absolutely no way out. He stood before the brightly-colored fish tank and was not aware that he was over-feeding the fish. He was powerless to resist Sarcany's logic. Fate had dealt the hand, and they must play it out.

"We will depart tonight for Catania. Sava will not speak to anyone," remarked a now composed and determined Silas.

25

The Double Reunion

Mme. Toronthal's letter arrived the very next day at the home of
Mme. Bathory. The postman dropped it in her mailbox where Borik
retrieved it. Pierre's death had left Mme. Bathory in despair, feeling
there was no reason to go on living. She opened the letter almost
disinterestedly. As she read the note, her expression changed and some
color came back into her cheeks. She realized she could do something
for her departed son, Pierre. She could repay Dr. Sandorf's kindness
and help the woman Pierre had loved. She ordered Borik, "Make
arrangements to leave for the International Hospital at once."

When Mme. Bathory arrived at the International Hospital, she
found Dr. Sandorf with Confucius by the shore where the enormous
aquarium was situated. She had to wait for several minutes because
they were engrossed in an experiment with an octopus. They finished
and left the water. Dr. Sandorf was speaking to Confucius and did
not immediately see Mme. Bathory.

"I have no alternative but to take the pearls to Catania within the
next few days," said Dr. Sandorf."

"My friend, it would be certain death for you, Luigi, and Maria.
What is to keep Carpena and the rest of those cutthroats from
breaking their word? There is another way, if you wish me to help,"
advised Confucius.

Just then, Dr. Sandorf saw Mme. Bathory and went quickly to her. He embraced her warmly. "I have been thinking of you and was planning to send for you. You have not been taking good care of yourself as you promised. Come, I have a surprise for you, better than any medicine. First, we better go to my office where you can sit down."

They entered the office and Dr. Sandorf gave her and Borik a tranquilizer. Meanwhile, Confucius went to get Pierre.

After Mme. Bathory was seated, Dr. Sandorf continued, "You recall that many believed Pierre had committed suicide. Well, I believe he was set upon by his enemies. They wanted his death to appear as suicide. In order to reduce the risk of another attempt on Pierre's life, it was necessary to deceive everyone, including you, into believing he was dead."

Mme. Bathory's face was transformed in astonishment at this statement. She tried to control her trembling body. Borik was also shaken. Reaching out to her, Dr. Sandorf said softly but reassuringly, "Yes, Pierre is alive and recuperating nicely. He'll come through that door in a minute. The nature of his assignment to uncover the identity of Regent made it imperative for us to keep him out of sight."

Words failed Mme. Bathory. Tears of joy overflowed from her as Pierre walked in. For several minutes mother and child were locked in an embrace. There was no adequate way to describe her joy.

Pierre apologized for the deception. "Mama, if they had informed you, you would not have been convincing at the funeral. We're all sorry; it had to be done this way."

"Pierre, Pierre. Dr. Sandorf, you did right. The safety of my son is all that matters to me."

"You have succeeded in fooling Pierre's enemies and in giving him a new lease on life," said Borik.

In her happiness, Mme. Bathory had forgotten why she had come. Dr. Sandorf now inquired politely, "Have you not been feeling well? Why did you come?"

From her expression, they gathered that it was a distasteful reason of some sort.

"Oh, Dr. Sandorf, you have brought me the greatest joy ... I have only tragic news for you." She handed Dr. Sandorf the letter from Mme. Toronthal. He read it.

Dear Mme. Bathory,

As one mother to another, please accept my deepest condolence for the loss of Pierre. When you receive this letter, I will no doubt also be dead. I am sorry to burden you at a time like this, but I have no one else to whom I dare entrust this errand. Please, please go to Dr. Mathias Sandorf and beg him to forgive me for my silence. Show him this letter, please.

Dear Dr. Sandorf,

You may not believe what I have to say. For years, it has seemed a horrid nightmare. I never wake up from it. First, let me assure you that I love Sava dearly and have always wanted only her happiness. What I am revealing to you must never be told to her, since it can only cause her grief.

When you escaped from Pisino, Commandant Von Brun was absolutely enraged and had your wife arrested. They thought you would return and try to rescue her. They placed her under special guard day and night and abused her constantly in an effort to get her to reveal whatever she knew. As the months went by and you did not come, Von Brun tried harder to get her to divulge the names of the other partisans. She never did.

Then, it became apparent that she was with child. Von Brun decided to withhold the services of a doctor unless she cooperated. She never spoke again. Von Brun was certain that she would break down and talk. I overheard him speaking to Silas about it.

Your wife gave birth in prison with no one to help her. She delivered the child herself and died because she was refused medical attention. Your little baby girl lived.

To hide what he had done, Von Brun asked Silas to take the child. Even he did not desire to destroy the baby girl. Since I could never bear children, I accepted the child as my own and named her Sava. As God is my judge, I raised her with all my love.

Now Silas plans to wed her to Sarcany in order to get his hands on her inheritance. Actually, half of your original estate, which was confiscated by the Germans, was put in a trust in a Swiss bank. Sava has no love for Sarcany, and you must not let this wedding take place.

Madame Toronthal

Dr. Sandorf sat heavily in his leather chair for a long time. He handed the letter to his friend, Confucius, and said nothing. Slowly, Dr. Sandorf unraveled the mystery. Obviously, Silas was in close communication with the Germans for them to have made the custodial arrangements.

Dr. Sandorf recalled Sava's face with her hand on his arm the last time they had been together. He saw, as through a veil, his wife's face. Surely, they were the same. How could he not have known? Confucius permitted him his silent reflections while the others left the room.

Some time later, a newly invigorated Dr. Sandorf emerged, bursting with joy, "Confucius, I have a daughter."

Confucius shared in his joy, saying, "We shall go together and see to it that there is no wedding. Afterward, we shall talk about Maria and Luigi and the plan I have for their safe return."

Dr. Sandorf's joy was contagious as word spread among all his friends. In response to Confucius's advice, he agreed, "Yes! Yes! I must see Sava. We'll go at once."

The Andrea Ferrato sped through the calm waters. They docked in Trieste and took a horse-drawn coach to the Hotel de Stradone. There, they were informed by the concierge that, after Madame Toronthal's funeral, Silas and Sava left without informing anyone where they were going. Dr. Sandorf was perturbed and did not believe the manager. He insisted, "May I see their apartment?" He thought that there might be a clue to Silas's whereabouts in the apartment suite.

However, the manager informed him, "It is not permitted, sir. It is out of the question."

Confucius stepped quickly to the desk. His sudden approach got the manager's undivided attention. As the manager looked into his eyes, he was instantly hypnotized. Confucius asked politely, "Please, sir; we would like very much to examine the Toronthal apartment."

The manager's demeanor changed. Falling totally under Confucius's power, he said almost mechanically, "Right this way, sir. Right this way."

The manager secured a passkey and led them up the stairs to the Toronthal quarters. There, the manager unlocked the door and permitted them entry. However, the apartment was deserted, and they found no evidence that would suggest where Silas and Sava had gone. Then, just as they were about to leave, Confucius asked the manager, "Do you know where Silas Toronthal has gone?"

The response was, "No, sir. He left but did not indicate where he was going or when he might return."

Dr. Sandorf inquired, "Did he say anything at all when he departed?"

To this, the manager reflected briefly, then recalled, "I remember asking when they would return, but I got no reply. However, when he mounted the coach he asked me, almost as an afterthought, to remember to feed the fish."

Confucius swiftly assimilated these words and eagerly instructed the manager, "Take us to the fish." Then, they entered Silas's private study where the fish tank was handsomely displayed. Inside, the brightly colored fish swam about contentedly. Confucius went to the fish tank and extracted some special food he had in one of his pockets. As he sprinkled this delicacy into the tank, the fish consumed it with obvious delight. Slowly, Confucius made contact with the fish and secured the information he and the doctor wanted.

Only when they returned to the lobby did Confucius release the manager from his hypnotic control.

When Dr. Sandorf and Confucius were alone in the coach returning to the pier, Confucius explained, "The manager will not remember we were ever there. They have taken Sava to Catania. There, she will be forced to marry Sarcany. We must hurry."

"We?"

"My friend, my plan includes going with you to Catania."

"By the way, do you know what species of fish were in the fish tank?"

"No."

"The fish are scalare, better known as angelfish. While outwardly beautiful, they have been known to eat their young."

Dr. Sandorf understood only too well that the characteristics of the fish were just like those of the owner, Silas; outwardly, a legitimate banker and loving father; and inwardly, ruthless enough to harm Sava and betray Austria.

26

The Rescue

The very next day after making their plans, *The Andrea Ferrato* sped toward Catania. They planned to arrive off the coast under cover of darkness. Dr. Sandorf, Pierre, Pescade, Matifou, Confucius, Kumiko, Nato, Miko, and Chuan were all attired in loose-fitting black Shaolin garb. Andrea Ferrato navigated the *Vengeance* well away from traditional shipping lanes so that no one would know they were heading for Catania. Andrea prayed that both Luigi and Maria were still alive. He also thought about Sava and Dr. Sandorf. After all these years, he anticipated that this reunion would be an extraordinary moment.

By nightfall, he brought the *Vengeance* to within three miles off the east coast of Catania and anchored her there. All the lights on board had been extinguished. The *Vengeance* swayed with the waves like a shadow. In the distance, they could see the pirate fleet and the night lights of Catania. The Roman fortress dominated the island and looked dark and frightening. These were anxious and restless moments waiting for the signal from Confucius to begin their rescue mission.

At roughly midnight, as dark clouds veiled the moon, they entered the water. Immediately, all were picked up by Ying and Yang, the dolphins, Tooth, Oden, and the other fish selected for this undertaking. With their marine escort, it took very little time for them to reach the shark-infested area below the fortification. Confucius and

Kumiko arranged for the normally hostile sharks to give them safe passage. Within minutes, they were within the subterranean caverns of Catania. Confucius and the others patted their escorts, knowing they would wait for them.

So far the plan was working fine. Now began the more dangerous part of their operation. Dr. Sandorf said, "We've absolutely no idea where Maria, Luigi, and Sava are being held. The longer we take to find them, the more precarious their situation will become."

They began slowly and carefully to climb a series of long staircases that were very dimly lit. This was an indication that there were no guards strategically placed in this part of the fortification. However, they nearly stumbled into the opposition after ascending three levels. Dr. Sandorf almost stepped into a corridor that was under the surveillance of armed guards. Confucius's quick thinking prevented the group from being detected. Without words, Confucius indicated that there were more lights in the corridor than in the stairwells. It took only a few seconds for Dr. Sandorf to register his friend's warning. To Confucius, the additional lights signaled people used this level far more than those below. Cautiously, they moved along the darkest wall until they noted two guards leaning against a great door, chatting about nothing in particular. Dr. Sandorf and the others braced themselves for a fight. Once again, Confucius stayed them with a gesture.

Confucius walked briskly out into the light of the corridor, strolling leisurely toward the guards. His manner was so casual that the guards merely stared at him as he ambled up to them. Since Confucius held no weapons, the guards did not know what to do. As Confucius approached, they regained their composure and acting on their orders to kill any strangers, clutched their spears and charged.

Confucius never broke his stride. Just when the guards' spears looked like they would impale him, Confucius dove headfirst between them, jumped high into the air, and kicked both guards in their heads. The guards dropped their spears as their knees buckled.

As the guards began to regain consciousness, they found themselves looking deeply into Confucius's eyes. Then, Confucius conveyed to the group, "It was simple to obtain from them a detailed description of the fortification and the exact location of all three prisoners." As the rescuers advanced, they left the two guards at their posts still under hypnotic control.

"It's just as the guards had indicated. In order to get to the chambers where the prisoners are being held, we will have to cross this open courtyard. There are eight additional guards posted here."

Since they had such success with their first encounter, both Confucius and Kumiko calmly approached the eight guards, who could not believe their eyes. The guards attacked but were obviously no match for the Shaolin moves of this duo. Within seconds, all eight guards were sprawled about the courtyard, and no alarm had been given. Here, again, all were hypnotized and made to resume their original posts as if no one had passed by.

Soon they were crossing the uppermost parapet toward the area where the prisoners were being kept. Pescade peeked over the edge of the parapet into another courtyard from which raucous sounds floated up. He could see the pirates' late-night orgy, comprised of loose women and a mingling of nations: Turks, Arabs, Africans, Spaniards, French, Italians, Algerians, and numerous other international outcasts. Pescade's assessment was accurate, "Damn. It's a pirates' convention. Nowhere else could we find such a collection of misfits and social outcasts."

"There's no way down through these pirates to the prisoners. Instead, we'll cross over the parapet of the multitiered dwelling to that flagpole," said Kumiko.

Once at the flagpole, they uncoiled hefty ropes, tossing them over the side of the roof. Peering down from there, it was a long fall to the rocks. The sea crashed repeatedly far below.

Dr. Sandorf said, "Miko, Chuan, Nato, and Matifou, stay here atop the building while we scale down to the windows below."

The group demonstrated no fear of the staggering height and danger below. Within minutes, Pescade entered Sava's room and found her sobbing on a bed. Earlier in the evening, Silas and Sarcany had revealed their plans that whether she agreed or not, they would force her to marry. Therefore, she had to contend with this new nightmare, as well as the loss of her mother and Pierre. Her sobbing prevented her from being aware that Pescade had entered her room. She first knew she was not alone when he gently touched her shoulder. She was initially terrified as she turned to him. He simply held a finger over his own lips, urging Sava not to scream out. She understood and cooperated. She had not expected to see one of Pierre's good friends here in Catania.

Pescade whispered, "Shhh. You have nothing to fear. We came to rescue you."

"We?"

"We've come for you, Maria, and Luigi Ferrato. Your real father is here."

"I had no idea Luigi and Maria were here. My real father? I don't even know who he is."

"Your real father is Dr. Mathias Sandorf. He'll come through that window in a second, with Pierre." Sava stared in disbelief. She could not speak.

Meanwhile, elsewhere in the fortification, Kumiko had slipped quietly into Luigi's room and untied him. Only one guard stood at his door. Kumiko quickly hypnotized this guard as they had all the others. Within seconds, both Kumiko and Luigi had located Maria. Earlier in the evening, Carpena had paid her an unpleasant visit. Carpena had once again imposed his carnal desires upon her.

Maria had discouraged him with a swift kick to his groin. Enraged, Carpena had beaten her into unconsciousness. Hence, when they entered her unguarded room, she needed to be revived and cared for. They quickly sponged off her swollen face. Maria came to and within minutes was ready to vacate the premises. However, with the sound of footsteps in the hall, they waited. Since Kumiko had hypnotized the guard at this door, they listened as the footsteps receded.

Meanwhile, further down the corridor, Sava regained her composure, thinking some cruel joke was being played on her. "Pierre? Pierre is alive?" She was astonished as Dr. Sandorf and Pierre entered. She dashed into Pierre's arms as he rained kisses on her face. Then, she was compelled to release him and go to her father. She and Dr. Sandorf felt awkward as they stood face to face. Within seconds, each smiled with so much tenderness and love that no questions passed between them. Words were unnecessary. Their eyes and souls met in an embrace. Dr. Sandorf wrapped her gently in his arms and, for the first time, Sava felt safe.

Pescade had been listening at the door and now cautioned everyone that someone was coming. They had planned to leave via the window. Instead, they were about to be discovered. They could hear the soft footsteps echoing on the flagstones. Then, Pierre's brow curled up as he heard the unmistakable voice of Sarcany. Within seconds, the group hid in the room. Sava turned the lamp down low as Dr. Sandorf and Pierre hid behind the window curtains. Pescade rolled himself into the small carpet and lay right in front of the door, just off to one side along the wall.

Silas and Sarcany entered, leaving two guards just outside the door. Silas approached the bed where Sava sat. She clenched her hands tightly. Silas spoke tersely and matter-of-factly. "Sava, tomorrow you will be married. Everything is set. The priest arrived a little while ago. I really wish you would change your attitude and consent to the marriage, for your own sake."

"Never!"

"Listen to me, Sava. This is the last time that I shall ask you to consent."

"I will refuse so long as I have the strength to resist."

Sarcany interjected, "By now we had hoped you would mellow and accept the inevitable. Your defiance is unacceptable. You will be mine! You will be mine!" Sarcany had advanced threateningly, seizing Sava's arm forcefully. He shook her.

She protested.

"Beware! Don't push me away. My patience is at an end. Once married, you will certainly regret your present attitude."

Sava cried out, "Pierre! Help!"

Sarcany mocked her, "Pierre? You expect a dead man to help you? Ha! Ha!"

Pierre was only a few feet away as he stepped from the curtain in full view of Sarcany and Silas. Sarcany's laugh died abruptly. In the dim candlelight, Pierre's face had the appearance of a death mask. Sarcany froze and grew pale. For the first time in his life, he was at a loss for words. He released his hold on Sava as if in a daze. His knees began to buckle. Silas backed toward the door in sheer panic.

"I am Pierre Bathory, the man you tried to murder on Marinella Street." Pierre struck Sarcany mightily on the jaw. Sarcany staggered and fell unconscious. Silas drew his pistol, aiming it at Pierre. At that moment, Dr. Sandorf emerged from the shadows of the curtain and with a swift blow knocked the weapon from his hand. Silas stared dumbfounded. This was too much for him. He broke out in a cold sweat. His worst fears had come true. Dr. Sandorf, the real father of Sava, knew everything. He obviously feared for his life.

"Do not be afraid. Your life will be spared because you raised my daughter. Do I have your word that you will not cry out?"

Silas backed toward the door, stating emphatically, "Yes. Yes. Certainly." Then, he bolted for the door crying, "Guards! Guards!" At that moment, Pescade had begun to unroll himself from the carpet. As he did so, Silas stumbled over him and pitched headlong into the door, striking his head. The two guards entered with some difficulty due to Silas's great weight at the foot of the door. Yet, they managed to enter and fire at Pierre and Dr. Sandorf. Both dove to safety behind the large wooden table, which absorbed the impact of the shots. Pierre and Dr. Sandorf then engaged these guards with their swords, dispatching them quickly. Pescade said, "The shots will bring a thousand pirates."

The shots rang loudly throughout the building and courtyard where the pirates were carousing. Kumiko, Luigi, Confucius, and Maria joined Dr. Sandorf, Pierre, and Pescade in the corridor.

Above on the parapet, Matifou, Nato, Miko, and Chuan prepared for the worst. Below, Dragon was already assembling his forces, with various groups rushing toward the sound of the gunfire.

Kumiko sent her hypnotized guard running down the left corridor as if in hot pursuit, while they actually went up the stairs from the corridor to reach the parapet. This was a wise ploy, for the pirates would not think anyone would try to escape by going up higher into the fortress. Any logical escape would be down. Also, if they could get past the courtyard they had come by on the way in, then they would reach that part of the fortress that contained the subterranean caverns.

Carpena was very cunning and hoped to surprise whoever had entered the fortress by coming upon them from behind and above. Thus, he assembled thirty pirates and mounted the highest parapet from the courtyard. This group ran straight into the fleeing fugitives. They stood face-to-face for a split second, and then engaged.

"Take them," cried Carpena. Once again, he underestimated his foe. Because his forces outnumbered them, he thought they would be taken easily. However, this was not to be the case.

Pierre and Pescade led the fight by charging directly into the oncoming group. Both were agile and fast, and their swords cut a path through the pirates. Dr. Sandorf struck boldly at the bandits too, managing to get hold of Carpena. Just as Dr. Sandorf was getting the better of him, two of the pirates secured Dr. Sandorf's arms and pinned him against the wall. Carpena wiped the blood from his nose and advanced menacingly with sword in hand. Just as Carpena swung his sword, Dr. Sandorf let his weight drop to the floor. Carpena's blade scraped along the wall. Dr. Sandorf swung both his legs up, striking the two pirates in their faces while they still held his arms. He sprang to his feet and kicked Carpena in the midsection. Carpena doubled up and fell backward.

All the others had their hands full at the same time. Confucius and Kumiko sailed through the pirates smoothly as if they were dancing. Their movements were graceful and sure. They used their legs, knees, hands, elbows, and even their hips as powerful weapons. Nato, Miko, and Chuan also cut a quick path through the pirates using their Shaolin skills. Within minutes, they had driven this band back to the stairs of the courtyard. Others were hurled over the parapet. Those who remained alive on the parapet were quickly assembled. Confucius and Kumiko used their tactile hypnotic power—one touch converted these pirates for rear-guard action.

Dragon then appeared with several hundred men in the courtyard below, making for the stairs leading to the parapet. Matifou had lifted a cannon, aiming it into the courtyard. He cried out to Pescade, "Here, Pescade, light it." It only took a second for Pescade to light the fuse of the cannon. The cannon disgorged itself with a loud thunderclap, blasting a hole in the large group advancing below. Then the small group of fleeing prisoners raced across the parapet. Matifou hurled the cannon, knocking down everyone on the stairs. Meanwhile, Confucius had summoned all the original guards from the subterranean caverns. They appeared at the head of the stairs, which gave Luigi, Maria, and Sava pause. Confucius quickly reassured them, "Do not fear, these guards are within my power and will help us make good our escape."

These eight guards plus the most recently hypnotized ones on the parapet then engaged Dragon, Carpena, and the hundreds of others. Carpena stared in disbelief as pirates fought pirates.

Dragon ordered, "Cut them down." Then, the larger force with Dragon in the lead killed the rear-guard force and gave chase.

As the fleeing group raced down to the subterranean exit, the pirates were in hot pursuit. Dragon yelled, "The sharks will be well fed tonight." Meanwhile, Pescade noted that the entire roof of one of the lower chambers was supported by a large central column somewhat corroded by water and time. A huge anchor chain lay abandoned nearby.

Pescade quickly summoned Matifou. "Do you think you can move the column?" He wrapped the chain around the column and handed the other end to Matifou.

"I can try." Like Sampson, he braced himself and pulled with all his strength. The chain snapped taut, and the column began to tremble. As the pirates entered this chamber on a fast run, Matifou's herculean strength won out against the column. The column gave way and the chamber ceiling came crashing down on them.

While Dragon dug his way out of the rubble, the fugitives encountered no more obstacles. They reached the lowest level and dove into the shark-infested waters. Sava was terrified; she had no knowledge of the Shaolin's ability to communicate with fish.

Dr. Sandorf reassured her, "Trust me, Sava. They will not harm you. They are our friends." Now Sava noticed that all the others were being picked up by friendly dolphins, whales, and even sharks.

Confucius summoned Tooth to give her a ride. Tooth responded with a flip and a splash, coming to a halt at the bottom of the stairs. Dr. Sandorf gently placed Sava on Tooth and joined her. Tooth sped away, and Sava experienced the most awesome ride of her life.

Within seconds, Dragon and his men reached the waterline. The pirates froze. Dragon and Carpena stared in disbelief at the sight of the fleeing prisoners all riding sea creatures to safety. Dragon said, "I'll be damned." Almost on cue, a savage shark rose from the water and almost snapped his head off.

On board the *Vengeance*, Andrea had kept a worried vigil. He watched intently as the returning sea mounts pulled alongside with their precious cargo of freed prisoners. Andrea's face cracked into a broad grin upon seeing Maria and Luigi climb on board. He rushed to them, reunited in happiness. The last to dismount was Sava with Dr. Sandorf. Sava turned and said, "Thank you, Tooth!" Tooth blinked a happy eye, rolled over, and smiled as only a shark can smile. All the others waved in gratitude to their respective sea mounts. They had a lot to be thankful for. They had entered the stronghold of the pirates, and all had escaped without harm. As the *Vengeance* weighed anchor, Andrea smiled, confident in the knowledge that no ship in the world could catch them.

Back in Catania, the pirates quickly dispatched three ships with the hope of recapturing the prisoners. After a day of sailing with full sail, they abandoned the search. They failed to find any trace. Upon their return, within two days, another sinister meeting took place.

Silas, Sarcany, Carpena, Dragon, and the rest of the chieftains met to discuss what had transpired. They could not explain how their own men were turned against them. Also, they could not comprehend how it was possible to swim safely through shark-infested waters. They remained bewildered as to how Pierre, a declared corpse, had somehow been resurrected. In all, the bandits, pirates, and their leaders were thoroughly disgusted with the way things had gone.

Once they had all vented their collective frustration, they once again plotted revenge.

Silas and Sarcany held their own meeting, concerned with their immediate problem of financing the imminent invasion of Trieste. Their difficulty was simple: no money, no invasion. This would mean Silas's years of collaboration with the Germans so as to become Regent were over. Silas thought that were he unable to hold up his end of the bargain, Von Brun might even kill him.

It was not long before Silas suggested that they go ahead with the wedding as planned. Without Sava, Sarcany was perplexed until Silas explained his plan. "We will substitute Namir, who will pretend to be Sava. She is more or less the same size and behind a heavy veil, no one will know it is not Sava Toronthal." So they proceeded with a staged wedding using a local priest who had never seen Sava. Sarcany, nonetheless, almost choked on the words, "I do." Then, when it came time to kiss the bride, Sarcany was most unhappy, while Namir beamed.

Once the wedding was concluded, it was a simple matter to forge Sava's signature, enabling the transfer of funds from the Swiss Bank to the Bank of Trieste. No one questioned Silas the banker and father. In fact, this was a stroke of sheer genius. Also, once they had the funds, Silas breathed easier concerning Von Brun, and nothing stood in the way of the invasion of Austria.

27

The Invasion of Austria

Von Brun arrived off the coast of Catania with fifty ships loaded with German troops and armed to the teeth. Meanwhile, Silas had pooled all his funds, enabling the outfitting of thirty pirate ships. These combined ships were more than enough to launch a surprise invasion of Trieste. While Trieste had a small fleet, it was principally a seaport center of commerce.

Just prior to embarking on their invasion, all the German officers, Dragon and his leaders, and all the bandits and pirates assembled on the shore where Von Brun addressed them as a whole.

"Tonight we depart for Trieste. The day after tomorrow, the city will be ours. Our mighty armada is invincible." A great "Hurrah!" sounded along the shore. Indeed, the pirates were eager to capture Trieste. Secretly, Von Brun had decided to motivate the pirates with a deal enabling them to sack the city. They would take everything they could carry and inflict havoc on the citizens. This he hid, even from Silas.

In all, a force of twenty thousand had been assembled. With a land invasion across the Alps, which had already begun, General Hattersfield would of necessity be busy mobilizing ground forces to meet this challenge. The next day the silhouettes of the armada dotted the horizon as far as the eye could see.

On the second day, morning broke with the armada only thirteen miles off the coast of Trieste. As they expected, no one had seen the fleet and surprise was on their side. Unknown to Von Brun, the sea creatures were very much aware of the armada and notified Chang, Confucius, and Kumiko. They in turn alerted Dr. Sandorf. Dr. Sandorf instructed Andrea, "*The Andrea Ferrato* will warn Trieste. With her speed, she will reach Trieste before the armada, and some warning is better than none."

Dr. Sandorf peered through his telescope, spotting Von Brun and Silas together. In turn, Von Brun shared his telescope with Silas and both easily saw Dr. Sandorf on the shore. It was then that Silas slyly indicated, "We must pass close to the International Hospital to reach Trieste."

Von Brun replied, "So?"

Silas lied easily, "I heard they installed large cannons on the island."

Von Brun knew there were no cannons at the hospital. Still, Von Brun scanned the island carefully through his telescope while he replied, "I heard it was unarmed."

Von Brun focused on Dr. Sandorf and Pierre Bathory on the shore. In a flash, he recalled his humiliation at Rovigno when they tossed him overboard in front of the villagers and his troops. In Pierre he saw the face of the father, Étienne Bathory, like a ghost haunting him. Then, the face of Dr. Sandorf's wife, Savarena, refusing to divulge any information also seeped into his memory. The smiling face of Count Zathmar appeared. He recalled his disabled gunboat when he shouted to Dr. Sandorf, "We'll meet again." Last, he reflected on his hasty exit from the Triglav. Collectively, these defeats were like searing hot blades cutting into him. In his entire military career, these setbacks at the hands of Dr. Sandorf were his most humiliating.

He lowered the telescope, ordering, "Signal ten ships to line up for a full broadside. I want that fortification on the island completely destroyed." Within seconds, the lead ship signaled the others, and ten ships peeled away from the larger formation, heading straight for the island.

On the shore all had gathered, never once thinking that their hospital would be fired upon. It was unthinkable. Chang asked Dr. Sandorf, "Will Trieste and Austria fall?"

Dr. Sandorf replied with a heavy heart, "I don't think Austria can beat off such a force. Certainly, Trieste will be taken."

Confucius asked, "What will become of our hospital if the Germans are victorious?"

Dr. Sandorf stated, "We will not be spared when Silas becomes Regent. It is only a matter of time."

Chang said, "A group of ten ships is heading our way. It seems Von Brun and Silas are impatient to destroy us. They must know we have no cannons here."

Dr. Sandorf gave a chilling analysis, "The true face of evil. They know we have no cannons. They don't care. It is Pierre and I, and what we represent, that drives them."

Chang, Confucius, and Kumiko grouped together and immediately arrived at a consensus, which Chang expressed to Dr. Sandorf, "My friend, whatever happens this day, I am glad we shall face it together. There may be a way to help Austria. There is also a grave risk involved. Our secret of communicating with sea creatures may be revealed. Yet, we do not see any alternative."

Dr. Sandorf asked, "What can fish do against an armada?"

Chang mused, "We hope that someday men and nations will learn that war is not a solution to differences, but rather a great waste of human resources. This day will be a bloody day. Watch!" Then, he entered the aquarium with Confucius and Kumiko. Submerged up to their waists, they began the ritual of communication as they had done on top of the island many years before. An electric, flowing, mental energy-wave emanated from them outward to the reef and beyond.

From the deck of the ships, the energy-wave looked like a flash of electricity passing by harmlessly. The ten ships closed in formation to level the hospital. The first ship's volley of fire bracketed the hill as round after round fell closer to the hospital. Three rounds found their mark, tearing into the building and exploding within.

The undersea world rapidly communicated with one another, and within seconds the deep-sea creatures responded. Just as the first ship made way for the second, a team of nineteen-foot swordfish, led by Glad, cut two large holes in the ship just below the waterline. The sea began to flood into her hold, and she began to sink. Meanwhile, two sixty-foot whale sharks commanded by Tooth quickly spun the second ship around, preventing her from discharging her cannons. With a whale shark on each side pushing her forward at increasing speed, this second ship became a battering ram against the third ship. When these ships collided, there followed a tremendous explosion, and both ships began sinking rapidly.

It was this explosion that caught Von Brun's attention. He looked back at his ships in disbelief. It was inexplicable. "What the hell is going on?" He continued to watch as the fourth ship circled the others, closing in for a broadside against the hospital. Suddenly, he saw this ship rise out of the water. It was lifted into the air by Blue, the largest of all mammals, the blue whale. This whale had slipped under the ship and lifted it like a toy. By gently rolling to one side, the whale flipped the ship over.

Silas cried out, "It's some sort of undersea vessel. Like Jules Verne's *Nautilus* submarine."

Von Brun was skeptical about such an explanation. "I'll be damned. It looks like a whale to me."

The other six advance ships with ready cannons broke formation. Oden and his pod began a siege on these ships. There were the sounds of repeated thuds as the whales cracked open the hulls with great force. Then, Ray, a giant devil manta ray, sailed out of the sea and smashed another vessel flat. This fleet aimed at the surface of the water. Their rounds skimmed along the surface and made contact with their own ships.

More swordfish cut holes below the waterlines while the blue whale and Oden ensured that none of the other remaining ships were able to position themselves for broadsides on the hospital.

Soon, those who had not been killed or drowned immediately were thrashing about in the water. They were cut off from the shore by a variety of sea creatures that engaged them. Pirates who managed to draw their swords found they were no match for Glad and his squadron of swordfish, which easily out-fenced them. Others were harassed by twenty-foot manta rays. Stingrays, shocker electric eels, spiny batfish, three-spined sticklebacks, and Ying and Yang—the male and female dolphins—organized a cadre of mixed sea soldiers who joined the fray. Some species had erect spines, which pricked the pirates and soldiers on their hands, feet, and buttocks. Even some old snapping turtles, led by Tank, got into the fracas, taking pieces out of some of the enemy. The flying needlefish, Wings, with his team, hurled themselves through the air like javelins, seriously wounding or killing those they struck.

By the time Von Brun signaled for the remaining fleet to turn around, the ten initial ships were lost, with pirates and soldiers helpless in the water. Unable to swim safely to shore, many drowned, and others were so tired they were useless for combat. The continuous fish attack relentlessly caused them such annoyance that they found themselves in a frenzy. Then, to make matters worse for the invaders, a school of four-inch tadpole catfish joined the fight along with

Scorpio's group of sea scorpions. These were joined by Vip's crew of viperfish. These fish carried poison glands at the base of their pectoral spines. Their pricks were worse than the sting of a bee, followed by paralysis and death.

At Von Brun's command, the remaining seventy ships began to circle the island hospital. They were met head-on with a repeat of the onslaught that disabled the first ten ships. Moreover, even more sea creatures arrived like charging cavalry at the scene. Schools of ten-foot sailfish, striped marlin, Nar the narwhal, and Zyg the hammerhead shark attacked with precision. Each of these fish had long, pointed noses that were used to puncture holes in the ships' hulls. Hands, the giant octopus, led her family and numerous other octopi in the assault. They were able to grasp ships and pull them under the surface with a tug. Even tiny Tina organized the remoras that usually attach themselves to sharks. These remora now hitched themselves to ships, with the result that they slowed their progress.

From the shore, a fleet of dolphins were outfitted with explosive devices, which they carried to the hulls of many ships. They were deposited against the hulls with the use of sea glue and sticky sap secreted by cooperating creatures. These explosive charges tore through the hulls of numerous ships that were still loaded with munitions. Many ships erupted totally, destroying the fleet and their crews.

Von Brun knew that there were no undersea ships, just the fish of the deep. However, he had no idea how to combat them. There was no military precedent to guide him. Indeed, there was never such a battle recorded anywhere in history. Yet, Von Brun felt that the key to this behavior lay on the island. He sailed straight for her with all his remaining ships.

Dr. Sandorf had wisely set about evacuating the hospital with the help of attendants and medical staff. The small Shaolin force took up positions along the shore. In spite of the fact that with every passing minute another ship was taken out of commission, several of the ships, including Von Brun's and Dragon's, got within firing range and began to blast the hospital. The patients had been successfully moved to the far side of the island. As the ships began bombarding the hospital, many small boats, filled to capacity with troops and pirates, were lowered. These boats quickly attained the shore, depositing their cargo of trained troops and bloodthirsty pirates. Only the small Shaolin force was available to do combat with them.

In waves of hundreds of troops and pirates at a time, they advanced up the sandy slope. These forces surrounded the Shaolin and the others. Not one member of the small protective force broke ranks even though they were severely outnumbered. Von Brun, Silas, and Dragon felt victory was at hand.

When a large force gathered to assault Chang, they encountered another surprise. When they made eye contact with Chang, he emitted a series of hypnotic suggestions known as "the eye of the tiger." Thus, in rapid succession there were two, three, and five tigers attacking the force on the beach. These phantom tigers looked real to the troops, and they panicked and began firing randomly. They struck one another repeatedly in their panic. Through this phantom screen, Nato, Miko, Chuan, Confucius, Kumiko, and the others simultaneously launched their small flying stars with eighteen per hand in rapid succession. These flying "suriken" stars ripped into the oncoming force with deadly precision. The first wave of one hundred soldiers fell quickly on the shore. The other forces soon had to climb over their dead comrades in order to get within striking distance.

The second wave of roughly one hundred were spellbound, confronted yet by another apparition conjured up by Chang. They believed they were being attacked by a menacing group of giant crocodiles. Between the imaginary tigers and crocodiles, the force was rendered incapable of an orderly assault on the Shaolin and others on the beach. Then, to their further astonishment, the small group of Shaolin attacked them.

Suddenly, subsequent waves of attackers were set upon with weapons and techniques they had never encountered before. The larger force had no response to this attack. The Shaolin wielded the flails—twelve-inch hardwood sticks tied together with a short chain. Several used nineteen-inch rectangular beams with a handle. Still others used a seven-inch blade hooked into a seventeen-inch sickle handle. They also used another sickle weapon outfitted with a long chain. Finally, each Shaolin unsheathed swords, which, in their capable hands, were incredibly devastating.

In thirty minutes of intense fighting, the Shaolin had killed or wounded nearly two thousand of the oncoming soldiers and pirates. Von Brun could not believe what was happening. His force, designed to take the city of Trieste, was in shambles. His troops dropped like flies all around him. At sea, his ships continued to be devoured by the army of the sea. Indeed, the masters of the sea were its creatures. Von Brun was losing Austria without ever firing a single shot at Trieste. He realized he was throwing away an entire Navy. Von Brun was finished. Silas's plans to become Regent were doomed in an afternoon.

The Andrea Ferrato returned, having warned Trieste. The ship was armed with several cannons and machine guns and sailed into the battle well ahead of the ten Austrian ships that always guarded Trieste. *The Andrea Ferrato*, under the able guidance of her captain, was too fast for any of the remaining ships to even take aim. None of the German or pirate ships was a match for her. She dodged in and around the remaining ships, raking them with devastating fusillades.

Back on the shore, the arrival of the Austrian forces was reinvigorating. Now, the Shaolin were pelting the opposition forces with their water weapons and stun guns. Von Brun, Dragon, Silas, and Carpena soon stood toe to toe with their enemy. They still had roughly one thousand men, enough to engage in hand-to-hand combat. Von Brun knew that all had failed. Now, as he was face-to-face with his adversary again, he knew it was surrender or die.

Von Brun was safely entrenched in the middle of his forces. He marveled at the oldest member of the Shaolin, Chang, who seemingly danced through his trained elite troops as if they were twigs. Every time Chang's hands or feet touched a soldier, the man went down. So it was with Confucius, Kumiko, Nato, Miko, and Chuan. They penetrated his crack troops as if they were cutting down sugarcane.

Dragon was soon face-to-face with Luigi. His preferred savate technique was used. However, as he sailed up into the air toward Luigi, he was unexpectedly met by a graceful aerial counterstroke of Kumiko. Her flight placed her several feet above Dragon. Her foot-strike was enormously powerful. She delivered it adroitly to Dragon's throat. Dragon's windpipe was smashed, and he died before he hit the ground.

Carpena slipped behind Dr. Sandorf and advanced with a sword. However, Dr. Sandorf was too fast for him. Dr. Sandorf whirled, kicking Carpena's sword hand forcefully. His blade flew high into the air. Then, Dr. Sandorf doubled Carpena up with a fierce kick to the midsection. As Carpena doubled over, his own blade came down, piercing his back. Carpena tried to extract the blade, but his hands could not reach it. He twisted and turned briefly, then fell dead at Dr. Sandorf's feet.

Von Brun was confronted by Pescade. Von Brun knew he had the superior strength and went straight for him with his sword. The crafty Pescade dove into his feet, tripping him. With his face covered with sand, Von Brun swung blindly for several seconds at the place he thought Pescade would be. Then, he cleared his eyes and found he was face-to-face with the mighty Matifou. Matifou struck him with his fist. The blow was so powerful that it rendered Von Brun unconscious immediately.

Silas was not a fighter and was so overweight that he could barely move in the sand. When he saw all the others failing to effectively overpower Dr. Sandorf's forces, he knelt down and begged for mercy, "Please, please don't kill me. Please." He broke down in tears, trembling, and wetting his pants. Pierre, with sword in hand, took him into custody.

The remaining Germans and pirates were leaderless. They looked around at the carnage and dropped their weapons. They cried out, "Enough! Enough! We surrender!" Only then did the Shaolin permit the sea creatures to halt their relentless assault. The sea creatures disappeared within the waves. This permitted hundreds of exhausted and thoroughly beaten forces in the water to swim to shore.

Within minutes, King Ferdinand and General Hattersfield dropped anchor and made their way to shore with fresh Austrian troops. They rounded up all the prisoners. General Hattersfield, with a select group of his own forces, took personal charge of Silas and Von Brun. To Dr. Sandorf and the Shaolin he said, "I don't know how you did it. Austria owes you a great debt."

King Ferdinand echoed this sentiment. "Dr. Sandorf and Chang, Austria is in your eternal debt. We shall rebuild your hospital, and you will have perpetual autonomy. However, may I ask what you did to the sea creatures?"

Dr. Sandorf remembered his promise to Chang and his loyal followers. The Shaolin had become more than just friends. He now knew why the secret must be kept. He knew that any nation that could control the masters of the sea could rule the world. With such a force of creatures not a single ship could set sail from any port in the world. Indeed, he knew as he answered his king that Chang's secret must be guarded. Dr. Sandorf answered, "The fish were not controlled. Why, we were more surprised than the Germans. I think their first cannon fire upset the fish in the aquarium. They seemed to react to the ships and cannon fire. Why, your Majesty, no one can communicate with fish. God has spared Austria this day."

King Ferdinand had no choice but to accept this version of what had transpired. Dr. Sandorf winked at Chang. No one would ever know that they could communicate with fish. Chang was delighted and cracked a smile.

Chang, Confucius, Kumiko, Nato, Pierre, Pescade, Matifou, Andrea, Luigi, Maria, and all the others watched as the Austrian fleet sailed back to Trieste with their cargo of prisoners. Quietly, the masters of the sea said good-bye to the sea creatures who had come to assist them. Then, all the fish returned to the aquarium where they in turn received Chang's warm thank you. Their finny friends of the deep began to frolic and splash, for they had also protected their new way of life and their new home.

One week later, during the national holiday declared by King Ferdinand, Austria celebrated its first triple wedding. Pierre and Sava, Luigi and Kumiko, and Dr. Sandorf and Maria took their solemn vows at the Cathedral of Trieste, whose bells rang out across the mountains.

The sound of the church bells reached the prison where Silas and Von Brun had adjoining cells. Von Brun stared in disbelief when Silas said, "I have a new plan."

Epilogue

Silas's plan was to bribe the guards and make good his and Von Brun's escape. Like the shrewd banker he was, he had squirreled away funds in a Swiss account and in nearby hiding places for contingencies. Silas settled across the border in Bosnia-Herzegovinia for eight years. However, Austrian Emperor Franz Joseph annexed this territory on October 6, 1908. The Slavic people protested, forming ongoing rebellions and attacks for many years. In a bizarre twist of fate, under his new identity, Silas became the revolutionary. He helped finance the *Black Hand*, responsible for coordinating resources, training people, and supplying weapons for the failed attempt on the life of the Emperor Franz Joseph.

On June 28, 1914, a nineteen-year-old rebel, Gavrilo Princip, assassinated Archduke Franz Ferdinand along with his pregnant wife, Sophie. He was the nephew of Emperor Franz Joseph and heir to the Austrian-Hungarian throne. This assassination ignited World War I.

Von Brun returned to Germany where he advocated the development of the Unterseeboot (undersea boat or U-boat). Germany's first submarine was built in 1905. It was a "Karp" class submarine which had a double hull, a Körting kerosene engine and a single torpedo tube. By World War I, Germany had twenty-nine U-boats.

Chang and Confucius decided to honor their ancestor, Sifu, by returning to China on his behalf with firsthand knowledge of Europe. They believed the time was propitious having heard of Guangxu, the Emperor whose name means the *Glorious Succession*. For many years, against stiff opposition, Guangxu issued massive far-reaching reforms. Many of their aquatic friends simply remained submerged in their fathomless domain.

The real Austrian friend of Jules Verne, Archduke Louis Salvadore de Toscane, on whom this book was based, returned to a free Austria and kept in close touch with him until Verne's death in 1905. The novel *Mathias Sandorf* received worldwide attention being translated in more than thirty languages. It inspired Georg Ritter von Trapp, who was born in 1880. We know from Maria von Trapp's famous book, *The Story of the Trapp Family Singers*, which became immortalized by the blockbuster film *The Sound of Music* that Emperor Franz Joseph promoted her husband, Georg, to Lieutenant Commander of the Austrian submarine "U-6." Like Jules Verne's real life hero, Georg Ritter von Trapp was an Austrian patriot who refused to serve the German regime by escaping to Italy with his entire family. Georg said, "I have sworn my oath of loyalty to only one emperor." Clearly, Dr. Mathias Sandorf and Georg Ritter von Trapp were chiseled from the same Austrian marble.

* * *

It seems fitting to reflect on Verne's inspirational figure as writer, seaman, painter, and illustrator who wrote nine books on the Balearic Islands over a twenty-year period. In 1910, Juan Carlos, the King of Spain declared him "freeman" of Mallorca—one having the full rights of a citizen—where he chose to live. The king envied his home known as Son Marroig, still located between Valldemossa and Dejá. A Moorish masterpiece, it boasts of terraces, arcades, galleries, porticos, pagodas, gardens, and a view of the sea unequaled and beyond description. In fact, the Archduke brought this scenic wonder to the attention of the world and it continues today to be a major tourist attraction. It is no wonder that Louis declared it his "oasis of peace." In our twenty-first century, it is one of the homes acquired by the motion picture legend Michael Douglas. Louis left Mallorca with the advent of World War I. His father was Leopold XI, Great Duke of Tuscany and Imperial Prince of Austria. He returned to his beloved

Austria once again because "noblesse oblige"—his patriotism and desire to see Austria remain free are testimony to his love of country and royal blood. He died in 1915.

The End